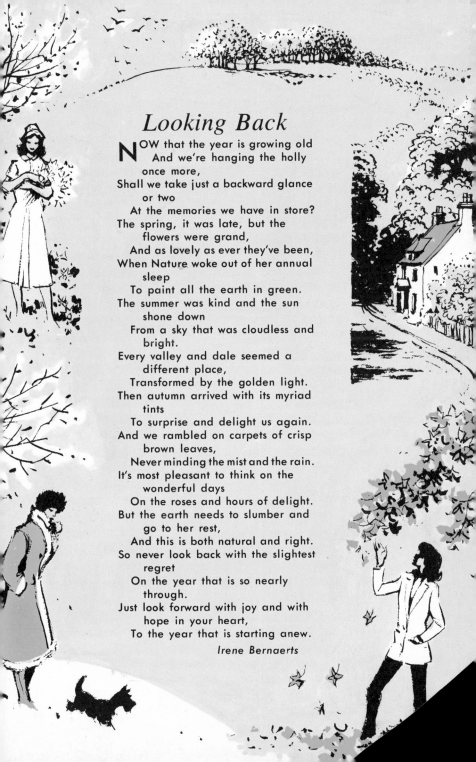

Looking Back

NOW that the year is growing old
   And we're hanging the holly
   once more,
Shall we take just a backward glance
   or two
   At the memories we have in store?
The spring, it was late, but the
   flowers were grand,
   And as lovely as ever they've been,
When Nature woke out of her annual
   sleep
   To paint all the earth in green.
The summer was kind and the sun
   shone down
   From a sky that was cloudless and
   bright.
Every valley and dale seemed a
   different place,
   Transformed by the golden light.
Then autumn arrived with its myriad
   tints
   To surprise and delight us again.
And we rambled on carpets of crisp
   brown leaves,
   Never minding the mist and the rain.
It's most pleasant to think on the
   wonderful days
   On the roses and hours of delight.
But the earth needs to slumber and
   go to her rest,
   And this is both natural and right.
So never look back with the slightest
   regret
   On the year that is so nearly
   through.
Just look forward with joy and with
   hope in your heart,
   To the year that is starting anew.

                              Irene Bernaerts

No home should ever be without them.

Marshalls

makes the meal

People's Friend Annual

•

CONTENTS

SCENIC VIEWS   J. Campbell Kerr

BACK COVER   A beautiful summer setting near Oban, Argyllshire

Where The Heart Is

by Constance Kay

I T was well over two years since Rachel Forbes had ventured into
the part of Muirhead which had once been so familiar to her.
    She'd always felt that to go back to her old home would be too
painful.
    She could remember, as if it were yesterday, how her father, learning
that all his investments had failed, had suffered a fatal heart attack.
After the funeral, his lawyer had broken the news as gently as possible
to her mother and herself. Rachel had been in her late twenties then.
    "I'm afraid there's very little money left," Mr Henderson had
explained. "I don't think you can afford to stay at Whinshaws."
    "We could live very simply," Mrs Forbes had answered.

The lawyer had shaken his head sadly. Then he had replied carefully:

"There are so many other factors to be considered. The rates, for example — and the heating bills in a place this size must be enormous.

"And what about the garden? You wouldn't be able to afford to keep on your gardener. And I noticed there are slates missing from the roof — that should be repaired before winter sets in."

Mrs Forbes had gazed helplessly at her daughter. Rachel had known her mother didn't understand much about managing her finances. She'd left it all to her husband.

"He's right, Mother," Rachel had said as gently as she could. "I'd get a job if it would help but I've no qualifications and you know the doctor said you shouldn't be left on your own. No, we're going to have to make up our minds to leave Whinshaws."

"But where can we go?" her mother had asked plaintively.

"Well, the house will fetch a good price on the open market," the lawyer had said. "It's in a nice central position. And then there's the land — that must be worth quite a bit."

He had scribbled down a few figures.

"There should be enough money for you to buy a small house anywhere you chose. The balance, sensibly invested, would bring you in a useful income."

B UT if we sold the land, what would happen to the house?" Mrs Forbes had asked.

"Well, if the buyers were developers, they might well pull the house down and build smaller houses or flats in its place. Or, as it's in a very central position, perhaps some shops or offices."

"No!" Mrs Forbes had cried in horror. "Never! I won't *hear* of Whinshaws being pulled down!

"My grandfather built the house for his bride. All the wood panelling and plasterwork was specially commissioned. He even went to Venice to choose the design for the stained glass window on the stairs! No — whoever buys the land must promise to leave the house standing."

"Well, a restriction like that would definitely limit the property's saleability," the lawyer had pointed out.

But Mrs Forbes had been adamant. No argument would shake her. Secretly, Rachel had been rather glad.

At last, after many months, a large insurance company had made an offer for Whinshaws. They wanted to make it their local headquarters.

Rachel and her mother had found a pleasant cottage on the other side of the town and settled down to make a new life for themselves.

O NE morning in May, two years later, Rachel walked to the local park and noticed that the lilac trees were in bloom. Catching the scent of the blossoms as she passed, she remembered her own lilac tree, planted at Whinshaws on the day she was born.

She had to go into town anyway, so why shouldn't she go and see how Whinshaws was faring in its new role? She might even go inside and ask for some information about insurance, just to see what it was like now.

The front of the house looked very much as she remembered it. Then she realised it was far smarter. The brickwork had been recently re-pointed and the woodwork was freshly painted.

The garden had been tamed, too. The once rampant herbaceous border had disappeared and the lawns extended. The grass was like green velvet, edges meticulously trimmed.

Here and there were geometrically-shaped flower-beds, all planted with rose bushes. They weren't in bloom yet, but the borders of blue and yellow pansies made an eye-catching splash of colour.

Rachel wandered among them, trying to recall the location of the lilac tree.

A T last, through a little wicker gate, she saw it.

An elderly man was forking up spent daffodil bulbs and putting them in baskets. He paused when he saw Rachel.

"Sorry, ma'am," he said. "This part of the garden's private."

Rachel stared at him. "Ben Pringle! Don't you remember me?"

He blinked at her in the spring sunshine.

"It can't be Miss Rachel, can it?" He faltered.

"It certainly *can*," she assured him with a smile. "So they kept you on as gardener? I'm so glad!"

"Yes — and all thanks to your lady mother, Miss Rachel. She put in the conditions of the sale that I was to stay as long as I cared to work."

"I really came to see my lilac tree," she told Ben.

"I've looked after it for you, Miss Rachel. When those landscape gardeners wanted to cut it down, I told them they'd have to cut *me* down first!"

He led the way to the tree, now in full bloom.

"I'll cut you a spray," he offered, producing a knife from his pocket.

N OW Pringle," a masculine voice said in mock reproof. "You mustn't give away our flowers."

A tall, distinguished-looking man had approached unob-served. His dark hair was greying over the temples and his piercing blue eyes were filled with amusement rather than anger.

"Begging your pardon, sir," Ben Pringle spoke with confidence. "The lilac tree used to belong to this lady. Her father and I planted it the day she was born."

"So recently? I should have thought it was older."

He gave a slight bow towards Rachel, who found herself blushing. She was saved from further embarrassment by a telephone ringing from inside the house.

The newcomer glanced at his watch. "Please forgive me. I must go."

He was about to walk away when he turned to her again.

"Please come to the garden whenever you wish, Miss Forbes," he said. "And bring your mother, too. You'll both be very welcome."

His smile was friendly and sincere.

"One day when the office is closed I'll show you round inside. Then you can see for yourself that we haven't caused too much havoc. My own office is on the first floor and still has a charming fresco of baby deer," he added.

"That was *my* room!" Rachel blushed again. "I loved those fawns."

"Then it will be my privilege to look after them for you," he said with another slight bow. "Goodbye for the present."

He seemed reluctant to go, but eventually he strode off across the lawn, his long legs rapidly covering the distance.

"Now," Rachel asked Ben Pringle, "who was that?"

"That's the boss, Mr Christopher Ogilvy. Regional director I think they call him. He's a real gentleman," the old gardener replied.

After a brief pause he asked: "And where are you and your lady mother living now? I trust she keeps well."

"Yes, apart from her rheumatism, that is. It always causes a few grumbles! I'd like to bring her here as Mr Ogilvy suggested, but it's an awkward journey from where we stay now. Torridon Cottage is right at the other side of town."

A FEW weeks later, on a bright Saturday morning, a large cream car stopped at the gate of Torridon Cottage. A tall man got out, looked at the name on the gate and came striding up the path to the door.

Mrs Forbes hastened to open it.

The stranger handed her his card. *Christopher Ogilvy, Foinhaven Insurance Company, Whinshaws, Muirhead.*

Mrs Forbes returned the card with an apologetic smile.

"I'm sorry," she said. "We don't need any insurance."

By now Rachel had heard voices and come to the door.

"Oh, Mother," she hastened to explain, "this is the kind gentleman I told you about. He says we can visit the garden whenever we like."

Christopher Ogilvy smiled at her.

"Ben Pringle said it was an awkward journey from here, so I've come to offer my services as chauffeur."

"Oh, how kind," Mrs Forbes replied. "Shall we go now?" she asked in quite a flutter.

"Well, if it suits you," he said gravely. "The office is closed today, so you could see inside the house as well — if it wouldn't be too painful."

"No," the old lady replied. "I'd like that."

S O they all set out. Mrs Forbes thoroughly enjoyed seeing all the familiar landmarks as they passed through the town. When they entered the drive of her old home she gasped with astonishment.

"Why, it looks just the same," she observed. "In fact, it's better than ever. It's all smartened up — and how tidy the garden is!"

Ben Pringle came forward to say hello. He was delighted to see his former employer looking so well — and he told her so with a grin.

"You're looking fit, too, Ben," Mrs Forbes replied. "But we're neither of us as young as we were and times have changed. Your boys must be grown up, now —"

"The boys are apprenticed to the parks department," Ben told her proudly. "But they still give me a hand in their spare time."

Mrs Forbes glanced towards Rachel and Christopher Ogilvy. What a handsome couple they make, she thought to herself with a smile. They had strolled on ahead of her along the path and the pair were now waiting for her outside the front door. Saying goodbye Mrs Forbes hurried to catch up.

Christopher Ogilvy opened the heavy oak doors.

"Oh, Rachel . . ." She glanced round the entrance hall. "It's hardly changed at all."

THE morning sun was streaming through the stained-glass window above the landing. It still threw fascinating shapes of different colours on to the massive oak staircase.

"I used to love sitting on the stairs," Rachel spoke up. "I had a white dress and I used to sit for hours watching the colours. I would pretend they were fantastic jewels . . ."

Daddy's Boy

OH, you are just a little one,
      And life for you is so much fun,
For simple things bring you more joy
Than some exotic, dearer toy.
The pleasures that you seem to find!
The things that occupy your mind!
That sparkle there within your eye
When Mum says, "You're a Daddy's
      boy!"

Yes, you are just a little one,
The world for you is full of sun,
Is full of snow and fairies too
And lots of magic things to do.
A world of make-believe and fun,
While you are yet a little one,
The world, a twinkle in your eye,
God bless you, darling Daddy's boy!

                                L. J. Wells

He led the way up the stairs to the first floor and into the drawing-room. Mrs Forbes ran her fingers along the polished wood of the table and looked around her thoughtfully. Meanwhile Rachel wandered around the room recalling her childhood memories.

"Very impressive," was Mrs Forbes' verdict. "But I prefer my pretty chintz-covered chairs and settee!"

They peeped into several smaller rooms now transformed into business-like offices. One, rather larger, contained gleaming metal and glass cabinets.

"Our computer room," their guide explained. "I don't imagine this will interest you very much."

Rachel shook her head. "They're just overgrown tape-recorders worked by black magic as far as I'm concerned!"

"Where do you stay, Mr Ogilvy?" Mrs Forbes enquired.

He seemed amused at the question.

"Oh, I leave Whinshaws behind after office hours. I have a small flat about half a mile away," he answered. "But if you mean which room is my office —'' He threw open a door and stood politely to one side.

Rachel turned her head away. She didn't want to hear her mother's inevitable comment on his choice of room.

THEY went down to the basement next and inspected the staff canteen which had once been the old kitchen. There was also a staff social room with a snooker table, dartboards and table-tennis equipment.

A notice board told of other activities — a music club, swimming, tennis and camera competitions.

Christopher Ogilvy noticed Rachel's interest.

"Are you fond of classical music?"

"Yes, very," she replied.

"There's an evening of Viennese music at the town hall next week. I have two tickets. Would you care to come?"

Rachel thanked him but said she couldn't leave her mother.

"Nonsense!" Mrs Forbes declared. "I'm sure Mrs Martin from next door would come and sit with me. Rachel, you should go with Mr Ogilvy, you don't get out enough."

When they arrived home again, Rachel turned to her mother indignantly.

"How could you? Fancy throwing me at the man like that!"

"He asked you to go with him, didn't he?" her mother protested, quite unrepentant. "I can tell he likes you and he's a bachelor, so why shouldn't you go out with him? You've never had a man friend since that John Gordon vanished when we lost our money."

John Gordon. Rachel had been sad and hurt at the time, but the memory was less painful now.

"Mother, I'm over thirty! I'm too old for your match-making!"

THE Viennese evening was followed by further invitations. A visiting opera company, a schools' orchestral festival, a flower show . . . Christopher Ogilvy seemed to have a permanent booking for any of these events at the town hall.

Rachel remarked on this one evening.

"Well, large commercial enterprises like ours are expected to support local cultural activities," he explained.

They got on very well together. In a remarkably short time they had slipped into an easy companionship and Rachel thoroughly enjoyed their outings.

But everything changed when, in early autumn, Christopher's managing director came north on a brief visit of inspection.

Christopher had to break a date. He did it very apologetically but Rachel had been looking forward to the piano recital.

"These V.I.P.s have to be entertained when they descend on us," he explained. "He's only here for three days; after that I should be free again. We could go out one evening next week, although it's getting close to balance time. We all have to be on our toes then."

"Don't bother about me if you're busy," Rachel said stiffly. "I have plenty to do; a mountain of letters to answer and a lot of sewing.''

S HE knew she was behaving badly. Her conscience pricked her
when she saw the hurt look on his face, but she was too
proud to withdraw her words.

Her mother scolded her. ''You'll lose him,'' she warned.

''I can't lose what I've never had,'' Rachel replied. ''I count for very
little in his life. I'm just someone to take to concerts.''

She shrugged.

''What else have we in common? His real life is in his work and I'm
right outside that. I don't even understand what he does. He never talks
about it to me.''

''Maybe he *can't* talk about his work — it might be too private,''
her mother suggested. ''Or perhaps he thinks you wouldn't be interested.''

The old lady smiled.

''On the other hand,'' she went on quietly, as if to herself, ''if he had
a wife or a fiancée, they could have entertained his managing director
together. Maybe that's what he really wants . . .''

''Now, Mother, don't start match-making again. A spinster of my
age, with very ordinary looks and no outstanding talents — what could
he possibly see in me?''

''You sound like Jane Eyre,'' her mother said sharply. ''Just
remember even *she* found romance!''

''Well, I don't see anything like that in store for me,'' Rachel replied
flatly.

''In the meantime,'' Mrs Forbes continued, ''his friendship is something to be treasured. Never under-rate a good friend, Rachel. I think
you should write him a note and apologise for your bad-tempered
remarks.''

''And have him think I'm running after him!'' Rachel answered. ''I
couldn't do that, Mother.''

''Well, maybe he'll call to see us soon when this balance thing is
over,'' Mrs Forbes observed hopefully.

But the weeks went by and autumn set in with its darker evenings
and changeable weather. Still he did not come.

I T was raining heavily when one day a few weeks later, the cream
car appeared outside the gate of Torridon Cottage.

Rachel hurried eagerly to open the door.

''Good morning,'' Christopher said with a slight smile. ''It's actually
your mother I came to see.''

Somewhat taken aback, Rachel showed him in.

''I've come about poor Ben Pringle,'' their visitor explained. ''He
collapsed while doing some digging — I'd warned him it was too stren-
uous for him, but you know what he's like!''

He sighed deeply.

''Anyway, he's in hospital and asking for you, Mrs Forbes. I've just
come from there.''

"I'll get ready at once. Will you get my outdoor things, Rachel?"

"May I come, too?" Rachel asked.

"Certainly," he replied gravely. "If you're quite sure you can spare the time from your letter-writing?"

"I deserved that," Rachel confessed. "I was really horrid to you after all your kindness. I was ashamed afterwards and thought you'd never want to see me again."

"That would punish *me* more than *you*," he remarked with the old twinkle in his eye.

He held out his hand and she took it. At his warm touch Rachel felt herself trembling with an unaccustomed emotion.

"Friends again?" he asked.

WHEN they reached the hospital the ward sister told them that only one visitor was allowed in at a time.

Mrs Forbes went to chat to Ben. Rachel and Christopher went out and sat in the car.

"The garden's been lonely without you," Christopher said. "You'd better come again soon. I think the weather will break any day now. It might be your last chance before spring."

"There are masses of snowdrops round the lilac tree," Rachel told him. "I used to rush out every morning to see if they were through the snow. I called them my snow-bells."

"What a delightful little girl you must have been," he remarked. "So lonely, too."

"Yes. My father and mother were completely wrapped up in each other. But I had the flowers and trees and the birds. I even made up stories about the baby fawns!"

Mrs Forbes came to join them and reported that Ben was doing well. He'd thanked her again for persuading the company to keep him on as gardener.

"He's loved the garden since he came to work for us as a lad of fifteen," she concluded.

"Well, he'll have his pension now," Christopher promised. "He can take it easy and tell others how things should be done."

The night following their hospital visit the weather broke. Gale-force winds swept over the town leaving a trail of broken slates and toppled trees.

Rachel lay awake in bed listening to the rain lashing down and the wind howling round the cottage. She thought of the old gardener in his hospital bed and hoped he was sleeping and not worrying about his beloved plants and shrubs.

She thought of Christopher, too, and how thoughtful he was about others. "A real gentleman," Ben had called him, admiring his concern for his staff. And he was so ready to show kindness to two lonely women who had lost their home through no fault of their own.

Is that how he regards Mother and me, Rachel wondered. Or do his feelings go deeper? She wished she knew . . .

Finally she dropped off to sleep to awaken to a freshly-washed world.

JUST after lunch the cream car with its driver appeared. He looked very serious.

"I'm afraid I've got bad news," he said after he'd greeted the two women.

"Not about Ben?" Mrs Forbes' voice was shaky with concern.

"No, not Ben. He's holding his own very well."

"No — it's your lilac tree, Rachel. The storm was too much for it. We've got it propped up now, but the tree surgeon I called in couldn't promise it would recover. Would you like to come and see it?" he invited.

The cherished lilac tree was a sorry sight indeed. Rachel couldn't control the tears which came to her eyes. Christopher took her cold hand in his.

"Don't cry, love," he said tenderly. "I can't bear to see you sad. We'll get a replacement."

His smile was encouraging.

"Oh, I know it won't be the same but your tree has fulfilled its destiny. It's brought us together."

Rachel gasped. Had he really called her "love"? Now the tears could not be held back but they were tears of mingled sorrow and joy.

Careless of any possible watchers, Christopher put his arm round her and led her back to the house. They climbed the staircase together and walked into the room with the fresco of baby deer.

He slid a plaque across the door so that it read *Engaged*. Then took Rachel in his arms.

"We *are* engaged, aren't we?" he said.

"What if one of your staff wants to see you?" she asked.

"Well, they might as well know sooner as later," he said with that twinkle in his eye.

"Even a middle-aged executive must have some privacy to propose to the woman he loves. Now when can we be married? Don't let's wait very long; we've so much lost time to make up!"

"But what about my mother?" Rachel queried.

"Oh, we'll find a nice house with a granny flat," he promised. "Have you any more excuses, or are you turning down my proposal?"

"Oh, Christopher," Rachel murmured from the shelter of his arms. "I never dreamed I could be so happy. Of course I'll marry you. As soon as you like!"

So Lonely Without You

E LLEN MILLAR was not usually a clock watcher, and she normally found her work enjoyable.

She had been a cashier in the Rob Roy restaurant for almost ten years now and knew all the regular customers by name; knew about their families, their work and their problems. It was part of her job, part of her life as well, she often thought, to chat to the customers and to listen when they lingered to talk after they had paid their bills.

Sometimes it was good news that they shared with her. More often than not it was a worry or anxiety which seemed to loosen even the most reticent of tongues.

Mrs Cameron, the hairdresser's assistant, for instance, who was getting up from her table and putting on her coat, had never been in the habit of talking much to Ellen. She usually sat at a corner table and read a book while she ate her lunch.

Yes, she was always civil enough, Ellen thought, just not the talkative type. Until yesterday, at least, Ellen reflected, trying to recall what she must have said in order to prompt Mrs Cameron to confide in her. There must have been something, she thought, recalling the other woman's shadowed eyes and the pinched lines around her mouth. Perhaps she'd asked if Mrs Cameron was feeling all right.

She certainly wouldn't have dreamed of asking that question today, she thought, as she returned the other woman's radiant smile as she came over to pay.

"I was just thinking," Mrs Cameron said, "that I went back to work yesterday afternoon feeling much happier. I couldn't tell any of the girls at the shop about my daughter going into hospital." She smoothed her youthful hairstyle self-consciously.

"Nobody there even knows that I am old enough to have a married daughter. Do you know I actually have two girls, and a son at college?"

"You'd never think it to look at you, Mrs Cameron," Ellen said sincerely.

"I try and keep up to date. I have to in my line of work. Grey hairs and wrinkles would look quite out of place in a beauty salon. The emphasis is on youth these days."

She paused, putting her head on one side, and smiled.

"So you can imagine what a relief it was to talk to you yesterday."

There was no hint of a question in Mrs Cameron's tone but Ellen intuitively guessed that she should say:

"Your secret is safe with me," and then almost at once, she realised she could have put it better and she added swiftly:

"It was very nice of you to tell me about your daughter — I hope you won't mind if I ask about the baby sometimes?"

"Not at all." Mrs Cameron's face beamed with pleasure. "I'll be able to tell you what he looks like tomorrow. My husband is meeting me from work and we are driving to Edinburgh this evening."

by Peggy Maitland

A FTER Mrs Cameron had gone, Ellen thought about her for a moment or two. She'd come immediately to the cash desk before sitting down to her lunch to whisper the happy news to Ellen, adding in a hasty undertone, that she hadn't told anyone else.

Well, even if she is a bit vain, Ellen thought, it seems a shame that she can't tell all her colleagues that she's just become a grandmother. Ellen's eyes flickered back to the clock.

Another hour and five minutes to go, she sighed inwardly, wishing that the time would go more quickly. She longed to put on her coat and hurry away to collect Jim at the hospital.

"Dreaming today, are you?" Mr Reynolds, another of the regulars, was smiling pleasantly as he pulled his wallet out of his pocket.

"Oh, I didn't notice you there, Mr Reynolds. Yes, I must have been dreaming."

As she picked up his bill and his money, she asked:

"Did you enjoy your lunch today?"

"Not bad, not too bad at all, thank you. At least your prices are reasonable. You know, I took my wife out to dinner last night —" He paused to pick up his change.

"Yes, I remember, you told me yesterday that it was your anniversary," Ellen said.

"Seventeenth." He nodded. "I asked my wife, what was so special about seventeen years of marriage? But she would have a night out. I wouldn't like to tell you what it cost me!"

With another headshake, he turned to go.

A GAIN Ellen's eyes flew to the clock. Her heart sank when she saw that it was still only five-past one.

Jim would be anxiously looking at the time, too. She visualised him sitting up in his hospital bed, waiting for her to bring his clothes. The suitcase was in the boot of the car.

She had thought about taking time off work while Jim was in hospital, but in the end she'd decided it wasn't necessary. Anyway, work stopped her worrying about him.

Today work was a strain. It was a real effort to ask people if they had enjoyed their meal or to agree that it was warm for the time of year, or cold for the time of year, whichever they said.

Still, as she handed elderly Mr Langlands his change, she heard herself asking:

"How did you enjoy your lunch today?"

"Dinner, lass, dinner," he corrected her in his loud strident voice.

Why, oh why hadn't she said meal?

"Lunch is for the gentry," he was telling her. "And that I'll never be. I'm a plain man."

There was a queue forming behind him but Mr Langlands seemed unaware of this. He wasn't going to stop until he had finished.

"I may be well dressed and my hands clean and I admit I've a bob or two to my name. But you know, I'm still one of the working class . . . ." He glowered at her as if daring her to say anything.

"And you eat dinner at dinner-time. I'll try to remember." Ellen struggled to be pleasant.

"Ay, you remember." He was nodding, as he made his way unsteadily towards the door.

What do you care what I remember and what I don't, Ellen was thinking resentfully. What do you really care?

She continued to sit at her place, a smile fixed on her face. She exchanged small talk, performed her duties, but all the time she seemed to be shaking inside and saying over and over again to herself, what do you care, what do any of you care how I feel. None of you think of me as a person with worries and problems of my own.

A T last, at long, long last, Mrs Pringle, the manageress, came to relieve her.

"Is your husband keeping better now?" Mrs Pringle asked.

But she wasn't looking at Ellen as she spoke. Her eyes were on the two waitresses who were standing chatting instead of clearing the tables. Her tone was casual, as if she asked the question out of duty or curiosity, rather than genuine interest.

Ellen felt her earlier resentment boiling to the surface.

"Yes, thank you," she replied in a taut, stiff voice before she turned on her heel and walked smartly away towards the cloakroom. At the same time, she sensed that Mrs Pringle, unaware of Ellen's anger, had turned her attention to the chattering waitresses.

All she cares about is running this stupid restaurant efficiently, Ellen muttered under her breath. She doesn't care, in fact, she doesn't even know that I almost lost my husband!

It was a different story ten days ago, though, she told herself as she snatched up her coat and bag. Mrs Pringle hadn't been offhand the morning that Ellen had arrived late.

In the early morning, when she had been sent home from the hospital to wait, she had been planning to stay off work. At nine o'clock she had heard that Jim had wakened from the anaesthetic, and that the operation to remove his appendix was a success.

She had been told not to come and see him until six o'clock in the evening, and the day had then stretched long and emptily ahead. So, despite all the disturbance of the night, her frantic call to the doctor followed by a journey through the darkness in the ambulance, she just knew she would not be able to sleep, not until she had seen Jim for herself.

She decided to go to work after all, to take her mind off Jim. In the end, she had arrived almost ten minutes late for work.

Breathless she had explained to Mrs Pringle that Jim had been taken ill and she apologised for being late.

"Don't mention it, Mrs Millar." Mrs Pringle had seemed as if she wanted to hug her with relief.

"I'm just so thankful to see you — I've a waitress off and we are short-handed in the kitchen, too. I'd never have managed without you! You're always so reliable — not like some of the others." She sighed.

Naturally Ellen had been pleased and flattered at the time. Now, thinking back, she realised that Mrs Pringle hadn't even bothered to ask her about Jim until today.

It wasn't really me she was pleased to see that day. I'm just a cog in a machine.

THE roads were quiet. As she drove she was looking forward to seeing Jim. It was wonderful to know that he'd be home in a while, sitting in his favourite chair at the fireside.

She'd often heard people say that their house seemed empty with one member of the family absent. She had never before experienced the sensation. Now, everywhere she looked in the house there seemed to be something tugging at her heart-strings; his empty chair, his place at the table, even the empty ashtray.

Her daughter, Lynne, had made one or two remarks about such reminders. But at sixteen, she had lots of interests outside her home and she didn't appear to be unduly upset by the fact that her father was in hospital.

Andrew, her youngest, appeared to be showing signs of stress. Ellen hadn't be able to persuade him to finish his breakfast this morning. He was serious minded and sensitive for a boy of twelve.

"He'll come all right once Dad's home." Lynne said.

Since Andrew was listening she added, "He's only worried because he's the man of the house and he wouldn't be able to defend us against burglars."

Andrew hadn't answered that. Before he went off to school, he had promised: "I'll be home early, Mum, I'll run all the way."

Lynne had looked at her mother with an I-told-you glance before she too had set off for school. She hadn't said she would hurry home. No doubt she'll be walking home with Arthur Sturrock, Ellen thought. Hand in hand, by all accounts.

As she drove into the hospital car park, Ellen thought fleetingly of her daughter again. She hoped that Lynne wasn't thinking too much about Arthur Sturrock. She was too young to be getting involved in an emotional relationship with any boy, especially when they were both still at school.

As she reached the hospital doors, suitcase in hand, she was thinking only of Jim, imagining how his face would light up when he saw her.

Castle Stalker stands on an island in Loch Leich in Argyll. It was built at the beginning of the sixteenth century by Duncan Stewart of Appin and presented to James IV as a hunting lodge. The estates fell into ruin when the family took part in the '45. After lying in ruin for two centuries the castle was eventually restored.

CASTLE STALKER : J CAMPBELL KERR

She was almost at the door of the ward, when the ward sister came along the corridor.

"Ah, Mrs Millar, can I have a word with you? We would like to keep Mr Millar for another day or two."

She paused, as she saw that Ellen's face had turned white. Putting an arm around her, she said swiftly, "Come into my room and sit down and I'll explain."

Ellen sat down gratefully in the offered chair and Sister continued:

"I'm sure he'll be getting home tomorrow but his temperature rose slightly today, so to be on the safe side, we'll just keep him in. In fact, his temperature is down just now so I can assure you there's not a thing to worry about. Just leave his clothes here then he'll be ready when you come tomorrow."

Ellen tried to hide her disappointment as she thanked the sister.

JIM was sitting in the day-room with other patients watching television. He stood up at once when she walked in. He smiled at her ruefully as they went to sit over in a corner so that their talk wouldn't disturb the others.

She held his hand tightly, unable to hide her misery after the initial smiles and hellos. He tried, rather half heartedly, to cheer her up, reminding her that one more day wasn't so very long.

Although she believed what the sister had said, and indeed it was obvious that Jim was fine, Ellen's spirits remained low. She couldn't seem to rid herself of a deep despondency.

"I'll come back and see you at the visiting time tonight," she promised, managing to smile, although her face was stiff with the effort.

As Ellen stopped the old car outside her house, she knew what she was going to do. Without stopping to take off her coat, Ellen went straight to her phone and dialled the restaurant's number. Mrs Pringle answered.

"Ellen Millar here, Mrs Pringle." Ellen's voice was crisp.

"I just wanted to let you know that I won't be able to come in tomorrow. I have to collect my husband from hospital. As you can understand he will be convalescent for a week or two, so I'm not sure exactly when I'll be back." Then there was silence except for the thumping of her heart.

Mrs Pringle sounded puzzled and anxious. "I didn't know that your husband was in hospital . . ."

"Well, I'm telling you now," Ellen answered stiffly. "As I said, he'll be convalescent . . ."

"Yes, yes of course, I realise that," Mrs Pringle interrupted swiftly. "Just you take as much time off as you need . . ."

"Thank you." Ellen had never heard her own voice sounding so icy. "I'll let you know when he's better."

Without waiting for a response, she replaced the receiver with a clatter which satisfied her mood.

It was all very well to be reliable and dependable, but she had suddenly discovered where her priorities lay. Jim was the one who needed her most.

A NDREW, true to his word, came rushing into the house like a
hurricane, his face alight with eager anticipation. Then as he saw
the empty armchair and his mother still with her coat on, sitting
in the other chair, he was suddenly deflated and pathetically
apprehensive.

"I'd better go and get changed," he said in a dismal voice.

Ellen put her hand on his arm.

"What about a glass of milk and a chocolate biscuit first? I'm going
to have a cup of tea before I start cooking . . ."

"OK." He went with her into the kitchen and flung his schoolbag
on to one chair and himself on to another.

Ellen tried to think of something cheerful to say. In her present mood
it seemed to be impossible. Then, thankfully, she noticed Andrew
reaching out to switch on his transistor radio.

She busied herself pouring out his milk and fetching the biscuit tin
before she put the kettle on to boil. Hardly realising how deeply she was
frowning, she stood at the cooker with the teapot in her hands.

She wasn't even aware of the door opening until the blare of the radio
stopped abruptly. She turned to see her daughter and Mrs Pringle in the
doorway.

"I had to come over, Ellen." Mrs Pringle clutched at her handbag
in an agitated manner. "I hope you don't mind, I don't mean to
intrude."

"I was just making a cup of tea. Will you have one?" she said.

In a daze, she heard Lynne graciously inviting the guest to sit down
and saying that she'd put out the cups and saucers.

"Andrew and I will leave you two to talk in peace," she added
meaningly.

Finally the two women were facing each other across the table.
Ellen was wondering how to begin to apologise for her behaviour.

Mrs Pringle began to talk and gently encouraged the tight-lipped
Ellen to tell her all about Jim's illness.

"It was only appendicitis," Ellen began. "Once the operation was
over, he was fine . . ."

"Still, it must have been frightening for you," Mrs Pringle said
softly.

The words and the kindly tone seemed to release Ellen's voice and
she found herself recounting all her fears of the past few days.

"And then today, he was supposed to get home. I thought the nightmare was all over, but they've decided to keep him another day."

She covered her face with her hands and wept.

"That's just what you need, Ellen. A good cry," Mrs Pringle was
saying sympathetically.

"I simply don't understand how you've remained so calm. And I'm
vexed with you for not telling me, or at least someone at the
restaurant.

"Goodness knows, we all tell you our problems, even the customers
do, so why didn't you think of returning the compliment?"

Through her muffled sobs, Ellen blurted out:

"I thought nobody cared. Usually it doesn't matter, everybody has their own worries . . . But today I just looked at everybody and wondered what you all care about me? I got so angry." She wiped her tears and blew her nose.

"Well, I care." Mrs Pringle said firmly.

"I'm so sorry." Ellen was calm now. "I don't know what came over me."

"Something was bound to give. You can only keep tense for so long," Mrs Pringle assured her.

She finished her tea and rose to go.

"Now don't worry. The cash desk won't fall down without you. Your place is here with your Jim, for as long as he needs you."

AFTER she had gone, Lynne and Andrew came back into the kitchen.

Subdued, Ellen gave them the gist of the conversation which had taken place, adding:

"It wasn't that I was being secretive. It was just that there never seemed to be a chance to tell anyone . . ."

"I knew you were being too brave, Mum," Lynne said soothingly. "It's been hard for me to live up to."

"I'm not brave," Andrew confessed, quickly. "But I knew you were pretending. I thought you were pretending Dad was better than he is. I mean, he looks really sick . . ."

Ellen gathered him into her arms.

"He doesn't today. He was watching television. You'll see for yourself when we visit him tonight."

Lynne was opening the fridge door to see what was for tea.

"I've got a date tonight," she said. "But I think I'll call it off. Arthur'll understand that family comes before friends."

Ellen nodded, smiling.

On the following afternoon Lynne and Andrew came hurrying in from school, overjoyed to find their father in his armchair smilingly waiting for them.

"We're having a coming-home party." He indicated the laden trolley which Ellen was wheeling in.

Ellen was happy. As her eyes met Jim's she was telling herself that this was a moment to treasure, this sharing of such sweet harmony.

When the doorbell rang none of them moved. None of them wanted to have their party interrupted. It rang again and Andrew rose with a shrug.

"Don't worry, Dad, I won't let anyone in to interrupt our party."

The three who were left silently looked at each other as they heard rustlings and murmured voices in the hall. Then Lynne tiptoed over to the window to look out.

"It's Mrs Pringle and another woman. They're getting back into the car . . ." she said.

Ellen put her hand up in dismay. In the same instant Andrew threw open the sitting-room door.

"Ta ra ra!" he sang out, half hidden by an enormous bouquet of flowers which he presented to his mother.

"Andrew, you should have asked them in," Ellen expostulated.

"They wouldn't come in, they said they'd come back another time," he answered. "They were only delivering this and that great big box in the hall."

Ellen went to look. Andrew and Lynne followed her and they carried the box back in.

"It's like a Christmas party! Look at all the parcels and cards too!" Andrew whooped.

The cards were for Jim, all with get-well messages.

"I can understand this one," Jim said. "It's from all the staff. But what about these? Who is Mr Langlands? And Mrs Cameron and Martha McLeod and Tom Reynolds . . . They're all sending good wishes to me and love to my wife!"

ELLEN gazed at them through a mist of tears.

"Some of my customers. Some of my good friends."

The parcels contained sweets, chocolates, fruit, biscuits and cake. Some of them weren't labelled, some were in paper bags.

Rubbing away her tears with the back of her hand, Ellen laughed.

SPARE A CRUMB . . .

MY parrot is a lordly bird. He toils not for his livelihood but his cupboard is never bare. He dines, when he pleases, from an abundant table which is freshly set each morning.

What remains of yesterday's fare is cast upon the ground outside. And there, the patient, hungry sparrows are happy to receive the crumbs from the parrot's table.

Are there not lonely, elderly folk of our acquaintance? From the abundance of our time, we spare them just the scraps of our companionship – a passing word in the street; a brief visit before we rush elsewhere.

What are they? Sparrows on the bough, waiting and hungry. Happy, like the birds to receive such crumbs of our attention.

Rev. T. R. S. Campbell.

"I'll never be able to thank them all. Fancy them missing me already!"

Jim was looking at her with a tender smile on his lips. He held out his hand to her.

"They must think a lot of you, Ellen —" he said gently "— to have taken all this trouble."

Ellen grasped his hand.

"I like all of them, too. In fact, I'm very fond of all my customers. But I'm not in any hurry to get back to them."

Her face was illuminated by a soft radiance as she looked into his eyes.

"I'll be staying right here with you, my love. You're the one I care about most of all."

Rainbow's End

by Elsie Jackson

"MY goodness! Look at this, Michael! Poor Cinderella's still washing up, and all on her own, too!"

Liz Mitchell turned round from the sink in the tiny kitchen of Springhill Community Centre. An attractive blonde girl and a dark-haired young man were standing in the doorway smiling in at her.

"I know!" Liz sighed good-naturedly. "Chief cook and bottle-washer to the Springhill Players. That's what I've become, Carol Gillespie."

"Well, it's not fair," Michael Gordon interrupted, eyes twinkling. "Carol lured you here to paint our scenery. It's definitely a case of false pretences. I should sue, Liz."

"Oh, don't do that!" Carol exclaimed, brown eyes widening in mock alarm. "I'm broke! I bought a new outfit for this photographic session I'm having next Tuesday. I'd have to flee the country if Liz sued me."

"Which would mean I'd have to find a new secretary," Michael commented. "So maybe it's not such a good idea."

"What's this about a photographic session?" A small grey-haired woman joined the pair in the doorway, obviously agog with curiosity.

Carol turned round to her, smiling.

"It could be my big chance, Mrs Menzies," she said, a little breathlessly. "A friend of Dad's suggested it. He thinks that with my face and figure, I could break into the modelling world. He's given me the address of an agent."

"How wonderful, dear!" Mrs Menzies clapped her hands.

"Do you hear that, Alex?" she called to a white-haired man out in the corridor. "We'll soon be seeing our Carol on the television."

"Very nice too!" Alex Robertson remarked, coming forward.

Then, winking across at Liz, he added: "Maybe in the meantime, though, Carol, you and Michael could come back and help to clear the stage. You've left me with all the work to do this evening."

As Michael Gordon steered the blonde girl out of the kitchen in Alex's wake, Mrs Menzies turned to Liz.

"Isn't she just beautiful?" she whispered. "So talented, too. She'll be the perfect wife for Michael!"

"Oh! But I didn't realise Carol and Michael were actually going out together!"

"Didn't you, dear?" Mrs Menzies looked surprised. "But then you haven't been with us for very long, have you?"

29

IT was another five minutes before Carol and Michael appeared, and Liz was standing waiting in the vestibule looking out at the night sky.

"Counting the stars, Liz?" Michael asked.

"I expect she's wishing, for fame and fortune." Carol laughed. "Like I do!"

Carol carried on talking as she slipped into the front passenger seat of Michael's car, and Liz, settling down in the back, listened enviously. Carol was never at a loss for conversation. She had an easy flow of chatter that seemed to cover every occasion. This evening she was fairly bubbling with excitement about her prospects in the modelling world.

It didn't seem long before they drew up at Carol's gate. The blonde girl wished her boss goodnight, then turned to Liz.

"See you in the morning on the usual bus." She smiled.

"How's art school, Liz?" Michael Gordon queried as he put the car into gear and pulled away from the kerb.

"All right, thank you. I enjoy it," Liz replied briefly.

Sitting looking at the back of Michael's curly head, Liz bit her lip in exasperation. It was always the same! She just could never find the words to talk to Michael Gordon naturally. And she wanted to so much!

She wanted to tell him that she had received a certificate of merit for a piece of sculpture last week. That she was studying the French Impressionists and loving it. But here she was, completely tongue-tied again, saying: "All right, thank you," like a well-trained little girl!

"How's the Gordon Staff Bureau doing?" she blurted out finally, as she saw the end of her street approaching.

"Oh, that's all right, too," Michael replied.

"I'm meeting the manager of the Redstone Hotel for lunch next Tuesday. If I can get his name on my books, it'll be wonderful. It's such a huge place, and they're constantly needing staff."

"Good luck, then," Liz told him, opening the car door, as they finally drew up outside her house.

LIZ switched the light on as she opened the front door . . . and found herself face-to-face with her own reflection.

What a fright she looked! There she stood in her training-shoes, her jeans frayed at the ankles, and her paint-stained shirt sticking out from beneath her brother's old anorak.

Even her short black hair looked untidy, sticking up in spikes and making her face look even rounder than usual. She also had a streak of blue paint on her right cheek.

Liz sighed as she took the anorak off and hung it on the hallstand. This always happened when she became engrossed in her work. She completely forgot about everything else.

This evening she had been working at the back of the hall for two hours, painting the opening scenery for the club's Christmas production of *The Wizard Of Oz*.

Still, she ought to have remembered to tidy herself up before the tea-break. What must the others have thought of her, she wondered.

"What's wrong with you, then?"

Liz's young brother, David, looked up from his homework with a cheeky grin, as she came into the living-room.

"Well, I just caught sight of myself in the mirror." Liz sighed and sat down cross-legged by the fire. "And I've just left Carol Gillespie. So you can draw your own conclusions."

"Carol Gillespie!" Red-haired David threw his pencil down on the table with a look of disgust.

"Honestly, Liz! You're always on about that girl. She's awful! She looks like a dressed-up doll with her dyed hair and her false eye-lashes and all that rubbish on her face."

"Oh, Davie!" Liz remonstrated. "Carol's hair isn't dyed!"

"Carol's all right," Mrs Mitchell interrupted, appearing out of the kitchen with the supper tray.

"She's just been spoiled by doting parents. She's a very attractive-looking, only child, and Myra Gillespie's convinced she's got a future Miss World on her hands."

"I seem to remember that Myra was a bit of a glamour girl herself." Liz's dad, sitting opposite her, looked up from his book.

"So she should have been!" Sheila Mitchell commented, putting the tray of cocoa mugs on the table. "She spent an absolute fortune on clothes!"

"At least we'll never accuse Liz of doing that!" David grinned, looking down at his sister's old shirt and jeans.

Seeing his sister's threatening look, David grabbed a mug of cocoa and a biscuit. Then, with an unrepentant grin, he headed for the door and went thundering upstairs. Liz followed him a minute later.

WHEN the door had closed behind the girl, Sheila Mitchell looked across at her husband.

"Am I imagining it, George?" she asked abruptly. "Or does Liz always look a bit dejected when she comes back from the Centre on Tuesday evenings?"

George Mitchell sipped at his cocoa.

"Yes. I must admit I've noticed it, too, Sheila," he said firmly.

"But on the other hand she's always full of beans every Tuesday tea-time, as though she's really looking forward to going to the drama club. So she must enjoy it."

"Well, I can't think that it's the beautiful Carol Gillespie that's making Liz look so downcast all of a sudden," Sheila said wryly. "Do you think there's a young man involved, George?"

"Now, how would I know!" George exclaimed, putting his mug on the table.

"Liz isn't exactly the forthcoming type, is she? She's always been a very private little person. Very sensitive."

"I know." Sheila Mitchell frowned. "Just the kind of lass that could be badly hurt, in fact. She's twenty, and she's never been in love yet. I could swear to that."

"What about this Sandy Dunn at the college? The lad who borrows her books and takes her to dances?" George queried.

Sheila smiled and shook her head.

"No. Liz says that Sandy's just a good friend. I believe her. There are no stars in her eyes when she talks about him."

LIZ'S room at the front of the Mitchells' semi-detached house was part studio, part bedroom.

Her father had gutted what had been a conventional bedroom and created something rather special. One of his innovations had been a padded window-seat where Liz could sit and sketch.

Tonight she crossed over to kneel on it and look out at the sparkling wintry sky.

What was it Michael had said to her in the vestibule half an hour ago? "Counting the stars, Liz?"

Suddenly the dark-haired girl gave a little groan of impatience and laid her head on her arms. It was too ridiculous!

She did this same thing every week. Wasted hours recalling every single trivial remark Michael Gordon had made to her. Remembered every glance of his that had come her way. And what good was it doing her? Absolutely none.

Michael wasn't interested in her. In fact, according to Mrs Menzies, he was all set for marrying Carol. Which was probably true, since, as well as being a super-looking girl, Carol was also a very efficient secretary. Liz had heard Michael say that several times.

Liz raised her head. Yes, these were all the hard facts. She recounted them to herself frequently, yet they just wouldn't sink in.

Liz lifted a velvet cushion from the seat and punched at it viciously with her fist. Oh, what an idiot she was! What a fool!

In fact, Liz reflected, she had been a little in love with Michael before she had even met him.

That had been Carol's doing. On their morning journeys into town Carol had often entertained Liz with stories about her young boss.

The young art student's imagination had been captured. She had asked Carol what her boss looked like.

"Oh . . . good-looking. Dark curly hair. Nice eyes. Fairly tall," Carol had replied vaguely.

Not that Liz had ever expected to meet Michael Gordon. And when, last June, she had finally agreed to paint scenery for the Springhill Players, she had forgotten that Michael had recently joined them. Carol had brought the young man over to introduce him.

"Do you have far to come?" he had asked Liz, looking at the bulky bag containing her painting materials.

She had told him that she lived in the same district as Carol.

"In that case I can pick you up and take you home along with Carol," he had told her.

Liz had barely managed to thank him. For quite unexpectedly she was overwhelmed by a positive turmoil of emotions.

Michael Gordon was having a very curious effect on her indeed.

Looking up for a moment too long into Michael's dark eyes, she'd had butterflies in her tummy, her head had begun to swim, she had felt her legs turn to cotton wool and her heart hammering in her ears. It had taken two cups of tea to restore her calm.

All the following day she had wandered round college in a warm, happy daze. During their last class of the day, her friend, Tina McEwan, had given Liz a nudge.

"That's twice Mr Smith's spoken to you, Liz, and you haven't heard him," she muttered. "What's wrong with you? Are you in love?"

"Yes. I think I am, Tina," Liz had replied dreamily.

"Do you mean it? Is it anyone I know?" Tina's eyes had widened with curiosity.

"No." Liz had chuckled. "He has short hair, is tidily dressed, and sometimes even wears a tie. You won't know him, Tina."

"Then I shouldn't think there's much hope for you, Scruff!"

Sandy Dunn, unashamedly eavesdropping behind them, leaned forward to ruffle Liz's short hair. "You stick to your own kind!" he advised.

Sandy had probably been right, Liz thought now. What did a smart, young business-man like Michael want with a scruffy-looking art student?

When Liz looked out of the kitchen window the following Tuesday morning she thought that it looked like a typical November day.

"Best take your anorak, Liz," Mrs Mitchell called from upstairs.

The Return

TO our little village today I returned,
   For many long years just for this I
   have yearned.
There are houses now, where we used
   to play,
All the trees and bushes bulldozed
   away.

But the shop at the corner is still
   standing there
But there's no Mrs Roberts, with
   greying hair;
Instead, there's a youngster in faded
   blue jeans
Selling sweets and groceries, and ice-
   creams.

Wandering on, what a joy to see
The village green, and the old oak tree
Where we danced the maypole to the
   piper's tune,
And dallied and kissed beneath the
   moon.

And walked the lanes where the
   blackberries grew,
And sat on the stile to admire the view,
And ran through the grasses in joyous
   delight,
And laughed and played from
   morning till night.

The cottage is still there, wherein I was
   born,
And the church on the hill-top, by long
   fields of corn;
And I let a few tears from my eyelids
   flow
For the carefree days of long ago.

Dorothy M. Loughran

"It looks as if it might rain later on. You'd better be prepared."

"Yes, Mum," Liz called back, picking her case up from the corner. Then, glancing at her watch, she frowned. She had misjudged her time badly this morning. She had only a few minutes to run along to the end of the street to the bus stop.

Darting into the hall, she grabbed David's old anorak from the hallstand. Her own was up in her bedroom. Then with a hasty "Goodbye, Mum!" Liz flew out of the front door and along the road to catch the eight-thirty bus.

Since Liz's was the first stop past the terminus, the bus was always half empty. This meant that she could usually keep the seat beside her for Carol, until the other girl joined the bus two stops further on.

This morning Carol was the only one at her bus stop. Liz saw several of the passengers turn their heads sharply in her direction.

She was looking very glamorous with her blonde hair beautifully styled and wearing her black fitted raincoat.

She had to manoeuvre herself carefully on to the bus in her high heels. Not only was she carrying a holdall, but she had an elegant, long red umbrella, with black fringes, hooked over her left arm.

CAROL lowered herself gracefully into the seat beside Liz and gave a sigh.

"Oh, Liz!" she exclaimed. "Do you know I've been up since six-thirty this morning preparing for my big day!"

"What's in there?" Liz asked, pointing to the holdall.

"That's what I'm going to wear," Carol told her.

"I've got to be at the studio at two. So I thought it would be easier to change in the office. I won't be away from my work so long then. I can walk round to the studio in ten minutes.

"But it's probably going to pour, so I brought my smartest umbrella."

"Are you nervous?" Liz asked.

"Oh, no! I'm never nervous," Carol assured her blithely. "Don't you remember? That's why I always got the main parts in our school plays. No nerves at all!"

Liz nodded and smiled, only half-listening as the other girl rattled on and the bus sped towards the city centre. When Carol rose to leave, though, Liz looked up.

"Good luck, Carol!" She smiled.

"Thanks, Liz." Carol beamed, lifting her holdall and tripping off down the passageway.

"See you tonight at the club," she called back.

The art college bus stop was four stops further along the route. And it was as Liz rose to get off that her foot knocked against something. Looking down, she saw to her dimay that it was Carol's long umbrella.

"Oh, no!" Liz groaned, lifting the umbrella up. She realised immediately what an absurd picture she was going to make, dressed in jeans and an old anorak, and carrying an elaborate, fashionable umbrella!

For a moment she was almost tempted to hand it in to the driver.

Then she looked out at the sky. It was bound to rain before long. And what would Carol do at lunchtime?

THE rain had started at eleven o'clock. By one-fifteen, when Liz's morning session finished, it was a steady downpour.

"Oh, no!" she groaned to Tina McEwan, as they paused to gaze from a corridor window. "I'm going to be drowned!"

"Why not forget the stupid old umbrella?" Tina suggested. "It wasn't your fault that the silly girl left it on the bus."

"No. I couldn't do that." Liz sighed. "Carol has such high hopes of these photographs. I'll just have to walk into town. That's all."

"Well, I expect the umbrella will keep you dry," Tina said consolingly. "You'll look a bit odd underneath those black fringes."

"But I can't use it!" Liz exclaimed, as they turned into the cloakroom and she lifted the red umbrella from a peg.

"It would be dripping by the time it got to Carol, and it might spoil her hair or her clothes."

It was twenty minutes later before Liz finally plodded up to the entrance of the Gordon Staff Bureau.

She had never felt so wet and bedraggled in her life. Her jeans were so wet that they looked black, and David's anorak was obviously leaking in places, for trickles of rainwater were running down her arms and down her back.

But Carol's fancy umbrella, Liz noted with relief, was still more or less dry, apart from the handle, which could easily be wiped. She drew it out from the front of David's anorak as she started up the flight of steps that led to the Gordon Bureau.

To her dismay, however, when she pushed the door open, she found the outer office empty. Glancing at her watch she saw it was almost ten minutes to two. Surely Carol hadn't left already!

"Liz! Oh, Liz! You've got my umbrella! I've been searching for it everywhere! Did I leave it on the bus? Oh, that was good of you!" Carol Gillespie suddenly burst through the cloakroom door and came running forward to greet her friend.

"I've just changed into my outfit," she added breathlessly. "How do you like it?"

"Fantastic!" murmured Liz, her grey eyes wide. Carol was wearing narrow trousers of shiny red material with a jerkin to match. Her eyes were heavily made-up and dotted with little silver stars.

"I'll have to leave right now, otherwise I would have made you coffee."

Then, looking up, she saw Liz properly for the first time.

"You poor thing! You're absolutely drenched!" she exclaimed. "I've never seen anyone so wet!

"I'm sure Michael would have run you back to college," she added as they left the office, "but he's having a business lunch with Mr Reynolds, the manager of the Redstone Hotel.

"That's all right." Liz smiled. "I'll survive. I don't melt easily. I expect I can catch a bus back to college now."

The rain was still falling steadily. Liz, partly sheltered now by the red umbrella, walked with Carol to the end of the block.

THEN, as they waited to cross at the traffic lights, she happened to glance to her right. There was a car halted just beside her. The driver was leaning slightly forward staring at the girls across the elderly man, who was his front-seat passenger.

Liz's eyes lit up. It was Michael Gordon!

She smiled and started to raise her hand in greeting. Then, quite clearly, she saw the expression on Michael's face change from one of uncertainty into shocked dismay. He jerked his head away just as Carol, too, spotted him.

"Look! There's Michael, Liz!" she exclaimed. "He could give you a lift."

Even as Carol began to signal with her umbrella, the lights changed and Michael's car moved away.

"Oh! He didn't see us! Isn't that too bad!" Carol sighed.

"Yes. Too bad," Liz repeated dully.

A few minutes later she took her leave of Carol.

"By the way, I won't be able to come to the club tonight," Liz said. "Will you tell Michael I shan't want a lift."

"Oh! What a pity! You were going to paint the 'Oz' rainbow tonight," Carol exclaimed. "I was looking forward to seeing it."

"I'll do it next week," Liz promised, as she joined the queue at her bus stop.

At least she would try, she thought bitterly. At the moment she couldn't have painted a rainbow for a fortune!

LIZ was in the living-room alone at eight o'clock that evening when the doorbell rang. Her parents were at the theatre, and David was upstairs in his room listening to records. The girl walked listlessly into the hall and opened the door.

Then she froze! Standing on the doorstep, looking embarrassed and apologetic, was Michael Gordon.

"I'm not coming to the club tonight," Liz blurted out after a moment's petrified silence.

"I know." Michael swallowed hard. "Could I speak to you for a few minutes, Liz?"

"Yes, of course. Come in."

Once in the living-room with the door closed behind them, Michael swung round to face Liz.

"I've come to apologise," he said.

"It was a despicable thing to do and I'm really ashamed of myself. It was the fact that I had Mr Reynolds with me, you see. Not that that's any excuse," he finished miserably.

"That's all right. I know I looked a fright," Liz replied tautly.

"You! Did you think *that*! Oh, heavens! That's even worse, then!"

"No! It wasn't you I was avoiding — it was Carol," Michael exclaimed, running a hand through his hair.

"You see, I'd just persuaded Mr Reynolds that I could supply him with the kind of staff he wanted." Michael sighed. "Steady. Dependable. Sensible. Those were his three basic requirements.

"Then I looked out of the car window and saw my own secretary in all that red gear, and brandishing that peculiar umbrella!"

"Oh, dear!" A smile had started to play around Liz's lips.

"On top of that I knew how excited Carol was," Michael went on. "And how she would babble away once she was in the car. So I shot off and left you both in the rain.

"Then I started to worry about what you would think of me. When Carol said you wouldn't want a lift tonight, I thought that was that!

"Only suddenly I couldn't stand it any longer. I decided to come up and try to explain . . ." The young man's voice tailed off unhappily.

"Would you like a cup of tea," Liz asked quietly after a moment. "Or have you to rush back?"

"They won't miss me for a while," Michael assured her.

Half an hour later Michael placed his empty mug on the hearth and smiled down at Liz.

"Do you realise this is the first proper conversation we've had?" he said. "This afternoon I was convinced I might as well give up hope."

"Hope of what?" Liz queried, looking up from the hearth rug.

"Of ever getting to know you properly," Michael said quietly. "For months I've been trying to pluck up courage to ask you out."

"You needed courage to ask *me* out?" Liz exclaimed incredulously.

Michael nodded and sighed.

"Let's face it. I must seem pretty dull compared with all your artistic friends. A stodgy, nine-to-five office worker like me."

"There's nothing stodgy about you, Michael. Or dull either," Liz declared emphatically. "If you'd asked me out . . ."

"Yes?" Michael's face had lit up.

But Liz's brow had clouded suddenly.

"Michael," she said hesitantly. "There's something I must know. About Carol and you. Mrs Menzies seems to think . . ."

"Mrs Menzies! Oh, Liz!" Michael laughed. "Carol's a dear girl — and an efficient secretary. But she's not really my type!"

"I'm so glad!" Liz breathed, reaching her hand out.

Michael gripped it firmly.

"From the moment I met you I've had eyes for no-one but you, Liz," he said gently. "I still don't quite know what's hit me. I've never felt like this before in my life."

"It's the same with me," Liz confessed, her grey eyes brilliant.

"I tell you what," Michael said with a smile. "Come back down to the club with me. Afterwards we'll go for a bite to eat somewhere. We can both try to count the stars."

"That sounds lovely," Liz murmured, standing up.

Then, as Michael, rising too, pulled her gently towards him, she said, "But before we count the stars, I have to paint a rainbow."

"Fine!" Michael whispered, kissing Liz gently on the lips. "When it's finished we can fly over it together."

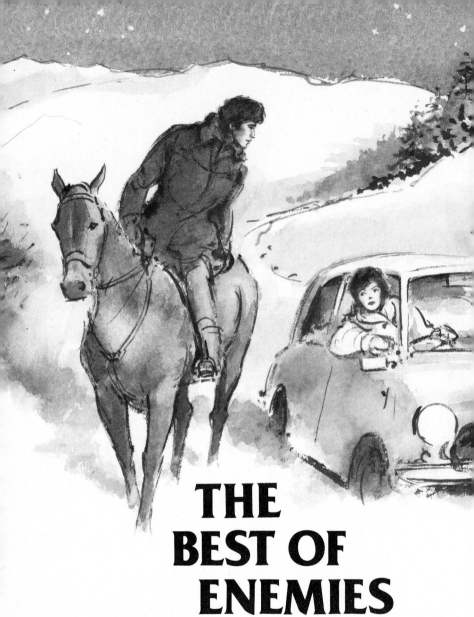

THE
BEST OF
ENEMIES

C OME on — move!"
Jen Grieve thumped the steering-wheel of the car with her fists
clenched in exasperation. Then, realising the absurdity of her outburst, she switched off the engine.

She knew there was no point trying again. Each time she revved up,
the engine whined and the wheels spun but the car would move neither
forwards nor backwards. She was stuck.

The force of the wind had lessened; she was sheltered here in this gully, between a high, rocky bank on one side and a stone dyke on the other. The snow was deeper, though, and piled up in drifts. In the beams of her headlights it was like looking down a long, white tunnel.

She switched off the headlights and sat back to consider her position.

Even if she had a shovel — which she hadn't — she knew she couldn't possibly dig the car out. To leave it and try to walk would be madness in this storm.

Besides, she wasn't too sure where she was. She'd been so busy peering into the driving snow and concentrating on keeping the car moving forward, that she was sure she'd missed the turning that would take her to Whiteburn. She could be miles from anywhere!

I'll stay put until daylight at least, she told herself. A snow-plough's bound to come along . . .

She shivered as the chill, eerie silence seeped into her.

by Margaret Cameron

It's like being in the centre of a snowball, she thought. Her nervous giggle broke the silence.

"You've got to keep warm," she said aloud, the sound of her own voice comforting her.

Should she switch on the engine again and run the car heater? Wait a minute, though! Hadn't she read somewhere that that could be dangerous if she fell asleep?

It was fortunate she had plenty of warm clothing in the car. She'd come well prepared for a stay in the draughty old manse in the dead of winter!

Her case was on the back seat. She twisted round and found her heaviest sweater, which she pulled over her head. Then she struggled into her anorak and wrapped an old rug round her legs.

She settled down to wait for morning light but that was none too easy. She was warm enough but her mind was still too active.

She should have been home in Whiteburn now, probably helping her mother with last-minute Christmas decorations. Thank goodness she had not said definitely she would be home this evening. At least her parents wouldn't be worrying about her . . .

T HE car was steaming up so she lowered her side window and looked out. The snow had stopped falling now and it was a calm, cold night with a star or two shining in the clear sky.

In the bright moonlight she thought she saw something moving on the road ahead — or where the road should be! She stared intently for a little, then decided she must have been mistaken.

Something prompted her to switch on her headlights. Instantly two eyes glared back at her out of billowing clouds of steam.

She stared, transfixed, as pictures of fire-breathing dragons came flooding into her mind. She felt fear prickle in the nape of her neck . . .

She switched out the lights and the eyes vanished. She waited and watched, and first a blurred outline and then a more well-defined shape appeared.

"It's a horse . . ." she cried aloud in relief. "It's a man on a horse!"

The approach of the horse and rider through the snow was practically soundless, almost ghostlike. As they came alongside the car, the horse blew great white clouds from its nostrils, and Jen had a momentary panicky urge to close the window.

The figure on the horse bent forward in the saddle.

"Hello," It was a deep voice. "Are you all right?"

"Yes. I haven't been here very long."

"That's good."

He slid out of the saddle, shuffled aside the snow and bent down. As she turned to look up at him, both their faces were palely lit by the glow of the interior light.

O H, it's you!"
They said it simultaneously but there was no pleased recognition in either voice. There was a long silence and the feeling between them was as icy as the night.

"As I was saying," Jen said quickly, to break the silence, "I haven't been here long . . . just long enough to get wrapped up. I'll be fine."

"I've no doubt you're fine at the moment. You might even fall asleep. But if the wind gets up again, and the snow starts drifting, both you and your car would disappear."

He stopped to allow his words to sink in.

"In that eventuality, many people would be given a great deal of hard work and worry — needlessly!"

There was another pause, then he added impersonally:

"So, to prevent all that, and for your own good, would you mind getting out of the car and coming with me?"

She stared out at him, her temper rising. Of all people, why did it have to be Archie Jardine!

But it was hard to focus one's anger on a shadowy figure.

"OK. Where am I going and how do I get there?"

"You're going to the hall at Myreton crossroads — you ought to know it. And you're going on my pony's back, sitting in front of me. The alternative is to tramp behind us."

Suddenly Jen had a desire to giggle at the whole bizarre situation. Taking a deep breath, she crushed the feeling down and answered with all the dignity she could muster.

"I prefer not to accept the alternative!"

"Right — let's get going."

Archie Jardine kicked away the snow from the door of the car and pulled it open.

"Bring the rug with you. You can leave your suitcase. No-one will be passing here tonight."

She locked the car and turned to him, waiting. He threw the rug over the pony in front of the saddle.

"Take hold of the saddle and put your left foot in my hands and I'll lift you up."

In a moment she was astride the pony and he was behind her. He reached round her and took the reins and the pony moved off back the way it had come.

"You won't be alone. There are two other people in the hall," he said over her shoulder. "A shepherd and his wife; Tim and Mary Ingram."

"How did you know I — or at least someone — was stuck here in the snow?" Curiosity had overcome her reluctance to speak to him.

"I saw your lights when I was on my way home from the hall after I'd seen Tim and Mary Ingram inside."

There was silence again as the pony plodded on through the snow. Slowly Jen relaxed, feeling safer than she had in the car. But she resolutely resisted the temptation to lean back against her rescuer.

They came round a bend and she saw the lights of the little hall, the centre of social life for the widespread community. She remembered being in it once, years ago, when her mother had been giving a toy-making demonstration to a gathering of women. Now she knew where she was — seven miles from home.

As they neared the hall, she felt Archie Jardine lean forward.

"Someone else has got here," he said almost to himself. "There's a van now."

At the hall he slid to the ground and helped her down. The door swung open and, silhouetted against the light, she saw a lanky, tousled young man.

"WELCOME, weary travellers," he said gaily and swept them a mock bow. "What guiding star brought you hither this Christmas-tide to our unworthy inn?"

Behind her Jen heard her rescuer laugh rather shortly.

"If some weary travellers would only have the sense to stay off the roads . . ." He didn't finish but what he had in mind was obvious.

A second young man, equally lanky and equally tousled, appeared behind the first.

"Nay, master, be not too harsh with us. We're but simple strolling players. Come in, and rest with us, poor company though we be!"

Jen couldn't help laughing as she followed the amusing twosome into the hall. Once inside, she saw instantly that they were identical twins.

The tanned, fit-looking young man who got up from a chair near the electric fire would be the shepherd, Tim Ingram, she decided. And the very pregnant girl beside him must be his wife.

But it was the old man, white haired and thin wearing an ancient coat, who caught her attention.

He was looking at her rescuer, like a dog with its tail down, waiting to be slapped and hoping it wouldn't be.

"Archie, I . . ."

"How did you get here?" His voice was brittle and accusing.

"Well, the boys . . . I was lucky they picked me up." His look took in the two youngsters.

"You'd no right to be on the roads at this time. You should have been here two months ago. Where have you been?"

"I know, Archie. I know and I'm sorry. I went to Ireland in the autumn — to Dublin. I wanted to go because . . ."

He stopped and didn't look at anyone. He seemed, for a moment, not to be with them.

"I didn't think it would take so long to get here," he ended lamely.

Jen looked up at Archie's face but it hadn't softened.

"Well, you can't come to Falbrae tonight. There's no place . . ."

"Yes, yes. I'm all right here, Archie. How's your mother?" His voice was ingratiating and Jen felt her resentment rise on his behalf.

"She's well. You can come tomorrow when the farm road's cleared. At the moment it's even worse than it is here."

He looked round the little group and turned to the two young men.

"Where are you from?"

"Aberdeen. We're Ron and Robin Crombie. There's no use telling you which is which! We're students, but we do some spare-time folk singing. We were on our way to sing at a concert in Whiteburn and then we were going on to Ballater and Banchory."

"Well, there won't be any concert for you tonight. The latest word I've had is that, providing there's no more snow, the plough should be here first thing in the morning. You'll just have to make the best of it till then."

GLANCING at him, Jen realised for the first time how tired he looked. Mary Ingram was apparently thinking the same thing.

"It's time you went home, Archie. You've done enough for one day. We'll be all right here. And thank your mother for the food."

"We hadn't reckoned on so many. I'm afraid you'll have to ration it."

"No, that won't be necessary," one of the Crombies said brightly. "We've got lots of stuff in the van. Always carry emergency stores!"

He grinned hugely.

"You're welcome to share tinned soup, beans, sausages, and some biscuits that have seen better days!"

"Well, with all that you should survive!"

Jen saw Archie Jardine half smile, then he said goodnight briefly and, without giving her the chance to thank him, he went off.

Jim Ingram and the Crombie twins went out to the van to bring in the food. Then they made a second trip to collect their sleeping bags, some old blankets and basic cooking utensils.

Jen sat down beside Mary Ingram. "Hello — I'm Jen Grieve."

"Yes. I recognised you. I've seen you once or twice at church in Whiteburn. Your dad conducted our wedding service."

"When's the baby due?"

Mary Ingram laughed.

"Oh, not for three weeks yet. But, today, when the storm got so bad, I panicked. Our house is very isolated and I kept thinking of us being snowed in for weeks. I made Tim get the car out to take us to Whiteburn, but we got stuck — until Archie pulled us out with the horse."

"What will you do now?"

"We'll still go into Whiteburn, even if the storm is past. I'll stay with Tim's sister."

She looked down at her rounded figure and laughed.

"I'm not risking any more storms! We were lucky the Jardines spotted us. They're very kind folk. It's not the first time they've done this sort of thing. But you'll know them?"

Jen looked away.

"Not really. I met Archie Jardine briefly a long time ago."

Even to herself her voice sounded stilted.

"He did seem, well, pretty sharp with that old man."

SHE nodded to the figure in the shabby coat who had found a newspaper and was sitting on the edge of the low stage turning over its pages.

The others had come in and had gone into the small kitchen to find out what facilities there were for heating the food.

"Archie's actually very fond of him." Mary lowered her voice, glancing at the figure by the stage.

"He saved the old man's life . . . let me see . . . well, I can't remember exactly how many years ago it is now. Archie found him by the roadside. He was ill and Archie took him up to the farm at Falbrae. The Irvines kept him over the winter until he was fit again."

"Who is he?"

"His name's Rupert Marshall. I believe he was once a very fine concert pianist and so was his wife. She died suddenly after a performance in Dublin. It was the end of his world."

She stopped for a moment, her kind eyes resting on the old man.

"He took to wandering and never played again. He comes here every winter since Archie found him, usually about the end of October, and stays in the bothy at Falbrae. He does odd jobs about the place and once the lambing's over he sets off again.

"I doubt that anyone knows where he goes after he leaves."

"I'm sure Archie was concerned about him not turning up as usual in October. That probably made him, well, as you say, a bit sharp when he found him here," Mary finished.

A FTER they'd eaten their meal, they sat talking. Rupert Marshall, who had been taking little part in the conversation, got up and wandered about aimlessly. He finally came to a halt on the small platform with the upright piano tucked away in a corner.

He stood beside it, looking down, unconscious of the silence that had fallen. He pulled out the stool, sat down and opened the piano.

He lifted his hands and began to play, tentatively, jerkily. Disappointed, he dropped his hands by his side.

Flexing his fingers, he tried again. This time they moved more and more confidently over the keys.

> *Mary had a baby, yes Lord.*
> *Mary had a baby, yes Lord.*
> *The people keep a'comin' and praisin'.*
> *Where did she born him, yes Lord.*
> *Born him in a manger . . .*

The boys had reached for their guitars and were strumming with him. The hall was full of the soft song.

When they reached the end, he put down the lid of the piano and smiled softly to himself.

"It's a long time since I played," he said apologetically, turning to his audience.

There seemed little more to say after that. They settled down to try to get some sleep and wait for the morning light.

Jen, through half-shut eyes, saw Mary Ingram asleep with her husband's arm about her. The twins were relaxed and snoring softly in their sleeping bags.

Rupert Marshall was wrapped in a blanket, his grey head slumped forward in sleep, his lined face almost saintly in the pale light of the one bulb they had left burning.

S HE wished she could sleep and forget it had been Archie Jardine who'd rescued her. Since he'd spoken so sharply to the old man she'd disliked him even more than ever!

Their first meeting was still crystal clear in her memory. It had been in the summer when she and her father and mother had come from Australia to Whiteburn.

She had been born in Australia, her parents having emigrated shortly after they'd been married. In many ways they had loved the life there but, deep down, her father hankered to minister to his own folk in his native Scotland. It was this which had finally brought them back to Whiteburn.

She hadn't wanted to come to Scotland and that first summer had been one of deep unhappiness. She missed all her friends, the sea, the sun, the great feeling of width and space and the eager throb of a young, exciting country. Though she hid her unhappiness, she made no secret of her intention to return to Australia as soon as she could.

One day she had walked along the bank of the little stream that gave Whiteburn its name. A few miles into the hills, it met another stream and formed a deep, quiet pool sunk between heather and rocks. She sat down to rest. Idly she began throwing pebbles into the pool as she tried to work out how many years it would be before she had saved enough to pay her fare back to Australia.

Her hand was poised to throw another pebble when she sensed she wasn't alone. She turned her head and the young man standing between her and the sun loomed tall and forbidding.

FOR a moment they gazed at each other, then, turning away from him, she lobbed the stone in her hand into the centre of the pool.

"Do you have to do that?" His voice was challenging. "You're spoiling the fishing."

She got up slowly and looked straight into the deep-set, blue eyes. She said nothing because, in her surging anger and resentment, she could think of nothing to say. She walked straight past him.

She said nothing to her parents about the meeting. Somehow it had got mixed up with her homesickness and that was something she didn't want them to know about.

Next day was Sunday. After the service she met the stranger as they were leaving the church. He moved towards her, plainly wanting to speak, but she looked through him and walked on.

In the seven years since then they had met only once, on the pavement of the main street in Whiteburn. He'd glanced at her without a flicker of recognition and walked straight past her.

After a careless question or two at home, she'd discovered his name was Archie Jardine. Since the death of his father, a year earlier, he and his mother were jointly running the extensive hill farm at Falbrae.

The snow-plough came with daylight. The menfolk soon got all the cars running, bringing Jen's to the hall door for her.

They were ready to go when Archie Jardine's mother arrived with the pony harnessed to a high-wheeled dog-cart. She laughed when she saw the boys' interest in her choice of transport.

"It's kept specially for occasions like this," she told them.

She turned to Rupert Marshall. "Archie was to try to come down with a tractor for you but he's out looking for some sheep. Get whatever you have and we'll go. It's too cold to hang around."

They thanked her and said goodbye to each other before they all went on their separate ways.

IT was three days since Jen had arrived home. Her mother was entirely engrossed in her annual frenzy of soft-toy making. Where all the toys went Jen had never been quite sure!

Standing by the window, she was trying to make up her mind to go out for a walk. Whiteburn had escaped the worst of the storm and there was only enough snow lying to give it a Christmas-card appearance.

She wondered if the road past Falbrae had been cleared. The snow-plough men had said they would probably go that way after the main road had been opened. Had Archie Jardine found his lost sheep and was Rupert Marshall comfortably settled in his bothy for the winter?

She shook away her thoughts and turned from the window.

"Jen, why are you so fidgety?" her mother called to her. "You've been back and forwards to that window I don't know how often."

Jen laughed and came across the room to kiss her mother.

"Sorry, Mum, I'm a sore trial to you. If you'd only let me help . . ."

"My dear Jennifer, you may be Edinburgh's most expert computer programmer — or whatever it is you do with these things — but you've never been able to put two decent stitches together!

"If you really want something to do you could tidy up a bit."

"Where shall I start?"

Jen laughed as she looked round at the confusion of material, stuffing, buttons, paper patterns and completed toys that littered the small room.

Her mother stopped sewing for a moment and followed her glance.

"H'mm. Just leave it. At least I know where to find things!

"I'll tell you what you can do. I'm running out of this brown nylon thread so you could walk to Alice Kerr's and get two reels. She knows what I use. Now, let me see, I'll have to do something with this giraffe's neck . . ."

Jen had bought the thread and was on her way home along White-burn's main street. It widened out into what had been a spacious market place and was now planted with trees and bushes. It's really most attractive, she thought, with its backcloth of snow-topped mountains . . .

H ELLO there! If it isn't our Jennifer!"

She swung round to find the Crombie twins bearing down on her, obviously having been in the baker's shop. She hadn't recognised their van parked by the edge of the pavement.

"Hello, it's nice to see you."

"Guess what. We've just seen your white knight!"

"My what?"

"Your Galahad, or is it Lancelot? The chap who rescued you!"

"You mean Mr Jardine?"

"None other . . . Archie Jardine."

"I see."

"No you don't. He's in hospital with a broken leg and a gorgeous black keeker!"

Inverness, long acknowledged as the "capital of the Highlands," takes its name from the River Ness — "Inver" being the Gaelic for river mouth. It grew up on the level plain at the best crossing point of the short river that flows out of Loch Ness at the northern end of the Great Glen of Scotland. Founded for strategic reasons, it was well placed for further development and is now the shopping, administrative and tourist centre for a wide area.

INVERNESS : J CAMPBELL KERR

She looked from one to the other, wondering which was which and if they were pulling her leg.

"Wouldn't it be simpler if you just told me what happened?"

"Well, we'd promised that after one concert here we'd sing for the patients in Whiteburn Hospital," Ron said — or was it Robin? "That's just what we've been doing. And . . ."

"— and now they're all demanding strong pick-me-ups!" his brother interrupted.

"And who should we see but Archie Jardine waving a plastercast at us and leering out of his one good eye."

"Fell off a tractor apparently. He must have been celebrating too soon!"

"No, that's not right! He was let down by his wellies. They were caked with snow and he slipped getting up on the tractor and down he came . . . yroomph!"

They had scrambled into their van while they'd been chattering on and now the side window was wound down. Like a pair of animated golliwogs, they grinned out at her.

"He's taken a tumble for you, too!"

JEN walked on home, her mind full of what they had told her. Her mother was still busy sewing when she went in. She knew she was only half listening when she told her about her meeting with the Crombie twins and Archie Jardine's accident.

"That was the nice young man who helped you in the snow. Well, you'd better go and see him or send him a 'Get Well' card or something. Now this stuff would be perfect for a zebra . . ."

Jen wasn't listening to her mother. She was looking at a bear; a beautiful white polar bear with big, black, sad eyes.

She picked it up without her mother noticing and walked to the door.

At the hospital she found no problem in getting in to see Mr Jardine. In such a small place, visiting times were kept flexible, especially so near Christmas.

When she stopped by his bed he put down the book he was reading and for a long moment they simply looked into each other's eyes. She went forward and sat down.

"I didn't have a chance to thank you the other day. Then I met the Crombie boys to-day and they told me you'd had an accident."

"I can imagine their lurid description!"

"They told me about your keeker!"

She reached into her bag and took out the sad, black-eyed bear and handed it to him.

He held it in two hands and then looked over it at her.

It was too much for her. She started to laugh and, in an instant, he was laughing with her.

"Oh," she said at length. "I'm sorry, but you . . . you . . ."

He touched her hand and smiled at her. "Please go on laughing. It's better than the cold war! And it really makes such a difference . . ."

They grinned stupidly at each other over the polar bear.

A Lesson In Caring

by
Elspeth Rae

"COME on, Debbie!"

"Don't keep the poor boy hanging about!"

Debbie Stewart, clearing the last invoice from her desk, grinned as her workmates' comments came sailing upstairs.

When Debbie finally ran upstairs and out into the June sunshine, it was to find Rory, scarlet faced, standing by the warehouse entrance.

"Honestly! Those girls are dreadful!" he exclaimed.

"They're a great bunch!" Debbie retorted, blue eyes smiling up at Rory. "You know, this is the third summer vacation I've worked here. I'm really going to miss this place when I'm not a student any longer."

"Well, I can't say I'll miss the grill-room!" Rory sighed, as the couple started off through the teatime crowds. "I thought I'd melt in there today. I don't think I'll ever want to eat beefburgers again!"

"Never mind, love!" Debbie gripped Rory's hand as they ran to cross the road. "Mum's making a meat loaf for tea," she told him, "with fruit flan to follow. And if you don't feel like playing tennis afterwards, we can just relax in the garden.''

"No, I think we'd better keep busy, Deb.''

Debbie nodded.

"I know. Whenever I think about tomorrow lunchtime I get butterflies. I'm sure my legs will collapse when I walk over to that Examination Results Board.''

R EALLY! I don't know why the pair of you are so long faced!'' Jean Stewart shook her head, as she brought the supper tray out to the patio at ten o'clock that evening.

"Mum!'' Debbie protested, as she drew up another chair for her mother. "Don't you realise how important these results are to us? If we get low grades I won't have a chance of this job in the university library — and Rory won't be able to stay on to take his Ph.D. degree!''

"I know all that, young lady!'' Mrs Stewart retorted, handing round mugs of tea. "But you've both worked hard and you've had good reports from your tutors all year, so you should have nothing to worry about. Now, if it were poor Kenneth Hunter . . .''

"Perhaps it's as well he's not going to be with us tomorrow,'' Debbie mused. "I'd hate to see him disappointed.''

"Why won't he be there?'' Rory queried, looking puzzled.

"Because he's spending the summer in Argyllshire, on his grandfather's farm,'' Debbie explained. "He's going to have to phone home to find out about his results.''

"I see!'' Rory's lips tightened into a hard, little smile. "Lucky old Kenneth!'' he said. "There he is enjoying a country holiday while the rest of us are working. It must be great to be well off.''

"Oh, Rory! Ken's *working* on the farm!'' Debbie laughed. "I'm sure you were there when he told me about it.''

The young man gave a non-committal grunt, then suddenly glanced down at his watch.

"Oh, dear! Time to go!'' he exclaimed. "I don't want to miss my last bus or Grandpa will start worrying.''

There was a moment of silence after Rory's departure. Then Jean Stewart looked across at her daughter.

"Rory's a good lad,'' she remarked quietly. "And I'm very fond of him. But . . .''

"I know, Mum!'' Debbie's blue eyes were troubled. "You're fond of Kenneth, too, And Rory never has a good word to say for him.''

"Why is that?'' Mrs Stewart was anxious. "Have they quarrelled?''

Debbie looked thoughtful. "Not that I know of.''

"Perhaps part of it is the fact that Kenneth's family are well off and Rory's always have to count every penny,'' she said at last.

"But you think there's more to it than that?'' her mother probed.

"Yes.'' Debbie sighed. "I think Kenneth's muddle-headedness irritates Rory. Rory's so efficient and hard working himself. He reckons Kenneth's just a big, spoiled child, who's wasting everyone's time.''

"But you don't?" Mrs Stewart smiled gently at her daughter.
"No," Debbie said gently.

L ONG after her mother had gone to bed, Debbie was wide awake.
She couldn't help thinking about the next day.

What her mother had said was true. She had worked conscientiously at her studies, and her tutors had been pleased with her. Still, one could never count one's chickens where exams were concerned.

Rory would be all right. Debbie was sure of that. He was a brilliant lad and very hard working. He would probably be awarded a first-class pass, and then he'd stay on at university to take his Ph.D.

Debbie's mind drifted back to her first meeting with the dark-haired, young man. It had been two years ago in the second-hand bookshop which was used by most of the students. Their hands had reached out for the same book — the only copy left in the shop.

"I'll toss you for it." Debbie had smiled.

When she had lost the toss, Rory had said, "I must treat you to a coffee, then. Come on!"

That had been the beginning of a friendship which had rapidly developed into a romance. During the rest of the vacation, they had met every week, and by October, when they had found themselves in the same small history group, they had been inseparable companions.

That was when Debbie had first become aware of Rory's single mindedness. He would allow nothing, not even their friendship, to interfere with his work. Slowly, though, she had begun to understand the reason behind his ambition.

Rory had no parents. They had been killed in a car crash when he was three years old. He and his elder sister had been brought up by their widower grandfather.

"Grandpa's never had much faith in further education," Rory had once told Debbie. "It was the headmaster of my school who more or less bullied him into allowing me to go to university. So I really have to prove to him that it was worth while."

D EBBIE had to chuckle now, as her thoughts switched to her other friend. For there could be no-one more different from Rory than Kenneth Hunter. Ken had come into her life last year. Though she had known of him beforehand, of course!

He would have been hard to miss. All six feet two inches of him, with that thatch of flaming red hair! And he always seemed to be getting into trouble with the university authorities!

That was how Debbie had first spoken to him. After the big lad had missed five class tutorials in a row she had hunted him out.

"Dr Watts is furious," she had told him. "You'd better show up next week, my lad, or you'll be out!"

To Debbie's surprise, Kenneth had taken her advice. And from then on she had found herself with a new and very likeable responsibility.

He had never wanted to come to university in the first place, he soon confided in Debbie. It had been his mother who had insisted upon it.

"Her family have been farmers for generations," he explained to Debbie. "She was different. She loved books, but she still had to work on the farm till she married, so she's determined I'll have my chance and end up a teacher."

"And what do you really want to do, Ken?" Debbie had asked.

"What do you think!" Kenneth had retorted, running an exasperated hand through his red hair. "I want to be a farmer!"

"And what does your dad say?" Debbie had asked gently.

"Whatever my mother says!" Kenneth had declared. "She can talk Dad into anything."

Kenneth, Debbie soon discovered, went from one crisis to another; a girlfriend broke his heart, he couldn't finish an essay on time, a lecturer was after his blood.

In recent months, though, his problems had been solely concerned with his work. With the final examinations approaching, Ken had begun to panic. He had haunted Debbie, appearing at the Stewarts' in the evening with his notebooks.

"Can I work along with you?" he would ask. "I think it helps."

"Only if you promise not to talk," Debbie had told him.

In April, Kenneth had gone off in his car for a few days, and had come back looking relaxed and weatherbeaten. He had found accommodation in a quiet cottage near Loch Lomond with a kindly, elderly landlady called Mrs McFadzean.

"She's a gem!" he had told Debbie. "I really got on well with her. She's someone I can talk to properly."

"But that won't get you through your finals, Ken!"

"What will?" the lad had asked harshly.

A FIRST, Rory! You've got your First!" Debbie flung her arms around her boyfriend's neck, as they pushed their way through the excited group in front of the Examination Results Board.

"And you've got a jolly good Second!" Rory declared, kissing the blonde girl exuberantly. "Well, done, love!"

But as Rory turned away laughingly to receive the congratulations of his friends, Debbie was still anxiously scanning the list of names.

"Rory!" she exclaimed, tugging at her boyfriend's sleeve. "I can't see Kenneth's name anywhere! They must have missed it out."

"Funny!" Rory frowned, as he too scrutinised the list. "Do you think I should tell them at the office?" he asked.

"Yes, I think you should, Rory!" Debbie urged. "Kenneth's mother's coming up to find out his result. She'll wonder what's happened if she can't find his name."

Rory vanished, to re-appear a few minutes later with a straight, set face. He took Debbie by the arm and drew her aside.

"There's no mistake, Deb," he murmured. "They haven't awarded Kenneth any degree at all. He's failed completely."

"Oh, no!" Debbie's face crinkled in disbelief.

"After four years' study! I didn't think they ever did that!" she said, looking straight at Rory.

"They don't very often," Rory replied grimly. "His papers must have been really poor."

"Oh, how awful!" Debbie's eyes suddenly filled with tears. "Poor Ken!" she whispered. "Whatever will he do, Rory?"

"I don't know." Rory tucked Debbie's arm into his, and looked down at her anxiously as they set off across the quadrangle.

Then, as they passed through the wide gateway, he said abruptly, "We mustn't let it spoil things for us, Deb. We have something to celebrate — and we worked hard for our degrees. I think we deserve to be happy."

"Of course we do!" Debbie agreed, blinking hard. "Did you want to do something special, love?" she added, smiling apologetically.

"How about dinner on Saturday evening?" Rory suggested.

"Sounds fine," Debbie replied rather uncertainly, "but won't it be expensive, Rory?"

"I've been saving up for it," Rory confessed, with a grin. "I'd an idea I might need a small nest-egg this weekend."

Debbie put her arm round the tall, young man and gave him an affectionate squeeze.

"It'll be lovely!" she declared. "An evening we can remember all our lives, Rory. I'll look forward to it."

"Good." Rory kissed the top of Debbie's head. "I'd best be off home now to tell Grandpa the good news," he added with a smile.

FOUR CREATURES

*H*AVE *you ever seen the four evangelists depicted in stained glass?*

Matthew is attended by the angel of inspiration, Mark by a winged lion, Luke by a calf and John by an eagle.

From early days each gospel has its distinguishing device.

For Matthew, the face of a man – denoting the Incarnation;

For Mark, the lion – proclaiming the royalty of Christ;

For Luke, the calf – signifying His sacrifice;

For John, the eagle – representing the Holy Spirit.

Where did they come from?

They were probably from the four creatures mentioned in Revelation. The first was like a lion, the second like a calf, while the third had the face of a man, and the fourth was like a flying eagle. Rev. T. R. S. Campbell.

"And I'll phone Mum before I go back to the office," Debbie told him. "They'll all be so happy!"

Yet even as she hurried off in search of a phone-box, the thought of Kenneth Hunter's failure returned to the young woman, and her blue eyes clouded. How on earth, she wondered, would the big, red-headed lad cope with such a blow!

Debbie was to receive her answer on Friday evening when she arrived home from work. Her mother came to meet her in the hallway.

"Debbie, love!" she exclaimed. "I've had Kenneth Hunter's mother on the phone for almost an hour this afternoon. She's distracted."

"Why? Whatever's happened?" Debbie's blue eyes widened.

"Kenneth's disappeared," Mrs Stewart replied. "He shot off in his car on Wednesday evening after he'd phoned home and found out his result."

"Oh, no!" Debbie walked slowly into the kitchen and sat down heavily on a stool. "It's just the sort of thing the great idiot would do!"

The girl sympathised deeply for her friend. "Oh it wasn't fair, Mum!" she burst out. "Kenneth should never have been made to go to university in the first place. It just wasn't his scene!"

Jean Stewart nodded.

"I know, dear, but I daresay his mother thought she was doing her best for him. As it is, all the poor woman wants now is to know that Kenneth's safe and sound. She wondered if you would have any idea of his whereabouts."

Debbie shook her head despairingly. Then suddenly she sat up straight.

"Perhaps I do, though!" she exclaimed softly. "Remember that cottage near Loch Lomond where Kenneth stayed in April? With Mrs McFadzean? That might be just where he'd run . . . Only I think I'd better go up there myself, Mum, before I contact the Hunters," she added. "I don't want to raise any false hopes."

"No. And I've an idea you think you can handle that mixed-up young man a lot better on your own!" Jean Stewart reflected shrewdly.

"Then I'll go down there tomorrow," the young woman said briskly. "I'm working in the morning, but I can set off after lunch."

Mrs Stewart was frowning.

"But haven't you and Rory something planned for tomorrow evening?" she queried. "Your celebration dinner? Will you be home in time, Deb?"

"No, I shouldn't think so," Debbie replied, as she crossed to open the back door. "We'll have to postpone it."

"Do you think he'll understand?" Mrs Stewart asked doubtfully.

"Of course he will, Mum!" Debbie exclaimed.

I N fact, Rory McLean had not understood — far from it! So that the following afternoon, as Debbie drove carefully through the city's western suburbs, she was still smarting from the previous evening's encounter.

For, when she had told him of her plan to look for Kenneth, Debbie had seen a side of Rory that she had never before suspected.

"So Kenneth Hunter's run off!" Rory had exclaimed, pacing to the Stewarts' sitting-room window. "I can't see what business it is of yours, Deb!"

"How can you be so heartless, Rory!" Debbie had exploded. "Kenneth's my friend. He must be feeling absolutely wretched at the moment. If I can find him, I might be able to help."

"Well, I must say Kenneth's helpless little boy act certainly pays off where you're concerned, anyway!" Rory had commented acidly.

"And just what does that mean, Rory?"

"Well, he certainly saw you a lot more than I did during the weeks before the exams!" Rory had exclaimed. "And now, just when I've planned a special evening for us, you throw it all back in my face!"

"I'm only asking you to postpone our evening out, Rory," Debbie had protested, tight-lipped.

"And I don't see why I should!" Rory's eyes had been angry. "You'll have to choose between your lame duck and me, Deb."

"In that case I'll have to choose Kenneth!" Debbie had blazed out. "I thought I loved you, Rory. I really did. But I don't think you need my kind of love."

Her anger had heightened.

"You're too self-sufficient. And you're rather complacent, too, I'm afraid. It's a pleasant change to realise that someone needs me occasionally. Is there anything wrong with that?"

Her answer had been the slamming of the front door as Rory had swung out and off down the garden path.

NOW, although her tears had dried up long since, Debbie still felt upset. She put her foot on the accelerator as she left the heavy city traffic behind her.

Once through Balloch, Debbie drove more slowly. Kenneth had given her a detailed description of the cottage he had "found" in April and of how he had arrived there.

Sure enough, it wasn't long before Debbie spotted the turning Kenneth had taken. Fifteen minutes later, she was pulling up in front of Mrs McFadzean's cottage.

A small, grey-haired woman was pegging up towels just outside the kitchen door and Debbie hurried up towards her.

"I'm looking for Kenneth Hunter. My name's Debbie Stewart."

The small woman's apple-face creased into a welcoming smile. "I've heard about you," she said. Then she nodded to the hill at the back of the cottage. "Ken's up there," she informed Debbie. "He's going home this evening. So he's decided to chop some sticks for me before he leaves. Run away up and find him."

Kenneth Hunter, however, had already spotted Debbie arriving. And as she started up the slope he came loping down to meet her.

"What on earth are you doing here!" he exclaimed, his face wreathed in smiles. "How did you find me?"

"It wasn't too hard," she said gently. "Oh, Ken!" she went on after a moment, "I've been so worried about you — and here you are, looking as though you haven't a care in the world!"

"That's Mrs McFadzean's doing," the young man said quietly. "I was in a real old state when I got here, Deb. But Mrs Mac has four sons and seven grandsons. She's had a lot of experience in helping young folk with their problems."

"So what are you going to do, Ken?"

But Kenneth nodded down towards the cottage.

"Mrs Mac's waving." He smiled. "That means she's put the kettle on. Come on, Deb! I'll tell you my plans over tea."

TEN minutes later, sitting in Mrs McFadzean's bright little front room, Debbie gazed down at the sunlit loch. Kenneth was explaining what he intended to do.

Of course he regretted his failure bitterly. Who wouldn't? Four lost years, after all! But that had to be put behind him now. He must go home and face the music. He'd phoned his parents that afternoon, to say he was on his way.

Then he was going to start on his true career — on the farm with his grandfather, who was only too anxious to have him as a partner.

"I should have stuck out for that right from the start," Kenneth said quietly. "That was my real mistake, Deb."

Debbie nodded, as she silently poured out two more cups of tea.

"And now," Kenneth suddenly exclaimed, "let me congratulate you. Miss Debbie Stewart! My mother told me your result, when I phoned. But what about Rory?" he asked anxiously. "Did he get his First?"

Debbie smiled faintly. "Oh, yes, Rory got his First."

THAT'S terrific! It really is!" Kenneth was fairly beaming. "He had such a lean time of it, when he was a youngster, Deb," he added quietly. "I expect he's told you, though."

"Not much," Debbie replied. "I don't think he enjoys remembering his childhood."

"No." Kenneth sighed reflectively. "It wasn't that he was kept in rags or anything," he added after a moment, "but Rory McLean was a brilliant scholar from the start. He loved his lessons, and he spent every spare moment reading."

Kenneth spoke softly as the memories came back.

"Neither his grandfather nor his elder sister understood that. They thought that when Rory sat down to read he was being lazy."

"Go on, Ken!" Debbie's eyes were suddenly very bright.

"We once had a sale at school," Kenneth continued. "And Rory's grandfather made him put all his books into it. He had a fine collection, too — mysteries, adventure stories, travel books. I always had plenty of pocket money."

The red-haired lad raised apologetic eyes to Debbie.

"And you don't have many finer feelings at twelve years old. I bought nearly all those books, a whole sackful, in fact. Just as I was leaving the stall, I looked up and found Rory watching me — or rather my sack. He looked absolutely sick, poor lad."

"Poor lad!" Debbie repeated shakily.

"But never mind!" Kenneth reached across the table and gripped Debbie's hand. "Rory has it all now." The tall lad grinned. "He has his First, his university career, *and* the prettiest girl in the class. Everything he needs!"

"Except that he doesn't need me," Debbie said quietly. "Or anyone. It's probably a result of his upbringing, but he's totally self-sufficient."

"What rubbish!" Kenneth stared incredulously at Debbie across the table. "Do you know," he went on more quietly, "I used to watch him every time I was in the reading-room. It was fascinating."

He grinned warmly.

"Rory could never relax until you were there beside him. He'd try to concentrate, but his eye would always wander to the door. Then he would look at his watch. Finally you'd appear, and he'd be able to get down to his work, as though he were complete. I never think Rory looks complete, unless you're by his side," he finished matter-of-factly.

"Oh, Ken, maybe you're not the academic type," she whispered, as she rose from the table, "but you know a good deal more about human nature than some of us bookworms."

H E'S gone to the park."
Rory's grandfather smiled when Debbie rang the doorbell at half past seven that evening.

"He's pretty down in the mouth for some reason. Maybe you'll cheer him up."

And Rory did indeed look dejected, Debbie thought, when she spotted him sitting on a bench beside the tennis court. His hands were thrust into his jacket pockets and his shoulders hunched.

"Hello there!" she gasped, collapsing breathless on to the seat beside him.

"Debbie!" Rory looked as though he couldn't believe his eyes. "Did you find Kenneth?" he asked after a moment. "Is he all right?"

"Yes, he's OK," Debbie whispered. "On the right lines at last, I think. He's going to be a farmer. By the way, he sends you his congratulations," she added hesitantly.

"That's just like Ken," he said wryly. "He's a real decent sort. I've always liked him, you know. Until . . ."

"Until when, Rory?" Debbie probed softly. Rory stood up, then turned to face Debbie.

"Until I suddenly thought he was going to take you away from me," Rory said, carefully plucking a rose from a bush. "I could see it happening — and I even knew why it was happening."

Rory groaned.

"Ken needed you, and you couldn't help but respond. The absurd part of it was that I needed you just as much, but somehow I just couldn't tell you . . ."

"And I couldn't see it," Debbie confessed. "But Kenneth saw it, Rory, and he told me . . . this afternoon."

"And we're supposed to be the clever ones! Good old Ken!" Rory smiled broadly and presented Debbie with the slightly-opened bloom.

"We should ask him to be your best man," Debbie murmured after a moment, her eyes soft and dreaming.

"Do you know," Rory said, bending to kiss her on the cheek, "I should think that's the most unromantic proposal a man's ever had. Shall I show you how to do it properly?"

"Please," Debbie giggled.

"Debbie, I love you," Rory whispered. "Will you marry me?"

"Most certainly," Debbie replied softly.

For Better... For Worse...

by Helen Daviot

PENNY CAMPBELL frowned as she heard the raised voices from the house next door.

"There they go again," she said, sounding more worried than annoyed. "Len, isn't there something we could do?"

Her husband looked at her over the rim of his spectacles.

"There's nothing anyone can do, except keep their noses out of other people's business," he warned, smiling to show that he didn't really believe she would interfere.

"But we've been friends, for so long . . ." she protested. "It seems wrong to sit by and let their marriage break up."

"Nay, love! It's a long way from that."

"But they row so much. They're tearing themselves to pieces — and all because they love each other."

Len got to his feet and came to stand by her, his hand on her shoulder.

"Don't fret yourself. Didn't we have our troubles when the bairns were small?"

"It's not just that. Anyway, Johnnie and Christine aren't babies anymore.

"I think that's partly the trouble. If Johnnie was younger; too young to understand his father's trouble, perhaps he'd just accept the fact that he can't see."

Len nodded, his face sober.

"You're probably right, but I can't honestly see what

we can do about it. People have got to sort themselves out."

Penny went back to her knitting, unconvinced. If Len was so sure he was right, why did he find it necessary to spend so much time in the greenhouse in the back garden? He only does that when he's troubled about something, she thought. Just as I knit . . .

NEXT day, Len returned home in the afternoon to find Penny banging around in the kitchen. A sure sign that she was upset.

"I'll say I'm sorry now, shall I?" he cried, hoping to jolly her out of her temper. "Then we can forget all about it!"

Penny turned from stacking the pans on to the pan-rack.

"Haven't I enough to worry about without you making silly remarks?" she snapped, then her expression softened as she saw his hurt look.

"I'm sorry, my dear. It's nothing you've done, or not done," she apologised. "It's just those two next door."

"What's happened now?" Len sighed.

"Well, you remember Pat was going out and I said I'd check the casserole she'd left in the oven was all right?"

Len nodded.

"Well, Brian got back a bit early and . . . and . . . Oh, Len! It was awful!

"His face went sort of tight, when he heard me, and he asked what I was doing there. Me! I've been giving Pat a hand as long as we've been neighbours."

"That doesn't sound like Brian. I've always found him easy going."

"I know. That's what was so horrible. He's different, Len; not at all the man he was before the accident."

"Well, I suppose that's understandable, love. A fellow can't lose his sight and not be affected."

"But he wasn't like that when it happened," Penny protested. "It's only since he came back from that training place!"

"They've made him so independent he can't bear anyone to give him a hand. He thinks Pat's trying to turn him into a baby!

"And poor, little Johnnie — he was just trying to be helpful, pouring his dad a cup of tea. Brian nearly bit his head off."

Penny's voice broke and she sat down on the kitchen stool.

"It's all so . . . so useless; so unneccessary. Pat just wants to help him. We all do."

"Happen that's the trouble," Len said quietly.

PENNY'S mind went back over what had happened next door. Once she'd explained why she was there, Brian had calmed down. With a muttered apology he'd gone through to the living-room and sat down by the fire. Penny followed him and stood by the door.

"The kids wouldn't have touched the stove," he said. "They're not babies. I'm the only baby around here — or so some people seem to think!"

He fell silent, turning towards the warmth of the fire.

"You can never be sure what children will do," Penny ventured, desperate to comfort him. "Mine were always up to something.

"Pat's so careful, so conscientious, and she knows I never mind popping in. She's only gone down to the shops," she explained. "Something she forgot."

Brian turned towards her.

"Ay, something she forgot. Why couldn't she have asked me to pick it up? She knows I pass the shops; it wouldn't have taken me a minute."

"Well, I suppose she . . ." Penny floundered, trying to rescue herself.

"You're a good friend, Mrs Campbell." Brian sighed.

*   *   *   *   *

"Of course, I knew what he was getting at," Penny told her husband now. "Pat went for the shopping herself because she didn't want him wandering around so near the main road. And she asked me to be in so he wouldn't have to light the gas under the kettle."

Len nodded.

"I suppose it's hard on a chap not to be able to do all the things he used to."

"But he can!" Penny said eagerly. "He can manage a treat. I was amazed at the way he gets around the house, almost as if he can see.

"He even goes to work by himself, and Pat says the job he's got takes a lot of doing; many a sighted man wouldn't be able to do it! It's wonderful what blind people can learn nowadays."

"A minute ago you were condemning the school he went to."

"Oh, Len, I'm so mixed up. I don't know what to make of it.

"If you could have seen the way Pat looked when she came in and saw Brian sitting there. And the way he spoke, telling her he hadn't needed me to brew him a cup of tea . . .

"I was in the kitchen then. Young Christine had come in with a scraped knee and I was washing it. I could hear every word."

"I hope you came back here sharpish," Len told her, and immediately felt ashamed when he saw Penny's hurt expression.

IT was over nine months since that terrible day when a man had arrived to tell Pat that her husband had been involved in a minor explosion in the chemical plant, where he worked.

When the doctors told her he would live she was too relieved to take in anything else. She had sat on the edge of the narrow hospital bed, his bandaged hands resting in hers and knowing only that he was going to get better.

Later, the doctors told her Brian would never regain his sight, but what did that matter? Wouldn't *she* be able to look after him?

As soon as Brian was physically strong again, it became clear he was not prepared to sit back and let her look after him. Encouraged by the doctors, he began to talk of retraining.

Pat's heart had contracted. She was convinced his gaiety was forced. She did not want him to be brave, she wanted him to take things easy.

"They said you'd get a pension," she ventured.

"Pension!" Brian almost spat it out. "I'm not an old man. I've got nearly thirty years of working life in front of me. I can't just sit about for the rest of my days."

Pat wanted things to continue as they had been when Brian had first come home from hospital, when she and the children had done everything for him. The friendship, which had blossomed between Brian and his son from the moment of Johnnie's birth, had grown.

Johnnie was marvellous with his father, nothing was too much trouble. He seemed to enjoy fetching and carrying for him.

Although glad to see how close they were, Pat was saddened when she thought of all Brian would miss of his son's development because of his blindness. Brian's dreams of helping Johnnie become a good footballer were shattered. Brian would never watch his boy play, nor even kick a ball about with him as he'd used to. But, surely, something even more precious was filling the gap?

B RIAN was determined to go to the Rehabilitation Centre. Despite her misgivings, Pat did not stand in his way and with every visit to the Centre she became more and more excited with his progress.

Remembering the shuffling, hesitant steps he had used when he'd been home, she watched proudly as he confidently walked about the grounds at the Centre.

When Brian returned home he quickly took charge of the situation.

"No-one is to move anything. All the furniture must be left just as it is, that way I know where I am," he instructed.

Pat knew Brian had always been determined and independent. It seemed he hadn't lost these qualities, and as a result, there were many incidents when their attempt to help conflicted with his desire for independence.

One day Pat had tried to put things right.

"You'll have to be patient with us, dear. Remember you've not been home long. We've got to get used to how clever you are."

As soon as she said it she knew how wrong it sounded. She had spoken to him as if he was a child who had to be humoured.

But he is like a child, Pat thought. He needs to have things done for him, and we don't mind helping him. In fact, we love it.

She tried to explain this to Brian, but he had cut her short.

"You've got to forget I ever needed your help," he said, smiling warmly as he put his arm round Pat's shoulders, and pulled her close.

"Don't think I don't appreciate what you did for me. But things are going to be different from now on. I'm not helpless."

Pat and Johnnie looked at each other, their gaze full of a kind of sadness mixed with pride.

"Of course, there'll be times —" Brian continued. "And then I'll ask you, I'm not a proud chap." He grinned. "But I must be allowed to try and manage for myself. I'll be OK, wait and see."

"Of course, darling," Pat had said.

"But we won't know when you need our help, so bear with us a while, won't you?"

Brian had laughed, contentedly and said it might have been better if they all could have gone to the centre with him, to be retrained.

"We'll get along, just you wait and see," he said confidently.

THINGS hadn't worked out nearly so well, though. The worst thing Pat had to bear was the unhappiness of her son's face, when his father shouted and stormed at him, and refused his help.

Father and son had been so close, they had shared so much. Now they were growing apart. If Pat were honest she had to admit that there was an ever-widening gap between Brian and herself as well.

The boy didn't speak of the times when he missed his father's presence.

"You never tell Dad about the school matches," Pat said one day, "Why don't you tell him about that last game you played so well in?"

Johnnie's face sobered.

"What's the use, Mum? He can't come and watch me. He was always so keen on sport himself. It seems just to be rubbing it in when I talk about it. Best to keep quiet, I thought."

Pat wasn't too sure, but she could see it embarrassed the boy to speak of things his father could no longer enjoy. He was obviously very sensitive about his father's disability.

Pat was saddened when Brian complained that she treated him like a child. She couldn't seem to make him understand that it was out of love that she tried to help him.

Pat confided often in Penny.

"We worry that he'll get hurt, or hurt himself," she told her.

"You remember how it was when your children were little."

Penny nodded. "But children grow up, and you've got to let them try new things. Sometimes they get hurt, but they soon learn," she added, wisely.

Pat quietly reminded her that Brian would never learn to see and Penny fell silent.

"Brian seems to be throwing our love back at us," Pat said hopelessly.

Penny thought a moment.

"It seems Brian needs to see things a bit more clearly in more senses than one," she said. "At the moment, he's concentrating so hard on becoming independent. But I'm sure he'll soon come to understand that you only mean well."

Penny said as much to Len the next time they talked of their young neighbours.

"If only he'd realise that loving works two ways. It's like giving," she said. "You've got to learn to receive as well as give. But how do you tell a man in Brian's position that?"

Len nodded sympathetically and, patting her shoulder, he went to brew a cup of tea before strolling out to the greenhouse.

Perhaps there was a way but he couldn't see it. He didn't like Penny being upset like this. With their own two children married, and living some distance away, she had taken this couple under her wing.

SATURDAY was a lovely warm, sunny day. A refreshing change from the cold, windy days they had been having. Feeling the sun on his face, Brian urged Pat to hurry up with her chores.

"We can't waste this beautiful day," he told her.

"I won't be long, dear, but I want to wash these blankets. Put on the radio and listen to that talk you said sounded interesting, while I just finish off," she suggested.

Brian flung out of the kitchen and she heard him stumble against an easy chair, a thing he seldom did these days. She opened the door cautiously, to see him sitting glowering at the radio.

"Are you all right?" she asked.

"Of course, I am. Don't fuss!" he snapped back.

"I . . . I heard a noise."

"Have I got to creep about like a mouse, now? I'm not likely to kill myself simply bumping into a chair," Brian said, sarcastically.

"Look, if you're not ready yet, I'll go on out to the park. I might as well be sitting in the sun."

"But, Brian, there's the road and . . . and . . ."

"So what! Don't I cross the road every day? What do you take me for? I'm not going to get myself killed if I can help it."

The last words were said from near the open front door and Pat bit back her reply. Didn't the neighbours hear enough of their squabbles?

She dashed back to her washing, fighting back tears and set to her work with a vengeance, determined to follow Brian as soon as she finished.

As it was, Brian had company on his bench in the park. As he sat, letting the heat of the sun soothe away the tension inside him, he heard footsteps he thought he recognised.

"Hello, Len," he called. "Enjoying a stroll in the sun, are you?"

"You don't miss much, do you?" Len Campbell sat down beside him.

Brian laughed. "It's surprising what your ears tell you if you let them," he agreed.

"Pity folks don't listen more," Len said, in a meaningful way.

After a moment he said: "Show me how good you are. There's someone coming up the path. What can you tell me about her?"

Brian listened carefully. The steps were light, and every now and then they broke into a hop and skip.

"It's a little girl," he said, and chuckled. "She's got long blonde hair and she's bouncing a ball."

"Right about the ball, but her hair's short," Len said, chuckling.

"Oh well, you can't win 'em all," Brian added.

There was a shout and the scurry of feet, and suddenly Brian felt a small body bump against his legs.

"Sorry," came a child's voice. "My ball's gone under your seat and I can't reach it."

"Here, let me," Len said, and Brian felt the struts of the bench lift as Len rose to his feet. The subsequent scuffles told him that Len was struggling to get at the child's ball.

"Whew!" Len said at last. "I'm getting too fat for crawling about under seats. Here you are. Now mind you look after it."

The child's steps began to move away. "Hey!" Len called. "What do you say?"

There was silence for a minute then the girl answered: "That's a jewel in your crown."

"A what?" Len asked, leaning forward.

"You're supposed to say 'Thank you.' What's all this about jewels?"

"It's what my gran says when I do anything for her. 'That's a jewel in your crown,' she says. I'm not sure what it means, but it sounds nice, doesn't it?"

"Yes, lovie, it does sound nice. It means you'll get your reward for helping, I suppose. So I've got to wait for mine, have I?"

"Thanks." The child laughed, as she ran nimbly away.

B RIAN sat thinking about the incident. A jewel in your crown! What a strange expression. And yet he supposed most people wanted to earn a jewel by helping someone else.

"You don't hear those old expression much now," Len broke in on his thoughts.

"I remember my old mother used it. I remember she used to say people didn't get enough opportunities to earn the jewels in the crowns they would wear someday. Funny idea, really." Len added.

Brian heard the strike of a match and Len puffing away at his pipe, and guessed Len was sitting contentedly, thinking about what he had just said. His own fingers went to the Braille watch.

It was beginning to look as if Pat wasn't going to join him, after all. But he had been pretty rotten to her. Not many jewels in your crown, my lad, he told himself. He stood up abruptly.

"Come on, Len. How about earning a jewel for your own crown by seeing me back home."

Chuckling, the two men made their way out through the park gates, both feeling rather pleased with themselves.

Brian was quiet on the journey back, wrapped up in his own thoughts. Had he been selfish, and unthinking?

He knew Pat and the children loved him, knew that was behind all their help. Perhaps he wasn't the only one who needed help to come to terms with the situation. Maybe I'd be storing up some jewels for my own crown if I could bring myself to accept their help, he pondered.

The house was warm and welcoming when he opened the front door.

Stifling his disappointment that Pat hadn't joined him, he whistled cheerfully as he went through to the kitchen. The sounds and scents there brought him up with a start. Antiseptic?

"Who's been hurt?" he asked, his tone betraying his anxiety.

"It's Johnnie, but nothing much." Pat's voice was reassuring. "He got a nasty cut on the football field; I was just bathing it. Luckily he's had his tetanus jab."

"What on earth were you doing, son?" Brian asked roughly, masking his concern.

"Falling over somebody's big feet." The boy laughed. "The ground's pretty hard!"

"It's obvious I'll have to show you how to fall." Brian laughed. "They taught us that at the centre. It was one of our first lessons. Came in useful too, not only on the games field."

"You played games?" Johnnie's amazement was apparent.

"We certainly did. Football was the game I liked best, it always was my favourite. They put a bell in the ball so you'd know where it was. It was a laugh, I can tell you. We really blundered around at first."

"Gosh, Dad! That sounds hard. I bet I couldn't do it."

"No, I don't suppose you could," Brian said, thoughtfully.

He turned towards Pat's voice.

"So that's why you didn't come out, looking after this clumsy lump. It was lovely out. Given me quite an appetite.

"When you've finished playing the wounded soldier you can put some jam on some of that bread your mum made, Johnnie. Give me a chance to put my feet up."

He heard the scuffle as the boy ran eagerly to do his bidding, and he felt Pat come close to him and slip her hand into his. Drawing her with him he made for his favourite chair.

"Mm! It's great to be home," he said, sinking into it, and pulling Pat on to his knee.

She snuggled against him.

"It's lovely to have you," she told him, her lips against his forehead.

The Tangled Web

by Ailie Scullion

I PROMISED myself I should never again return to Crombie Bay. Never did I want to set eyes upon the old cottage we used to rent from Mr Gow, the local farmer, with its breathtaking view of the sound, or the rolling hills at the back door.

That cottage held too many painful memories for me.

Before we married, Johnny Marshall and I both taught at the same school. Afterwards, it was taken for granted that I should go on teaching for a short time, until the family came along. We were desperately keen to have a family of our own, even though it would mean sacrifices.

We loved that cottage. It was our safety valve, Johnny always said.

The minute school ended, we used to pack the large wicker hamper and set off for our "retreat."

Five years later we had almost given up in despair. I had been to several doctors and there were several false alarms, but still we remained childless.

Then, on the last day of term, I received a letter from the clinic where I'd gone for a routine check-up the week before. This time, my hopes were realised. The test had proved positive.

I thought of all the ways I should tell Johnny and watch his face light up with joy. Then I glanced down at the wicker hamper standing on the floor ready to be packed for our annual holiday.

Wouldn't it be the perfect start to our holiday if I were to tell him once we arrived at the cottage? I would keep my secret just a little bit longer.

That evening, between waves of nausea, I helped pack our hamper and tried to share my husband's boisterous enthusiasm, but failed.

"Gosh, Julie, you are in a strange mood tonight," he said.

Next morning I followed him out to the car and we drove along in silence for miles. I kept telling myself not to be foolish, then remembered something my old granny used to quote.

"Oh what a tangled web we weave when first we practise to deceive," she used to say.

But surely it was not deceit. I was just picking the correct time to tell him about the baby. If I told him right now, it would be to gain his sympathy. No, much better we wait until the cottage.

That first day I felt moody and ill at ease, for the moment we arrived in Crombie Johnny made off down to the Pettigrews' house to thank them for delivering the box of groceries.

He finished up waiting there for what seemed like hours getting up to

date with all the local news. And there I was in the cottage, desperate to impart my news.

Eventually, my nerves gave way and I began to cry, and it was then Johnny returned.

"You silly little ninny," he kept repeating as I told him the reason for my strange behaviour. "Fancy wanting to keep that good news to yourself so long? Here, use my handkerchief, sweetheart."

Everything should have been perfect after that. Our shared joy should have been enough, but Johnny seemed to want to share that joy with everyone. He went off and told George and Molly and Farmer Gow up at Lea Farm.

"Really," I told him edgily. "Why don't you put an announcement in the paper?"

He had looked at me so strangely, and when I said I was feeling rather tired and wanted to lie down for a while, Johnny seemed crestfallen. We always went for a turn along the beach before going to bed.

"I won't be long," he assured me rather coolly. "I might just take a walk up to Lea Farm and back."

The holiday had got off to a bad start, but never would I have believed it would end in tragedy.

THAT was six years ago, and now my son Timothy was a schoolboy himself, lively as a cricket and a pocket edition of his father. I had but to look into his bright eyes to remember Johnny.

I loved my son dearly but each time I would look at him he served as a reminder. Life was no longer easy for me. For one thing I had to earn a living. I gave up my home, went back to Edinburgh and lived with my parents. When Timmy was old enough to be left I went back to teaching.

Then Timmy found the photograph album, the one in which Johnny and I used to paste our holiday snaps.

"Where's this, Mummy?" he demanded.

The photograph showed the cottage by the sea, with sea-gulls hovering above the roof.

I tried to explain why I'd never spoken about the cottage before. He had been too young to travel, and it was so far away. But my excuses sounded so trivial and Timmy was looking at me ever so strangely.

"Let's go this year, Mummy," Timmy begged.

I took one look at him and knew I had been unfair. Timmy's holidays had always been spent at home with his grandparents.

"All right. If you like, we could go as soon as school finishes. I'll phone Mrs Gow to see if she can let us have it again."

Old Mrs Gow was delighted and surprised to hear from me after all these years and she assured me the cottage would be free.

The moment I committed myself I realised just what I'd let myself in for. The place would be full of memories, and what should I do if I ever had to face . . .?

Daisy Caldwell! There was no use fooling myself any longer. Daisy was the true reason I had never returned to Crombie Bay. I should have gone back and faced her years ago. Why hadn't I? Perhaps, because I didn't wish to hear her explanation of what happened that night six years ago.

I was still driving Johnny's old car, although it was now less than dependable, but the night before we were due to leave, Timmy and I began to pack the wicker hamper to place in the boot, ready for the morning.

Next morning the sun was already high in the sky as we set out on our marathon journey. I had promised my son that we would stop half-way to picnic, perhaps opposite Seal Isle on the coast.

The cottage stood at the top of Crombie village with views of the sea. There were safe beaches and shallow rock pools where my six-year-old would have fun with his shrimp net. I had been selfish, I kept telling myself.

All memories of Crombie were not bad. There had been wonderful times too, and the locals were so friendly. I wondered if George and Molly Pettigrew still lived in the cottage along the path. They had always been very nice to us.

W E ate our picnic and watched the seals cavorting on the rocks off Seal Isle. Timmy couldn't keep still, and as we climbed back into the car he asked me for the umpteenth time how much longer it would be.

"Less than an hour now, lovie," I told him.

I was trying hard to keep the nervousness from my voice, for before we stopped for lunch I had been noticing strange sounds from the car engine.

Now I began to think about the Lea Brae, the steep hill we had to climb before the descent into Crombie.

When I saw the roadsign for the Lea Brae and its warning for motorists to select a low gear, my fears returned. On the flat the car had been behaving reasonably well.

With trepidation I began the arduous climb. The sound I had been dreading returned when we were more than half-way up.

In panic I pressed down hard on the accelerator. No sooner had I done so than the engine petered out completely. Quickly, I switched off the ignition and pulled on the handbrake.

I sat quite still and prayed that the engine would start on the hill. But as I was about to turn the key in the ignition I heard the sound of a horn blaring.

Puffing up the hill was a bright red tractor, and driving it, a man with unruly, dark hair.

"Having trouble?" he yelled over the noise of the tractor.

His grin seemed to put the finishing touches to my ragged nerves and I found myself answering sarcastically.

"No, I always stop on steep hills to enjoy the scenery."

The man's grin widened as he leapt down on to the roadside and without another word dragged a rope from under his seat.

"Ask a silly question," he said cheerfully. "Never mind, I always keep my rope handy for the Lea Brae. You've no idea how many veteran cars I've had to drag up behind my tractor.''

I sat rigidly behind the wheel and watched as he fixed up the tow rope, then listened in silence as he uttered instructions in the painstaking manner I myself sometimes adopted when dealing with rather slow-minded children.

With another wave, the dark-haired man jumped back up on to his tractor and drove off. After this, I was too busy following his instructions to think much about my deliverer, but later, on the flat, I began to speculate from which farm he had come.

Above Crombie, there was only Lea Farm owned by Mr Gow. Perhaps this man was one of his casual workers. Yet, what I would never understand was how the stranger knew exactly where to stop, directly outside Rose Cottage!

What was more, he began to manhandle the wicker hamper from the luggage rack and before I could stop him, had carried it into the cottage.

''I'll just leave it here in the kitchen, Mrs Marshall,'' he said. ''Sorry I can't wait, I'm needed up at the top field, but I'll probably see you around.''

I felt too stunned to reply. A stranger, and he knew my name. I guessed that the Pettigrews must have told him of my arrival. I had written to Molly to prepare her for my surprise visit.

As I made my way inside I almost tripped over a huge box of provisions propped against the sink unit. The cottage didn't run to a fridge but I noticed two pints of milk standing inside a pan of cold water in the sink, and a fire was burning in the hearth.

It could only be the Pettigrews, I thought warmly, then I caught sight of a card. It was balanced against a vase on the windowsill.

Please call across and see me once you are settled in. Daisy Caldwell.

I felt as though I'd been drenched by a cold shower. How dare she! The woman who had caused me so much misery all those years ago. Did she really expect me to go and visit her?

D AISY CALDWELL lived in a solitary fisherman's cottage on the tiny isle of Inchdhu. To reach it you had either to row across from Crombie pier, or, if the tide was right, cross by the causeway.

The causeway! The word sent a shiver down my spine. It was on the causeway that my Johnny had died, swept away by a sudden squall, cut off by the tide.

I tore the card into tiny pieces and threw it into the heart of the fire as my young son came skipping across to me.

''This is super, Mum. I don't know why you never brought me before.''

I watched as the last tiny scrap of card caught light and knew the reason why. It was because of Daisy Caldwell, a woman I had never even met.

Strange, too, for Johnny was always at me to cross the causeway with him to meet the Caldwells. Old Sam, Daisy's father, was a real character, my husband would recount after a visit.

He would return always with freshly-caught fish and tales of the sea. Sometimes, he would mention Daisy, too, who earned her living making garments for the craft shops on the mainland.

But I had always a fear of that narrow strip of land which seemed to stretch for ever.

"Perfectly safe," Johnny would inform me blythely. "So long as you watch the tides."

But I remained adamant. I preferred to watch the sea from the safety of Crombie Bay.

"When can we go down on to the shore, Mummy?" Timmy suddenly asked.

"After we've had some tea, love," I replied, feeling a wave of tenderness pass over me as I watched his eager face.

From the kitchen window I could see activity in the Pettigrew's garden. George was mowing his lawn whilst Molly hung out clothes on a line. I smiled as I watched her.

Molly was one of those stoutly-built women who seem possessed of boundless energy. As soon as she had finished hanging out her clothes she began to hurry along the back path which led between our gardens.

"How are you, lovie?" she called from the door. She tramped across my kitchen and enveloped me inside an enormous hug. Then leaning back, she began to study me intently.

"You're thinner," she announced accusingly, then turned towards my son. "And this is the lad? S'truth, he's the very image of his dad."

"Do you really think so, Molly?" I said quickly.

Molly nodded her head to emphasise the point.

"Just like his dad, my dear. And now, tell me this? Why has it taken you so long? Don't you know we've all been anxious to hear how you were coping?"

S HE had always been a frank woman, Molly, but I couldn't help my next remark.

"Everyone, Molly?"

She took my meaning.

"Ay, lass. She most of all. You misjudged Daisy, you know."

I stared at her coldly.

"I don't think I wish to discuss Daisy Caldwell if you don't mind."

Molly was about to argue further when she discovered Timmy watching her curiously.

"Well, sonny," she asked him. "And when are you coming down to see my Sheona? She's a Labrador and has just had six new puppies."

"Puppies?" My son's eyes widened and he looked across at me.

"Can I, Mum? Please can I go and see the puppies?"

"Tomorrow, Timmy."

I watched his face fall but at once Molly spoke up.

"Your mum's right, laddie. She'll have lots of unpacking to do tonight."

When Molly left, I remembered that I had not thanked her for the groceries. Really, I was becoming so absent-minded. I could also have asked about the farm worker who helped me on the Lea Brae.

Oh well, we were here for six weeks. Molly and I would have plenty of time to chat and catch up with all the local news.

After tea, I took my son down on to the shore and watched him kick sand into the air. As I knew he would, Timmy discovered the rockpools and lay on his tummy to watch tiny hermit crabs and the shrimps which darted in and out through the rocks.

"You can bring your net tomorrow if you like!" I called to him.

I was glad my son seemed so happy, but later when he lay asleep in bed, whilst I tossed and turned in mine, I knew I could never share his happiness, not here in Crombie, and least of all in the cottage.

NEXT morning, I took Timmy along to see Sheona's pups. George Pettigrew explained to my son that he had chickens, too, at the foot of his garden, and, if Timmy liked, he could feed them later.

Meanwhile, Molly led me inside her spotless kitchen, where she had already masked tea. As she handed me my cup she spoke again with her usual frankness.

"You know, my dear, you should really go across to Inchdhu and have a word with Daisy. She doesn't keep well these days. You cannot go on punishing yourself, lass."

In an attempt to change the subject, I reached for my purse and offered to pay for the provisions she had left yesterday.

Molly's eyes widened.

"Provisions, lovie? Not guilty I'm afraid. I guess you must have a fairy godmother."

When I tried to collect Timmy he looked up at me pleadingly. In his arms he was holding three Labrador pups.

George Pettigrew winked at me.

"I'll bring the boy along later," he said.

And so I returned to my cottage and began to clean it from top to bottom. When at last I returned to the kitchen, I gazed once more at the empty box on the floor and wondered about those provisions.

I was startled by a sharp tap on the window, and, looking up, I recognised the dark-haired man who helped me on Lea Brae. This morning, he was dressed in a tweed suit.

"Can I come in, Mrs Marshall?" he called.

As he spoke, he began unlatching my back door, then stepped inside the kitchen.

"Glad to see you are settling in. You got the provisions then?"

I gaped at him.

"Then it was you?"

He didn't reply at once and I looked up. He was no longer smiling. His eyes seemed full of sadness as he spoke.

I couldn't help but feel puzzled.

"Actually, it was my sister's idea. As soon as I heard you were returning to Crombie, I went across and told her. I suppose you read her note?''

"Your sister?'' I repeated stupidly.

"Yes," he went on grimly. "My sister, Daisy Caldwell."

I knew who this man was now. Once, my husband had told me about him, after a visit to Inchdhu. This was old Sam's son, the boy who didn't care for the fishing, and who had emigrated to Canada in an effort to earn the money for a down payment on a homestead.

"You must be Harry?" I said at last.

I spoke almost accusingly, and for a moment a glimmer of his old smile returned.

"Yes," he admitted. "I'm Harry, Daisy's big brother."

There was a long pause, but the dark-haired man didn't take his eyes off me for a second. When he spoke his voice seemed choked by emotion.

"You were very unfair to my sister, Julie."

"Unfair!" I yelled. "Me, unfair!"

For answer, he caught hold of my elbow and more or less propelled me outside. We were looking out to sea. The tide was out and the causeway was clearly visible. I shuddered and he gripped my arm tighter.

"Don't you see, Julie? You cannot hide from the truth. This afternoon, I'll take you across to speak with Daisy."

"Never!" I began, but his voice repeated.

"This afternoon, Julie. Be ready at two. I'll bring the boat."

He arrived punctually at two, this time dressed in oilskins.

"Here," he insisted, "you must wear these."

Timmy came running across to hear what was happening and before I could stop him, the tall man hoisted my son on to his shoulder.

"How would you like to come for a boat ride, Timmy, lad?" he asked.

My son yelled with glee and allowed Harry to fasten a small life-jacket over his jersey.

There was no way I could avoid going with the man other than create

---

The Joy of Spring

NOW, once again, as fragrant Maytime calls,

Laburnum boughs are decked in golden shawls —

How often I have marvelled to behold

The sunlight glinting in their chains of gold.

How bountiful they are — so many there —

Enough to crown a thousand maidens' hair.

So soon their radiance will fade away —

But would they seem so precious, could they stay?

And though I may feel sad to see them go

If there forever, should I love them so?

Their transient beauty, fleeing, poignant, rare —

Makes them, to eyes and hearts, more deeply dear.

Elsie Campbell

a scene in front of Timmy, so I found myself following the pair down to the jetty, where Harry Caldwell helped me down into a small motor launch. Then we were off at a breathtaking pace, a wide white arc of foam following behind in the boat's wake.

The journey by boat took a mere five minutes. By foot, on the causeway, it could last almost an hour. I shuddered once more as I thought about Johnny and how he had misjudged the tide — Johnny who had always been so careful about such things.

DAISY was sitting outside her cottage as we arrived. I noticed she appeared to be crocheting something white and lacy. As we approached from the small jetty, she rose and came towards us, and I noticed for the first time that she was leaning upon a stick.

"Spinal arthritis," Harry explained quietly as we advanced. "She contracted it four years ago, but it has progressed rapidly, I'm afraid."

So this was the woman I feared? Her face, I realised, must have been beautiful once, but now seemed thin and haggard, and her once dark hair, which must have looked something like Harry's, was now turning grey. When she spoke it was a voice dulled by pain.

"So you have come to see me at last, Julie. I think it's high time we had that talk," she said quietly.

Her brother was speaking confidently to my son.

"How would you like to see over a lighthouse, nipper? I happen to know the keeper and I think he might show us around."

Timmy looked at me for approval, and once more I found myself nodding. I knew Harry was being diplomatic.

Daisy led me through to her back room, which she used as a workshop. On a long table lay a display of knitted goods and some beautiful crocheted shawls.

"I tried several times to get in touch with you, Julie, but the post office said you had left no forwarding address."

I nodded my head then watched the woman's eye tighten.

"Didn't you even care to know what really happened?" she asked.

"It's past and done with," I began lamely, for I had become aware of something since entering the woman's house. Daisy Caldwell was a desperately unhappy woman.

She crossed to the other end of the room and from a cupboard removed a brown paper parcel. This she handed to me.

"By rights, this belongs to you, Julie," she said. "Open it please."

I did as I was bid and shook out what appeared to be a baby's white shawl, worked with delicate threads of fine wool.

"I . . . I don't understand," I began slowly, but as I spoke I knew I was lying. As I examined the shawl, I realised what had happened that night six years ago, the night Johnny had told me he was walking to Lea Farm, but instead, crossed the causeway to see Daisy Caldwell.

Once again my grandmother's words returned to haunt me.

"Oh what a tangled web we weave . . ."

But my Johnny's tiny deception had been innocent enough. This shawl was to have been a surprise . . . for me! I drew in my breath

74

and waited as Daisy began to speak, her pale blue eyes very sad.

"Nothing but the best for my Timothy, that's what he told me, Julie. Paid for in advance too. He sat in this very room and talked and talked about the future, his future with you, Julie, and the boy. Oh, he was sure it would be a boy, you understand."

I nodded my head. Johnny had often spoken about having a son and how his name should be Timothy after his own father. But Daisy was speaking again, this time in short staccato sentences. I could tell by the tone of her voice how upset she was.

"Suddenly, Julie, I noticed the time. 'You can't go by the causeway,' I told him. 'The tide will be going back in less than an hour. Wait for my father. He won't be back with the boat until midnight, but it will be much safer.' But Johnny wouldn't wait . . . He said you'd been looking a bit poorly."

The woman's voice faltered.

"If it had not been for that squall springing up . . ."

HERE, Daisy's voice petered out and I found myself watching her in dismay. All these years I had been harbouring suspicions about Daisy, and, God forgive me, about my own darling Johnny, too.

"Oh, Daisy!" I let out a long wail and she came across and put her arms about me.

"There, Julie. Cry if you must," she comforted. "I did all mine six years ago, when it happened. You see, I have never forgiven myself, for, in a way, I was to blame for his death. I should have known better than let him use the causeway that night."

I brushed away the tears and looked mistily at her.

"Oh, Daisy. Forgive me!"

The older woman dropped her arms from my shoulders.

"I know what you thought, my dear, but you couldn't have been more wrong. Johnny loved you, the way a man should love a woman. You were the only one in his life. You . . . and the boy."

Once again we clung together, gathering strength and comfort from each other. Later, as we drank tea, I admired the beautiful garments

---

An Enchanted Time

*D*REAM *of a perfect Christmas! When softly the snow is falling, twinkling past the window, till all is sugar-coated, and every footstep muted.*

And through the snow's caress, a tryst is kept with Christmas Eve. Sweet singing in the valley Kirk to greet the Saviour's birth.

Christmas Day! Fun and feasting. Well nigh mediaeval. Crackling fire smiles from the grate on household and its guests. A carpet of presents round the tree, holly decks the festal board.

Such Christmas as on Christmas Cards. Yet better than dreams are memories of Christmas in the days of youth.

The nostalgic sweetness of the remembered past, like lavender retains its perfume. Like early memories that never lose enchantment.

Rev. T. R. S. Campbell

---

which Daisy crocheted for the very busy tourist trade, in the area.

"Harry's coming," Daisy remarked, her eyes on the window. I straightened and glanced at myself in the mirror. My eyes looked puffy and red but I was ready to face Daisy's brother. When he came in he looked first at his sister, then at me. I watched his face relax.

"Well, if you girls have had your chat, I think we should be heading back," he said cheerfully. "Remember, some folk are not on holiday. I have a farm to run."

I turned and gave him my full attention.

"A farm, Harry?"

The familiar grin reappeared.

"Why yes, didn't you know? Lea Farm. Old Farmer Gow took me on as a partner three years ago. He can't manage it all on his own."

"Well I never!" I said in amazement. "Mrs Gow never mentioned it when I phoned."

My eyes sought Daisy's. There was so much that I did not know.

On the return journey, I watched Harry handling the small motor launch, but now I watched with a new awareness.

He was a kind man, how else would he have shown such patience towards a woman who had almost broken his sister's heart?

But there were six long weeks stretching ahead. Six weeks in which I would attempt to make up for the past. I would go across often to see Daisy and become her friend. Although, after today, we were friends already, I told myself. Trouble shared could draw people close.

And what of Harry? This man who had been so determined misunderstandings should be cleared away? Yes, what of Harry?

As I sat opposite him, hugging my son to me, I thought about the future, perhaps for the very first time. Until that moment, I had never allowed myself to look further than next pay day.

Between Harry and myself there remained a large question mark. Through his sister Daisy, he already knew a great deal about me. Over the next six weeks, I intended to get to know him too.

Sandringham Hall is the country home of the Queen. It is an impressive building and is particularly famed for its delightful gardens — the Rose Garden, Dutch Garden and Water Garden as well as an interesting bronze statue of Buddha, dated 1698.

The house was bought by King Edward VII when Prince of Wales in 1861. The elaborate iron gates at the main entrance to the grounds are known as the Norwich Gates and were a gift to him on the occasion of his marriage in 1867.

The grounds are open to the public during the summer, if there is no member of the Royal Family in residence.

SANDRINGHAM HALL : J CAMPBELL KERR

Her Uncertain Heart

by Barbara Cowan

I HOPE your grannie doesn't nag you too much this time." The friendly oil rig worker grinned at Judith.

He had taken a fatherly interest in her during the train journey from Aberdeen. Now he manhandled her two large suitcases on to a platform luggage trolley.

"Good luck with your promotion," he said as he lifted his own luggage. "My wife usually shops in your Glasgow store, so I'll tell her to watch out for Judith Sutherland, the new assistant in Personnel."

Then with a cheery wave he strode off carrying his own huge suitcases as if they had no weight.

Judith waved back, then pushed her trolley towards the barrier of Queen Street Station, where she saw Stan Fisher, her grandmother's neighbour, waiting.

He hadn't changed since she last saw him three years ago in his student days. His hair was still shoulder length and he still wore casual, student garb, although he had graduated two years ago.

She felt a little ashamed of the flicker of disappointment that it wasn't his older brother, Dennis, who had come to collect her.

"Wow! What a transformation!" Stan shouted uproariously, and Judith felt herself go pink as everyone nearby turned and stared at her in her slim skirt, neatly-belted jacket and pink blouse with a flouncing bow at the neck.

"You look like an advertisement for office efficiency," he chortled, but made no attempt to help her with the heavy trolley. "Come on, the car's outside."

Judith followed him, trying to get the trolley to go in a straight line, but the two front wheels were buckled and she ended up pushing it sideways to get it to go forward. By the time she reached the car she was feeling disgruntled. Stan was already sitting behind the wheel.

"Just throw your cases into the back seat," he said.

Judith felt her temper rising. Stan always made a great thing about believing in equality of the sexes, but she felt this was just plain laziness.

He glanced at her as she got into the passenger seat.

"I think training shoes and jeans would have been more suitable for travelling down from Aberdeen. But your grannie and fat cousin, Felicity, will approve of your crease-proof appearance," he mocked, as if this was the last thing she would want.

She didn't retort. Three years ago this is exactly how she would have felt. In fact, up until three minutes ago the thought of deliberately pleasing her outspoken Glasgow grannie or her silent, morose cousin, Felicity, was farthest from her mind.

Certainly during her stay with them in the semi-detached Corporation house in Carntyne, while she worked as an assistant in a large Glasgow supermarket, she seldom won their approval. But her widower father, who lived in Ayrshire, insisted she stayed with them then.

"Working on computers suit you?" she asked pleasantly to change the subject.

"Fine!" Stan said lightly. "Let's me afford to run a car like this."

"Very comfortable!" Judith murmured, then added, carefully casual, "And how is Dennis's 'Do It Yourself Shop'? Thriving, I hope!"

Stan shrugged before replying.

"Never see him much. Always seems to be working." He was dismissive about his joiner brother's first venture into business.

THE journey to her grandmother's house took less than half an hour, but in that time Judith realised Stan was changed. He used to be a lively, humorous companion and they were inseparable.

Now he was boring. All his conversation was about himself. And when he pulled up at his own gate she wasn't surprised. He was lazily, self-centred now too.

"Thanks for the lift," she said shortly, pulling her cases into the pavement.

"Don't mention it!" Stan replied, slowly getting out of the driver's seat. "How about going for a curry tonight? But I'm a bit short of cash, so we'd have to go dutch."

"Thanks, but my grannie will probably have a meal prepared."

"Never stopped you going out in the old days," Stan said huffily.

"Three years of cooking on single, bedsitter gas-rings has taught me never to pass up a meal cooked for me," Judith said, lifting her suit-cases.

"Here, let me!" A voice came from behind her, and she found the cases being taken from her grasp by the slight figure of Dennis Fisher, Stan's older brother, still in his working overalls.

Immediately a happy smile lit Judith's face. Seeing him again she knew he was the real reason she'd applied for the Glasgow position.

"Watch out, Sir Galahad! Your knees are buckling under the weight!" Stan roared with malicious humour.

"One thing is certain," Dennis called coolly over his shoulder. "No-one would mistake you for a dashing knight!"

Judith laughed at his quick retort. His quiet ability to cope with most situations was the one thing she'd noticed immediately when they'd met by chance a few months ago when he was visiting relatives in Aberdeen.

Yet, it was strange. She'd hardly noticed him on her last stay. Then all her attention had been for his flamboyant brother, Stan.

A S they reached the side entrance to her grandmother's house the door was flung open and her cousin Felicity's plump face smiled warmly at Dennis. But when her glance moved to Judith the warmth evaporated, her smile was wary, almost fearful.

It jolted Judith, for as children they'd been friends. This was the look she recognised often in new employees who were apprehensive and scared of her.

Yet, in the ensuing bustle of getting settled, Judith found her glance going constantly to Felicity. She was different somehow.

Maybe it was the badly-applied make-up. But Felicity was almost cheerful. So different from the scowling memory Judith had stored from last time.

"Never thought you'd be back," her grannie greeted with her usual bluntness, "but you're welcome and looking much improved."

"My father still insists I stay in Glasgow with my grannie." Judith laughed. But she knew it was only partly to please her father that she had come back to lodge here.

"Aye, you've been a sore trial to him." Her grannie sniffed. "But it's his own fault. You're his only wee lamb and he's let you have too much of your own way. Still, I suppose it's young Stan Fisher next door that's the real attraction."

Judith laughed. She would stay pleasant no matter the provocation.

"No, I don't think Stan and I have much in common now," she replied gently.

"That's one blessing," the old woman muttered as Dennis came out

of the bedroom after carefully depositing the cases, inside the room.
He took his leave and Felicity showed him to the door.

When they left the room together, Judith found her grandmother watching her, her old eyes, shrewd and humorous.

"You've noticed the difference. Felicity's slimming!" She gave a little laugh. "Great what love does for you!" Then she added practically, "But maybe you'd give her some help putting that stuff on her face. She makes an awful mess of it — though she spends pounds on all those wee jars of cream."

Felicity came back into the room and overheard her grandmother's remarks.

"Oh, Gran, give me a chance." She sighed.

"Why not! Let's have a facial session before tea. It was part of my training to advise assistants," Judith offered.

"Do her in the next half-hour and that'll suit me," Grannie remarked as she made her way to the kitchenette.

"That's plenty of time for Felicity," Judith said. "Then afterwards I'll do your face, Grannie," she quipped.

Old Mrs Sutherland was highly amused, and for five minutes, as Judith applied cleansing lotion to Felicity's face and removed it with wet cotton wool pads, she could hear her grannie chuckling gently every now and then.

After a little Judith became absorbed. Felicity's skin was good and it struck her that if she really slimmed down she could be a beauty. The bone formation in her face was excellent. As she stood back admiring her own handiwork she remarked on this to Felicity.

"Do you really think so?" Felicity said anxiously. Then she lowered her voice. "There's someone . . . I think he likes me," she whispered in an unexpected burst of confidence.

"Do I know him?" Judith whispered back.

"Yes, he's . . ."

"Whispering is rude!" their grannie interrupted, laying the teapot and cosy on the table. "My, we'll have Dennis queueing up to take you out looking like that."

Her grandmother's innocent remark startled Judith. Surely it wasn't Dennis. But she remembered the warmth of Felicity's greeting for him. And he'd seemed extra jovial and good-natured in the half-hour he'd stayed after her arrival.

She'd thought it was for her. But there was obviously a growing bond between him and Felicity that had suddenly blossomed after a lifetime's acquaintance. They'd even been at school together. The thought chilled Judith.

THEY sat down then to tea and Judith marvelled how rigidly Felicity adhered to the diet laid down by the slimming club she attended. She was interested, thinking of advising employees about their weight problems. It was a subject most people were keen to learn about.

But Felicity was still wary of her, so Judith gently questioned her, using all her personnel training to put her cousin completely at ease.

Soon she had Felicity explaining at length, with all the fervour of a new convert, the necessity of changing the eating habits of a lifetime.

"Och, it all boils down to what I've said for years — eat less!" their grannie said, rising to clear the meal.

"Right, Felicity, let's clear up for Grannie. Then we'll give her a facial."

"Me — oh never!" the old woman declared.

"You'll love it. It's so relaxing." Felicity cajoled.

"And I need practice on the more mature woman," Judith coaxed.

"Oh well, if it helps you in your job," the old woman grumbled. But Judith knew she was secretly pleased. Grannie loved a new experience.

Judith began again the process of cleansing and moisturising, giving the little professional explanation of each step as her trainer had done. She set out deliberately to be amusing for she wanted to rid Felicity's eyes once and for all of that strange apprehension.

And she felt happy too that coming back was proving much more pleasant and easier than she'd expected especially as life had seemed one long row when she'd left. She'd promised herself then, never to return.

> ### The Lowliest And The Highest
>
> *SAID Christ: "The last shall be first." I know where above a Cathedral's great west door, this truth is carved in stone.*
>
> *Long ago when the shrine was being built, the Bishop visited the site. He observed a young girl standing at the bend of the road where the oxen halted, before they dragged loads of dressed stone up the hill.*
>
> *To each she offered a handful of grass!*
>
> *Bishop, designer, masons, craftsmen combined to raise the Cathedral. But the lowliest of them all – the girl who fed the oxen – was the one they chose to honour. They carved her tale upon the enduring stone. Even as Christ exalted the humble.*
>
> Rev. T. R. S. Campbell

But perhaps after three years of living in bed-sitters which had the bare minimum of comfort, sharing flats with other girls who borrowed her tights, forgot to wash up, and even pay their share, she looked on life differently, and didn't take anything for granted. Then there was Dennis, too, next door, to bring her back.

But she felt a small ache. She'd banked a lot on getting to know him better, but now there might be something between him and Felicity. It was disappointing, and yet when she looked at Felicity the difference in her was startling.

She took the towel from round her grandmother with a flourish.

"And now madam is ready to face her public!" she said, holding a mirror in front of the old woman.

"Oh my!" she gasped. "It really makes a difference, but I couldn't go out with this on my face." She examined Judith's handiwork.

"Oh my!" she kept repeating, for it seemed to be a new person who stared back at her.

JUST then the doorbell sounded and Felicity answered it and ushered Dennis in again. The two cousins giggled helplessly at their grandmother's consternation being caught wearing make-up for the first time in her life.

Dennis was quick to see Judith's handiwork on both Felicity and her grandmother. He looked from one to the other and shaded his eyes with his hands as if overcome.

"Such ravishing perfection twice over. I'm dazzled!" he gasped. "It's more than a poor mortal can take."

"Och, wheesht your nonsense!" the old woman said, struggling up from her seat and making for the kitchenette. "I'll need to get this stuff off."

Oh, Grannie, after all my work," Judith cried.

"When my carriage awaits, too, to take you specially to the Brownie display," Dennis said, bowing low, then added ruefully. "Actually I forgot, but a certain anxious little Brownie came in at tea-time to remind me of a promise given weeks ago to take you."

Mrs Sutherland clapped her hand over her mouth.

"Oh, I forgot all about it, and wee Sheena Morran bought me a ticket out of her pocket money so I would go. Her mother and father can't be there — and Judith just arrived, too!"

"Can't we all go?" Judith asked. She remembered the tiny Sheena who lived several houses down, as a constant visitor on her previous stay.

"Why not!" Dennis produced some untidily-printed pink pieces of cardboard. "Sheena sold me extra tickets when she heard you were back."

They all trooped out to Dennis's dilapidated old car in high good humour just as Stan came to the garden gate.

"Aren't you coming for a curry?" he asked in some astonishment as Judith prepared to climb into his brother's car.

"No thanks, I've eaten." Judith smiled. "We're going down to the church hall for the Brownie display. Why not come?"

"Brownie display! You!" Stan gasped. "You've changed! But no thanks," he finished sourly and got into his own new car, slamming the door behind him.

WHEN they arrived the church hall was a buzz of parents and they could not get seats together. Sheena's small, painted clown's face peeped through the curtains and grinned delightedly as they sat down. She waved wildly before she was hauled away unceremoniously, by someone backstage.

"Oh, I love the atmosphere of these things." Judith laughed to her grannie.

"I'm glad you're now adult enough to admit it," the old woman said dryly, and Judith looked at her in puzzled surprise. But she couldn't question the remark as the lights were suddenly dimmed, and the show started.

Each childish act was given generous applause. But to Judith's surprise after the interval she found Dennis sitting beside her. She had been careful in picking her seat to allow him to sit beside Felicity.

She felt absurdly glad. But she wondered what Felicity was thinking as Judith didn't want to hurt her. They had almost got back to the happy rapport they had as children.

Yet, she had come to Glasgow to be near Dennis — to see if the magic of the few days with him in Aberdeen could be recaptured. He'd seemed to hope then she might get a transfer.

When the display finished, little Sheena came and dragged them into the adjoining hall, where small square tables were set out, at which each Brownie was to entertain her guests. Sheena's eyes were shining at having a full table.

"If I do this well it will help me get my hostess badge," she breathed as she concentrated on pouring the tea, and gravely handed round sandwiches and some rather squint-looking cakes.

"I made them," she whispered.

"Delicious!" Judith proclaimed, accepting a second one. She remembered her own anxiety as a Brownie.

Later, when Dennis drove them home, Judith was aware that he contrived to have her leave the car last, and as her grandmother and cousin entered the house he detained her.

"I hope I'll be seeing a lot of you," he said quietly.

It was exactly what she wanted to hear, but the thought of Felicity dampened her enthusiasm.

"I'm sure you will," she said non-committally, and followed her cousin into the house.

Although they had had tea so recently, the kettle was put on again as a matter of course by her grannie.

"I'm going straight to bed," Felicity said wryly. "I've eaten all I'm allowed today."

"To think of the years I've tried to get her to think of her weight and this infatuation has made her take it seriously." Old Mrs Sutherland sniffed. "I only hope the man in question feels the same way about her."

Judith felt her heart go cold. So that was why Dennis felt free to speak to her. He didn't know. Poor Felicity! But what a position she herself was in.

SHE felt suddenly tired after her full day, and she sank down on a chair as her grannie came in with a loaded tea-tray. As she made to help, Grannie shook her head.

"Sit down, you've been all day on the go," she commanded.

Thankfully Judith accepted a scalding-hot cup of tea and one of Grannie's parkin biscuits.

"Now tell me all about your new position," the old woman said, settling back into her chair ready to listen. Judith was tired, and her body ached now for sleep.

But she saw Grannie wanted to talk so she explained carefully that the position was the same, but the Glasgow store was bigger so there was more responsibility.

"Great where a bit of ambition and hard work get you," Grannie murmured. "There's Felicity now, who was with the firm two years before you started with them, and she's still loading shelves. All the while you've climbed the ladder rung by rung. It says a lot for you, girl."

"It wasn't easy." Judith smiled, thinking of the times she'd wanted to give it all up, having to attend classes and study on top of her work load.

"I never thought you'd stick it," Grannie admitted.

Judith grinned.

"I know! Remember, you told me before I left."

"You did it to spite me then," Grannie said with dry humour.

"Partly." Judith laughed again. "And partly to prove to myself I could do it."

"Well, you've come back to us like the wee girl I remember visiting as a child — good-hearted and with a bit of fun besides." Grannie spoke now with satisfaction, but added, "Last time, you were well nigh unbearable, talked of nothing but yourself. You'd never have taken time then to give us facials, or please a wee lassie by eating her lumpy cakes."

Judith smiled uncertainly at this side of the story. She had been thinking all evening how much nicer her grannie and Felicity were now, compared with her last visit. She never dreamed the fault might have been with herself.

Yet thinking back honestly now she knew she'd made little effort to please them last time. She'd been totally absorbed in herself.

"But then, it was your age, I suppose." Grannie sniffed knowingly. "Your first job and you wanted to be independent. Maybe I should have been more tolerant, should have realised that it wasn't all your fault, with Stan next door egging you on. But he goes to London next month for a new job. The experience will make or break him." She gave a chortle of laughter. "But I bet it bobs his hair!"

Both women laughed.

"We all have to learn to conform to our changing patterns of living."

Welcome Signs

FEBRUARY brings cold comfort
    With its fogs, its frosts, its rains,
Yet it offers simple pleasures
    In the fields and country lanes.

Banksides starred with yellow colts-foot,
    Celandines just peeping through,
Daisies whitening the meadows,
    Snowdrops brightening the view;

Lapwings nesting in the pastures.
    Blackbirds flute a mellow tune.
Silver catkins on the willow.
    Surely Spring is coming soon!

Courtney Farmer

Judith murmured, indistinctly, trying to stifle a threatening yawn.

"That we have," Grannie said, rising from her seat with a sigh. "Even at my age I have to accept that my old legs don't support me up and down the hills to the Edinburgh Road as they did. So I'm for bed."

WHEN Judith crept into the bedroom she was surprised when her cousin's head came up from the pillow immediately.

"Sorry, did I wake you?"

"No!" Felicity whispered. "I've been waiting for you."

Unconsciously Judith braced herself for the confidence she felt was coming about Dennis.

"Do you really think I could be pretty if I lose enough weight?" Felicity asked anxiously, struggling up into a sitting position.

Judith's eyes were pricking with tiredness, but she tried not to show it as she smilingly replied.

"No doubt about it."

"Oh, I hope so. It would give me confidence with Robert."

Felicity sighed, then smiled at the mystified look on Judith's face. "Robert Glen — remember he was in charge of the delicatessen. He's given me a ticket for the brass band concert he'll be playing in next month, and he suggested we might go for a meal afterwards. In fact, he's going to book a table in the local hotel."

Suddenly a huge wave of relief swept Judith into wakefulness. It wasn't Dennis for whom all the dieting was being done. She listened joyfully as Felicity told her about the unexpected birth of romance with the rather solemn young man she remembered as Robert Glen.

Felicity talked at length of how they'd found they shared a mutual love of brass bands. Judith smiled as she listened, for Felicity was just as full of doubts, fears, joys and hopes as she herself was over Dennis.

And in return Judith found herself confiding in her cousin about Dennis being the main reason for her return. It was a wonderful relief to talk about it to someone sympathetic.

"So that's why he's been in and out of here so much recently," Felicity marvelled delightedly.

A loud series of thumps on the adjoining wall interrupted their confidences.

"Would the pair of you stop talking and let a body get some sleep," their grandmother's voice complained from the next room.

The two girls tried to muffle their giggles as they settled down.

Judith lay in bed happily drowsy. It was strange that just a few hours ago on the way down from Aberdeen she was almost dreading coming back here, remembering the tensions of her last visit, wondering about her reception. How oblivious she was then that it might have been partly her fault, until tonight's truthful look back at the past.

Love could be a painful process, to be sure, but at this moment there was no other place in the world she wanted to be — and tomorrow she could meet Dennis with an easy heart.

Share A Little Happiness

by MARY FAID

THE Mackays had just come to live in the bungalow next door. It was an especially lovely house, quite unlike Kate Allison's, which had been built fifty years ago at the time of her marriage. It was small and plain and lacked the modern luxuries she'd never had the money to indulge in.

One thing it did have was a sweet, old-fashioned garden, whose most intriguing feature was a wooden wind-toy that her granddaughter, Sandra, had brought home to her from abroad.

On this June day Kate was standing at her kitchen window, fascinated as always by the antics of the little wooden man turning a handle to bring up a bucket of water from a well. When the wind blew, he turned fast and furiously, bending and stretching.

When the wind fell he became still, but, at the least puff, he was at it again. Sometimes she felt sorry for him, never getting a real rest from his labours yet still looking cheerful and industrious, and the thought made her laugh. It was so silly to feel sorry for a little wooden man.

Kate peered forward, adjusting her glasses. Apparently she was not the only one to be fascinated by the toy. Through a gap in the fence a small boy had appeared, creeping up as if drawn by a magnet. He stood there watching, absorbed, and Kate in her turn watched him.

She had seen him before, this small boy from next door, and was drawn to him. The parents had spoken briefly across the fence, but they were busy people and Sarah was both shy and withdrawn — not, however where children were concerned. She opened the back door and looked out, smiling.

"Do you like my little wooden man?" she asked.

He nodded, hardly able to tear his eyes away. He had a round, thoughtful little face and straight blond hair, very like her own grandchildren when they were young. Now they were grown up and Kate, who loved small bairns, missed their lively chatter.

"What is your name?" She went on to ask.

"It's Colin John Mackay and I'm going to be four in July."

"Gosh, you're almost a man. Are you having a birthday party?"

"If I'm good," he replied. "Some of my friends are coming and so is Uncle Andy. You can come too, if you like."

"Thanks very much, Colin, but I don't go to parties nowadays. I'm too old."

He eyed her thoughtfully.

"Yes, you are old, but so is my mummy."

She smiled. His mother would be about twenty-five, Kate reckoned, but what was fifty years difference to a small boy's eyes?

A voice called him from next door.

"I'll have to go now, but please can I come and watch the wee man again?"

"Whenever you like," she told him.

"Oh, thank you." His manners had obviously not been neglected. "I think you're a very nice lady."

With that he vanished through the fence and Kate went indoors.

FROM then on it was as if a light had come into her life. She did not force the boy's friendship, just watched him at play and quietly answered his questions. She knew only too well that the mind of a child was a mystery to be fathomed only by great care and understanding.

Her granddaughter Sandra heard all about Colin John next time she visited.

Sandra's home was in the far north, but she had left to take up a post in Glasgow and came to see her grandmother every other Saturday.

She was an independent girl: had had several boyfriends, but her standards were so high it was difficult for many of the men she'd known to live up to them. Which would be sad, for of all the things that Kate wanted to be, a great-granny was the most important.

"I've got a new friend," she told Sandra, delightedly.

"He calls me Auntie Kate and his name is Colin John. He lives next door and will be four in July. I'd like to give him a present. What would you suggest?"

Sandra smiled affectionately. Trust Gran, if there was a child around, she would adopt him, and she was glad for her. She guessed her life was quite lonely, now that Grandpa was gone. They had been everything to each other and she needed something to fill the emptiness. An idea came to her.

"You once knitted me a darling pussy cat. We called him Whiskers — remember? I loved that animal. If you could do the same for Colin . . ."

"Funny," Kate said. "I was thinking along the same lines myself. But I haven't knitted anything for ages."

"Then it's time you started," her granddaughter replied, "before you forget how. I know what! Why don't you start on it tonight?"

Taking her at her word, Kate went to work, searching in the corner cupboard where she kept her bits and pieces. There in a box she found some old knitting patterns, among them the very "Whiskers" she'd made for Sandra so long ago. There were balls of wool, too, carefully preserved, and even knitting needles of the size required. At last they would be put to use!

With excitement and anticipation she sat down to cast on the first stitches. It wasn't easy. Her fingers had gone stiff and each stitch took twice as long as it used to do. Her eyes smarted a little at the type on the pattern. Peering at the instructions, she had to admit that the task wasn't so enjoyable as in the past. Still, she'd started and wasn't going to give up now!

Meanwhile, she made an effort to become more friendly with Colin's mother.

Joan Mackay was a busy woman with a part-time office job. In the forenoons, Colin was looked after by a daily help, but the boy preferred Kate's company and that of the little water-man in her garden.

I HOPE Colin isn't being a nuisance," Joan remarked one day over the fence.

"He loves your garden better than his own. It keeps him off the street, having somewhere to play."

"I admit he's company for me," Kate said. "I believe he's having a birthday soon?"

"On the twentieth of this month," his mother explained. "His dad and I are giving him a railway set with all the gadgets. It's very expensive, of course, but we want him to be happy."

It crossed Kate's mind that the boy was a bit young for such a gift and that it would surely make him happier if he had more of his mother's company instead. But she was old and not with it — perhaps the younger generations knew better.

She would have to hurry now to get his present finished. Every evening, out came her knitting needles, and the woolly cat's body, after much knitting up and ripping down, was at last ready to be sewn together and stuffed. The next day it was Colin's birthday, so it would have to be done that night.

She laid out the finished pieces: back and sides, head and ears, four legs and a tail. The main part was white and the appendages brown and black; when ready, she would embroider the nose, eyes and mouth.

Going to work with a will, Kate sewed and sewed, stuffing the parts as she went with small pieces of foam. Midnight came and still she stitched. Then, at last —

"There!" she exclaimed to herself, breaking off the final stitch. "It's not a bit like 'Whiskers,' but at least it's a cat."

Unfortunately, it was then she realised with a sinking heart that the "thing" was not even a cat. In fact, it wasn't like any known animal.

The face had a funny, lamb-like expression, one ear went up, the other down, the body flopped and the tail wobbled, and when she tried to stand it up, its little narrow legs completely collapsed beneath it.

She gazed at it in despair. There was nothing she could do now to mend matters. She would go to bed and perhaps it would look better in the morning.

M ORNING came and in her dressing-gown, Kate went into the sitting-room. There the creature lay, flopped on the table, still looking as pathetic as it had the night before.

Dejected, she did her housework and went out to hang some washing on the line. Even the water-man, in the absence of any wind, looked dejected.

Only one thing kept her cheerful. This was Sandra's Saturday — she'd be here for tea. Kate started to prepare the sausage rolls and soda scones she was noted for. But even they did not turn out as successful as usual. The face she presented to Sandra was quite care-worn. She really felt her age today.

"What's the matter, Gran? Somebody steal your scone?" Sandra queried, with a grin. Gran herself always said that.

Kate smiled shakily.

"Well, somebody or something kept my scones from rising."

"Too bad. Perhaps you were feeling low to begin with — that always affects one's baking." Sandra said, sympathetically.

She ought to know, being a Home Economics teacher.

"Well, I wasn't too bright. I was up half the night finishing a version of your 'Whiskers'."

"Really?" Sandra said, excitedly. "Oh, do let me see it!"

"All right, but prepare yourself for a shock," she said grimly, producing the strange object from the cupboard.

Sandra took one look at the floppy creature and started to laugh.

"Oh, Gran, it's priceless!" the girl giggled.

"That's right, laugh. That's all it's good for, a laugh! And to think of the hours I spent on it! I ought to have known. I'm just not up to anything like that, any more. In fact, I'm not much use to anybody."

This was so unlike Kate's usual attitude that Sandra immediately felt contrite.

"What are you talking about? You're my gran and a very super person. I don't know what I'd do without you. I'm sure that Colin loves you too. As for this cat you've knitted — well, he's super!"

She hugged it to her.

"Look how cosy and lovable he is. Even his floppiness is endearing!"

"That's all very well," Kate declared, "but it simply won't do for a birthday present. I can't think what to do."

Sandra gave her a kiss.

"I'll tell you what. Wrap Floppy up in a parcel and take him to Colin this minute. He'll love him."

"How can I? He's a misfit. Colin's people would laugh at him, the way you did. That boy will have lots of expensive presents. He won't even look at my poor little offering."

Sandra refused to listen.

"Well, if you won't do it, I will!" She said, determinedly, and left.

Pressing the doorbell, which made a musical tinkle inside the house, Sandra stood on the red tiled step, waiting. She rang again, but no-one came. No signs of a party, either; it was very strange.

As she turned away, a car drew up at the gate and a young man got out. He was carrying a parcel, too. Colin's father, perhaps? He came up the path, smiling at her.

"Isn't there anyone at home?" he asked, and she could not help noting how bronzed and fit he looked and how his blue eyes twinkled.

"Afraid not. Aren't you Mr Mackay?"

"No, I'm his brother — Colin's Uncle Andy. I've brought him a present."

"Same here," Sandra said, indicating her parcel.

"But surely someone is in? I was told there was a party."

"Yes, it's strange. Perhaps we should try the back door."

"Good idea." They crunched over the gravel and round the side of the house, but found no sign of life. Simultaneously they both noticed a garden seat.

"Perhaps if we wait here someone will turn up," the young man suggested.

Sandra agreed, but as she sat down, the string of her parcel caught on the arm of the seat. It burst, and the cat came tumbling out.

"Is this your work?" he asked.

"No, it isn't, and don't you dare laugh!" she answered sharply.

He did laugh, however, but kindly.

"What is it supposed to be?"

"Well, it started off being a cat, then it became what you see in front of you. But I like it, it's interesting!"

"It certainly is. But if it's not your creation, whose is it?"

"My grandmother's," she told him. "She used to make lovely knitted toys, but her fingers are quite stiff now and she can't follow the patterns. She was so ashamed of Floppy she didn't want to bring it herself, but I think he's lovely, don't you?"

His eyes twinkled as he looked into her earnest face.

"Lovely," he murmured, and for some reason she blushed pink.

I T was so pleasant there in the garden that they sat and talked for quite a while.

Then they heard the sound of footsteps from the house, and Mrs Mackay opened the back door. Her husband was there, too, but no Colin.

"Hello there," Andy greeted her. "We've been waiting here with Colin's presents. Where is he?"

"Colin," Joan replied, a catch in her voice, "is in hospital. He's had an accident. Ran out of the gate into the path of a car."

"Oh, no!" Sandra exclaimed.

"Is it bad?" Andy asked, full of concern.

"He's pretty shaken and has a fractured arm but they say it's not too serious. Naturally we've cancelled the party. Please come in,

Andy, and bring your friend." She looked questioningly at Sandra, who explained.

"I'm Mrs Allison's granddaughter. I'm so sorry. I'll go and tell her what's happened."

"Yes, do, but please don't alarm her. She's been very kind to Colin."

Andy followed her to the gate.

"Have you transport to take you home tonight?" he asked.

"I'll be taking my usual bus."

"Please let me run you home. We've got a lot to talk about."

Sandra saw no reason to refuse, and they fixed a time to leave.

When Kate saw her granddaughter coming up the path, still with the parcel under her arm, she was concerned.

"I knew it was a mistake, Sandra! I shouldn't have let you take it across."

"No, Gran, you're wrong. Colin wasn't there to get it." And she explained what had happened. Kate was most upset.

"Poor little soul. On his birthday, too! I must go and visit him in hospital. I don't know quite how — but I will!"

A way was found. Sandra had only to mention it to Andy and he was at Gran's gate next Saturday, ready to take her to the hospital.

K ATE had asked after her small companion every day. It seemed that Colin wasn't getting on as well as was expected. The bruises and fractured arm were healing, but he seemed so listless; nothing seemed to rouse him.

Kate fancied that the little water-man was looking as sad as she felt herself. The garden wasn't the same for either of them.

Andy and Sandra were waiting in the car, and before she joined them she locked the front door behind her.

"Aren't you taking Colin his present?" the girl asked.

"He'll have enough without that. The best place for it is the dustbin and that's where it's going the minute I get the strength of mind to do it."

"Gran, give me your key! I'm going back for poor old Floppy."

There was no arguing with Sandra, so Floppy went, too. Sandra thrust him into Kate's arms at the door of the ward.

"You go first. Andy and I will take our turn later. Good luck!"

Kate looked round anxiously.

"Colin Mackay? He's over there," the nurse said. "Perhaps you can get him to smile. We can't! Not even his parents have succeeded."

Colin's eyes were closed, long lashes at rest on his pale cheeks. She stroked his forehead with her finger-tips and he opened his eyes in vague recognition.

"Hello, Colin John!"

"It's Auntie Kate," he said faintly. Then, with a spark of life, "How's the wee man?"

"Still working hard. I've brought you a present from both of us. Look!"

"It's a pussy cat!" The boy beamed. "He's great!"

Kate breathed a sigh of pure relief. Bless the boy, she thought.

"Thank you, Auntie Kate! Now I've got a friend to keep me company." he said softly.

SURE enough, the boy began to improve from that very moment. It was like a miracle. Soon he was home again and one Saturday in August Kate spied him through her kitchen window creeping through the gap in the fence, the woolly cat clutched in his arms.

She opened the door and went out to him. His legs were very thin, but already his face was losing its pallor.

"Glad to be home, Colin?" she called out.

"Yes, Auntie Kate. I brought Floppy round to show him to the wee man. See, he's still turning his handle! You'd think he'd be tired by now, wouldn't you?"

"He's the kind that never gets tired," Kate said.

While they chatted, two people came round the house from the front gate.

"There she is!" Sandra's face was glowing. She ran to kiss her grandmother, and Colin made a bee-line for her companion.

"Hello, Uncle Andy! I'm out of hospital now and so is Floppy. Come and see Aunt Kate's wee water-man. He never stops!"

Hand-in-hand they watched the little toy, while Sandra stood happily beside the old woman.

Kate felt her granddaughter slip her arm through her own and she turned to speak to her in time to catch her gazing proudly at Colin's uncle.

Sandra turned, aware of her gran's eyes on her.

"Andy's very fond of Colin," she said, a blush creeping into her cheeks.

The old woman smiled, knowingly, warmth filling her heart.

"And you, my dear girl, are very fond of Andy, aren't you?"

"I can't hide anything from you, Gran." Her voice was low and surprisingly intense, as she continued.

"I've never felt this way before — and, I might as well admit, I never expected to. Andy, well, he's just different from the other men I've known."

"I may be old-fashioned." Kate smiled. "But that sounds to me like love!"

The difference in their ages forgotten, the two women laughed together like schoolgirls.

"You could be right, Gran." Sandra giggled.

"I know I am," Kate replied, then, as a thought came to her, said, "The future looks quite exciting, doesn't it?"

"Yes, Gran — it does!" Her granddaughter answered.

She would look forward to Sandra's marriage, and, hopefully to the time when there would be children. Meantime, there were lots of happy times in store, for Colin, Sandra, Andy and herself. She smiled out at the little wooden man, who always kept going, no matter what. She would take her cue from him and do exactly the same.

Treasured

"ISN'T it great, Tina?" enthused Douglas Samson. "Our Eric, due home tomorrow?"

The couple were climbing Clunie Hill at the time, and had stopped to look down upon their town, hidden beneath an ochre pall. Beyond the town, the river wound like a silver snake, and they could see ships at anchor out on the estuary.

"I bet you are looking forward to seeing him again," Tina said.

Douglas and Tina stood with their backs pressed against the first-mile gate. She nodded her head and looked at the man by her side, as though waiting for a reaction. Douglas Samson stared straight ahead.

Tina Martin and her family had always lived next door to the Samsons in Lilac Avenue. Eric and Douglas were twins and the same age as Tina. Naturally, they went everywhere together. Folk used to call them the terrible trio when they were at school.

Eric had always been the agreed leader, Douglas and Tina content to tag along behind. Strange, too, because they were identical twins. Douglas and Eric looked alike, talked alike and seemed to do everything together, yet Tina knew there was a great difference. Naturewise, they were poles apart.

John Samson, the twins' father, ran a small building contractor's firm in town. It was expected that the boys would follow him into the business.

Eric had other ideas. As soon as he qualified as a surveyor, he was off to London. Douglas, who had qualified at the same time, stayed at home, despite much persuasion to join his twin.

Two years later, Mr Samson died. After Eric left home, he had seemed to lose interest and let his business run down. Douglas took over the reins and had been trying to get it back on its feet ever since.

That was six years ago and a lot had happened since then. Eric, for one thing, had his own firm based in London, but spent most of his time abroad. This visit home had come out of the blue.

Eric had never been much of a letter writer, but would send Tina postcards with glossy photographs of exotic places and signed flamboyantly "From Eric with love." Tina had pasted each one into her scrapbook.

It was impossible not to draw comparisons. Eric believed in taking risks, whilst Douglas was careful. Once, when they were fourteen, there had been a big fire in a warehouse at the far end of town.

Tina could remember Eric dragging them there to watch as the fire brigade fought the blaze, but whilst he stood on the edge of the pavement, his eyes alight with excitement, Douglas hung back in the shelter of a

Memories

by
KATE
HANNAH

shop doorway, his face ashen, hands trembling. When Eric chided him, he gave a quiet reply.

"There might be someone trapped in there, Eric."

It was Eric, too, who had defended Tina when Mr Armstrong's ferocious Alsatian came loping along the road barking. He had stood with arms outstretched in front of her. Eric the fearless, Tina called him in those days.

Of course, Eric was fond of his twin. As soon as his business prospered down south, he had offered Douglas a partnership in it. The latter declined apologetically.

He told Eric that he was beginning to see a light at the end of the tunnel. The family business was making progress at last.

NOW Eric was on his way home, having travelled the world, and made a name for himself, according to everyone in town. He was due a hero's welcome.

Douglas, Tina would defend loyally, had made his name also, even if it were only a modest new building in High Street, but he had his own office at last and his name above the door. He even employed Tina now as his secretary.

Tina stood at the window next morning and watched Douglas drive his mother to the airport to meet Eric's plane from the South. She waited impatiently for their return, and when the car drew up outside, stood on her tiptoes to watch.

Mrs Samson stepped out first, looking smart in her fur coat and hat. Eric came next. He was dressed in a light-weight suit and stood shivering on the pavement before his mother hurried him into the house. Douglas took up the rear, carrying three leather suitcases.

She waited for the phone to ring. When it did, it was Douglas's voice she heard.

"Mum says are you coming in for tea?"

She stopped in the hallway just to check her appearance. Tina had styled her hair the way Eric used to like it, in a neat French Roll.

"They're through in the lounge," Douglas advised, holding the front door open so she could slip in.

"Why, Tina," greeted Eric, "you look terrific."

He had been standing with his back to the fire, but now hurried across the room to sweep Tina into his arms.

She studied the twins carefully. It had been so long since she had seen them together. Six years had made a difference. Eric looked thinner than his brother, and, of course, bronzed by his travels.

Douglas never did have much colour, but it had been a bad winter, and he looked even whiter standing beside his twin.

"We must have an evening in town," Eric was saying purposely. "What do you say, tomorrow night?"

So like Eric, she thought. He never was one to let the grass grow under his feet.

Nevertheless, she was ready and waiting when he came next door the following evening to say that the taxi had arrived.

"Where's Douglas?" she asked slowly, but Eric shrugged his shoulders.

"Says he had to nip back to the office, Tina. Something to do with a phone call," he replied.

That would be the garage contract Douglas was hoping to clinch. She had been typing letters and estimates regarding this for weeks. Tina allowed Eric to drape her little fur cape around her shoulders.

They had a wonderful night in town, Eric proving he was still an excellent escort. They ate dinner at the brand-new restaurant which had opened opposite the theatre, and afterwards he spoke of his wanderings and plans for the future.

She felt glad he had been successful.

"It was grand seeing you again, Eric," she told him truthfully as they arrived back home and were standing at Tina's gate.

Eric leaned towards her, ready to draw her into an embrace, and it was at that moment they saw the glow in the sky. Orange sparks were flying high into the air above High Street where Douglas had built his new office.

They began to run together but even so, Tina reached the spot first. She could hear Eric's voice behind her.

"It's all right, Tina. It is not our Douglas's place. Just the old bakehouse."

Eric was right, she realised, but the bakehouse stood next door to Douglas's new building. Tina could see sparks landing on top of the roof, and the fire brigade, sensing the danger, had been hosing water on to it.

T HE policeman who was attempting to hold back spectators, turned, and Tina recognised John Brodie, another old friend. He came across immediately.

"Don't worry, Tina," he said. "Douglas isn't badly hurt."

She felt her knees giving way beneath her, then Eric took charge.

"My brother's injured, John?"

The policeman nodded.

"I believe he was working late in his office and smelt burning. It was Douglas who sent out the call."

"But you say he is hurt," insisted Eric.

Once more the man in uniform nodded.

"He remembered that old Simy, the watchman, would be on duty upstairs in the bakehouse, so he broke in through a window and managed to get him out."

Even as she listened to the explanation Tina felt sick at heart.

Eric was demanding to know to which hospital they had taken his twin, but the policeman waved his hand.

"You know Douglas," he replied. "They wanted to take him in the ambulance, but he insisted on going home."

They found him sitting in his father's old armchair.

Mrs Samson was holding a cup of tea to her son's lips when Tina ran across and looked into his eyes.

"Are you all right, Douglas?" she asked softly, taking his hand.

He looked up rather sheepishly and nodded.

Eric too was across, clapping his twin on the shoulder.

"Well done, Douglas. I never thought you had it in you. A hero at last, eh?"

Tina frowned as she looked up at Eric Samson. It was obvious that he was proud of what his brother had done, but Tina couldn't believe he would be so insensitive. Surely he knew what Douglas was going through right now?

It was true that Douglas was no hero, not in the accepted meaning of the word, anyway. He had confessed more than once to having a terror of fire. The sound of a fire engine made him cringe.

It was the thought of Simy the watchman, trapped upstairs, which had encouraged him to conquer his fear long enough to enter that blazing building and raise the alarm. Then he had gladly escaped home, where, his mother now informed them, he had been very sick.

As soon as she could, Tina went next door to tell her parents what had happened, but early next morning she went back to the Samsons' house and found Eric eating breakfast off a tray as he sat leisurely beside the fire. Mrs Samson was scurrying about the room, her face anxious.

"Would you believe it, Tina," she said, shaking her head in distress. "I've never heard of anything so stupid. It's Douglas! He wouldn't stay here — just insisted on going down to his office. Nothing I could say would stop him — he was so determined."

Tina nodded as she replied.

"He'll want to know if there has been much damage. You know he has bought in a lot of equipment for the garage contract."

"Garage contract" Eric broke in. "Why does our Douglas bother

---

GOOD COUNSEL

SON, these are thoughts to remember
    And check against every device:
Will the pleasure you're tempted to purchase,
    Prove costly or cheap at the price?

The thing which for nothing is offered,
    Is merely the bait on a hook.
Whenever you're prompted to take it,
    On all sides make certain to look.

'Tis nice to be told you are clever
    And wise as the books on the shelf.
'Tis nicer if others believe it,
    But never believe it yourself!

And here is a rule of behaviour:
    Be gracious whenever you can;
There's nothing in arrogant conduct
    That adds to the worth of a man.

An order gains nothing from shouting
    And meanness adds nothing to size,
Remember a man can be humble
    And still be both clever and wise.

Edgar A. Guest

himself about small fry like that? He could be well set up by now, if he had accepted that partnership I offered.''

TINA gazed at him sorrowfully. Eric, the fearless! The man who took risks! He would never understand his own twin. This morning he looked slightly put out, she thought, as though resenting that for once, Douglas had stolen some of his thunder.

She didn't wait to find out, but hurried towards High Street, her heart sinking as she saw what was left of the old bakehouse.

Douglas's office and workshop hadn't come off unscathed. The sign over the door looked scorched and the windows and the gable-end wall were darkened by smoke.

''How are you?'' she asked urgently, and drew his face down so she could kiss his lips.

''Fine,'' he told her shakily.

''I nearly fainted last night, Douglas, when I heard you had gone into that building,'' Tina admitted.

''There was no real danger,'' he began uncertainly, but Tina waved this aside.

''You must have been terrified, my poor darling, when you saw the flames.''

He nodded his head.

''Yes, I was scared stiff, Tina. I admit it. If it hadn't been for old Simy being inside, I should have ran home, as usual.''

''But you didn't,'' she reminded him softly, and kissed him again.

A month ago, Douglas had asked her to marry him, but even he was not wholly convinced when she said that she would. He had always been convinced that it was Eric she loved.

He knew all about Tina's scrapbook, about the postcards his twin sent regularly from all the corners of the globe.

What she couldn't convince him about, was the fact that she didn't need the scrapbook at all.

The memories she treasured of moments spent with Douglas were stored inside her heart and required no album.

''About Eric. Have you really got him out of your system, Tina?''

''A long long time ago, dearest,'' she told him firmly. ''You just refused to be convinced.''

Douglas leaned back against his chair, looking tired but contented, then, as he looked up again, his eye caught sight of the smoke-ingrained windows, the scorched sign above his new office door.

''Pity about all this, Tina, but I suppose it serves me right for trying to impress you. I shall never be Eric. I don't think I have the make-up to be a success.''

Tina put her arms around Douglas's neck, then rubbed her cheek against his.

''A bucket of hot water and some soap will soon get rid of the grime, Douglas,'' she told him. ''As for impressing me, there's no need. Eric's successes are just something to stick in our scrapbook. You, my lovely brave Douglas, you are reality.''

...TO BELONG, FOREVER

by IAN WILSON

FIONA GRANT gazed from her window across the valley, realising that this was the last time she'd be looking at her favourite view.

Circumstances had suddenly changed for her. Since the recent and unexpected death of her father, she'd found the market garden too difficult to run single-handed, and so decided to sell. But the deal had been carried through quickly, thanks to Iain MacAllister.

For the first time she was beginning to appreciate what a fine man Iain was. And too late, she thought sadly as she wandered round the house.

His recent accident had quietened his usually ebullient nature and shown her for the first time a sensitive nature underneath. So sensitive, in fact, that he'd offered to sell off her pieces of furniture for her rather than let Fiona go through the agony of doing it.

Idly she placed her fingers on the piano keys. This wasn't being sold but was going into store until such time as her new home in Edinburgh was fixed. Until then, she'd be staying with her sister, Muriel, and husband, Sandy Lawrence.

Conscious of someone beside her, she turned.

"I'm sorry, Iain, I was day-dreaming."

"How will you manage without your piano?" he asked, studying her face.

"Oh, one piano is much the same as another. Muriel has one, and I'm taking all my music with me."

Iain wasn't fooled by the tone of her reply. He knew that the piano had been a present from her parents on passing her first music exams.

Fiona smiled through a tear.

"How's your leg?"

"Coming on very slowly, but I expect I'll be back at work before I see you again. How many cases have you?"

"Just the two," she said, quietly.

A S he carried them to the car, she noticed just how badly he was limping.

"I came rather early," he told her. "So you wouldn't have to wait around till the last minute."

"I appreciate that, Iain."

"Shall we go then?" she said, trying to sound cheerful.

As they drove away, she steeled herself not to look back, but there was one memory she just had to take away with her.

"Will you take me round by the Water Mill?" she asked.

Iain smiled understandingly as they drove along the twisting lane, its shelter of overhanging trees a tapestry of red and gold autumn colours. At last they crossed the bridge over the rushing Mill Stream and stopped the car in front of Mill Cottage, where Iain lived.

"Isn't it sad?" Fiona said. "Such a beautiful mill should be alive, not lying silent like this."

Fiona shivered.

"How about some coffee before you go?" Iain asked.

"Please." She was grateful.

Iain busied himself in the kitchen and returned with two mugs of coffee.

"Fiona, what am I going to do with myself for the next few months? I'll go crazy just sitting about here."

"Why don't you renovate the mill?" The idea came to her, suddenly.

Iain smiled wryly.

"I've often thought about it." He smiled. "I suppose I just need something or someone to spur me on. Thanks for the idea." His mood changed.

"Now, we'd better be going," he said, brightly.

"You'll like Edinburgh," Iain said, as if sensing her indecision. Then he added, quietly, "I'll miss you, Fiona."

His compliment was unexpected as he didn't usually give way to emotion. Fiona turned away to dab a tear with her hankie. As she did so, Iain bent down to pick up something which had fallen.

"I almost forgot." She gasped. "That's my piano key." She held it out. "Will you keep it for me, Iain? My piano's my most precious possession, you know."

She smiled.

"You might even say that's the key to my heart you're holding."

As the bus drew away, she couldn't help feeling sad at Iain's forlorn, limping figure.

FIONA fell in love with Edinburgh at once. Though she'd visited often, she'd never explored, and Muriel and Sandy were on hand to help her.

It was a whole new experience, so enjoyable and different from life in Kirkstone. But, after a few weeks, she decided the time had come to settle down and earn a living.

Her doubts were accentuated by Iain's letters. Though not very informative, they reminded her that she was still just a step away from her former life and not yet absorbed into her new one.

Muriel noticed her change of mood as the days passed, and was determined to involve Fiona in the life of the community.

So Fiona found herself playing the piano for the old people at their weekly get-together in the Church Hall.

Mr MacBride, the young minister, was delighted with his new "find."

"You have a charming way with old people, and I was wondering if you might do me a favour?" he asked.

"If I can," she replied, with interest.

"One of our older members, Mrs Douglas, has turned her back on the Church since her husband died. Such a pity, too, she was one of our staunchest members. But she and her husband were very devoted, and I expect she's finding it hard to face people again."

"How can I help?" Fiona asked.

"You're sympathetic," he said, matter-of-factly. "You may be able to succeed where I've failed."

"Well I'll certainly try." She smiled.

FIONA wasn't worried when the old woman didn't answer the bell, as a slight movement of lace curtains showed that Mrs Douglas was up and about.

However, after two or three futile calls, Fiona took a piece of paper from her pocket, scribbled a message on it, then pushed it through the letter-box. Tomorrow she would return and see if her note had had any effect.

The next day the sound of her knocking seemed to echo through the old stone villa. Fiona waited, sighed and was about to turn away when the the door opened half-way and Mrs Douglas looked at her very cautiously, from behind the safety of the heavy wooden door.

"Well?" she asked in a rather uncompromising tone.

"Mr MacBride phoned to say I would be calling," Fiona said, quickly. "I'm Fiona Grant."

Mrs Douglas hesitated.

"Come in then." The older woman turned and led the way inside.

They sat down in large comfortable armchairs beside a huge fire. Fiona held out her hands to it gratefully.

"I like a good fire," Mrs Douglas said firmly.

"Me too," Fiona replied. "We used to burn logs at home. I loved the smell of the damp wood and those lovely sparks."

"So you're a country girl, Fiona?" Mrs Douglas asked.

Fiona looked surprised at her knowledge.

Mrs Douglas gave a faint smile.

"I made sure Mr MacBride gave me all the information about you."

Fiona began to feel slightly more at ease, in the presence of this tall, rather elegant woman.

"I'm a country girl myself," Mrs Douglas told her.

She stood up.

"I expect you'd like some tea."

"You're very kind." Fiona was pleased — it seemed the old woman had accepted her.

"While we're drinking it, you can tell me all about yourself," Mrs Douglas replied. "It's such a long time since I had a visitor."

FIONA told her all about Kirkstone and how most of the young people had to move away to find work.

"As for me, when my father died, I was heartbroken." She sighed, remembering. "But I also felt incredibly free for the first time in my life."

"And why isn't an attractive young woman like you married?" The old woman eyed Fiona speculatively.

The question was sudden and Fiona felt sure she blushed. She explained about Iain.

"Please don't think I'm trying to interfere," Mrs Douglas explained. "I'm just interested. He sounds such a nice man. I hope things work out for you both. Sometimes you should take your happiness while you can," she added, quietly. "My husband and I did, and I've no regrets."

"I've put my regrets behind me," Fiona replied. "Naturally I think of Kirkstone, but when I've found a job, I expect I'll think of it less and less."

"What kind of job are you looking for?" Mrs Douglas inquired.

"That's the difficulty." Fiona sighed. "I'm not really trained for anything."

Kate Douglas continued to regard Fiona thoughtfully.

"Would you like to work for me, Fiona? I've been toying with the idea of taking on a housekeeper/companion. I've often thought of advertising, but my courage has usually deserted me."

Fiona couldn't have been more surprised.

"I don't know what to say!" she gasped. "Can I think it over?"

When she told Muriel, her sister had no doubts, saying it would be a splendid opportunity.

There was a letter from Iain, too.

But in the quiet of her own room, she read it with less eagerness than the earlier ones. It was such a formal letter.

Suddenly she felt angry, not with Iain but with herself for ever imagining that Ian felt anything for her other than friendship.

"Very well, Fiona," Mrs Douglas said when Fiona accepted her offer. "We'll give your stay an initial period of six months, until the spring comes."

G RADUALLY the pattern of Fiona's life emerged, and autumn merged into winter, any reserve which Kate Douglas had, melted away under Fiona's companionship.

Fiona still wrote to Iain regularly telling him of her new life, and although she tried not to think of him too often, she did miss his undemanding friendship.

For Fiona, Kirkstone seemed a long way off, and yet, as February slipped into March, and the tips of the daffodils appeared, she couldn't help thinking about the Water Mill and the masses of daffodils surrounding it in the spring.

Kate Douglas, however, had other things on her mind.

"I would like a new spring outfit, my dear, I haven't bought any new clothes at all since Alec died."

Fiona felt glad. The older woman was taking an interest in life again, and the thought warmed her.

"Let's go on a shopping expedition tomorrow to Princes Street," Kate suggested.

P RINCES STREET was in one of its frisky moods with a gusty wind tugging and teasing at chilled limbs. Fiona was laden with parcels as she trailed in the wake of Kate, whose energy seemed unquenchable.

"I think a cup of coffee is called for," Kate said.

They weaved their way through the throng. Fiona banged into a woman next to her and turned to apologise. Both women looked at each other in amazement.

"Fiona!" The other woman exclaimed.

"Morag." Fiona couldn't believe the coincidence.

"Tom's brought me for a day's shopping. It's quite special, actually, I'm having a baby in September, so we're here to buy some things," Morag said, with a shy smile.

"Oh, Morag, that's lovely news." Fiona put her hand on her friend's arm.

"And what's your news, Fiona?" Morag asked.

She explained about Mrs Douglas, then asked after everyone in Kirkstone.

"Oh, they're all much the same, really," Morag said, then continued with odd bits of gossip which Fiona had missed hearing so much.

"Sorry everything fell through between you and Iain," Morag added, "especially now with the news about his leg. But then I expect he's told you all about it."

Fiona felt a sick feeling rising in her throat.

"No, he hasn't mentioned anything at all."

Morag's hand flew to her mouth.

"I'm sorry, I hope I haven't spoken out of turn."

"Tell me, Morag, please," Fiona pleaded.

"Apparently the leg was worse than they thought. Now, it seems he's going to be left with a permanent limp. And there'll be no chance of his going back to the oil rigs again."

"When did he find this out?" Fiona was shocked.

"Just after Christmas, so I understand," Morag said. "He's terribly depressed. I suppose he didn't tell you because he didn't want to worry you."

After Morag left her, Fiona felt stunned.

After they'd completed their shopping and returned home, Kate found Fiona in her room crying bitterly. She sat down on the bed beside her, gently cradling the younger woman's head in her arms, soothing her until the sobbing had ceased.

"It's Iain, isn't it?" she asked.

At first Fiona didn't reply but Kate persisted.

"Remember last autumn when a young woman came to my door? Well, she managed to help me when I needed it most, and I grew to love her as if she'd been my daughter. Now you need me — won't you tell me what's wrong?"

"I've been such a fool, Mrs Douglas," Fiona sobbed. "Iain's always made light of his injury."

She explained what Morag had told her.

"I thought he didn't care for me, but now I know the truth about his leg, I realise it was me he was thinking about. He didn't want me to worry."

"Are you sure?" Kate asked tentatively.

"Yes," Fiona was definite.

"I think I'm old enough to know the signs of a woman in love and you've been carrying a torch for Iain ever since you came to stay with me."

She took Fiona's hands in hers.

"Then off you go to Kirkstone, but remember, this will always be your other home."

I MMEDIATELY Fiona wrote to her friend Nan MacRae. The reply came by return of post to say that she could stay as long as she liked.

And true to her word, Nan was waiting at the bus terminal when she arrived.

"It's good to see you, Fiona." And she hugged her friend joyously.

As they drove home, Fiona noticed the usual slow pace of life in Kirkstone, so unlike the hectic dash in Edinburgh.

Yet, as the days passed, courage to visit the mill eluded her. It was only when she passed her old home with its bright new curtains and paint, that she realised the past was no longer important, the future was what mattered.

She walked quickly along the lane towards the mill, her heart beating just that little bit faster.

Iain was waiting at the gate, with a smile on his lips.

"Nan told me you were coming."

Fiona glanced at the silent mill before following Iain inside.

"Please excuse the mess," he said. "This is a bachelor establishment."

He sat down, stretching out his leg, gingerly.

"It's a bit stiff today, but the doctor says it'll be fine soon."

"Iain, why didn't you tell me about your leg?" Fiona said quietly. "I know all about it. You should know news travels far in Kirkstone."

"Then you know I'll be a cripple for the rest of my life," he said abruptly.

"You'll have a limp, that's all." Fiona couldn't conceal her anger.

"Why don't you stop feeling sorry for yourself, and face the truth? Why do you think I came back to Kirkstone? Certainly not to hear your self-pity. I'm here because I was worried and I want to help."

"I don't want your pity." He avoided her eyes.

"I'm not offering you my pity!" The angry words tailed off as her voice became softer. "I'm offering you my love."

She held her breath during the long silence that followed. Then Iain spoke.

"I wanted to tell you, Fiona, but I'd no right to interfere with your new life in Edinburgh." His anger had died now and was replaced by tenderness.

"Oh, Iain, you'd every right, every right in the world," she said.

"I need you to take me in hand," he said with a grin. "I always hoped you'd come back. That's why I kept your piano here."

Fiona looked at him in amazement.

"I couldn't stand the thought of it getting dusty in some store room," he continued, then.

"The key, remember what you said, the key to your heart, so I kept it close to remind me of you."

Fiona felt tears come to her eyes, at the tenderness in his voice.

"While you were away," he said confidently now, "I remembered what you said about renovating the mill. I've had some thoughts about it, even looked over it, most parts are in good order. We could renovate it together."

He looked across at her and there was no mistaking the look in his eyes.

"I love you, Fiona — I always have." And as he held out his hand to her she crossed the room, took his outstretched hand, and knelt beside him. As he leant forward to take her in his arms she knew that Kate Douglas had been right — she belonged here in Kirkstone, with the man she loved.

FREE TO LOVE

by
Agnes Kennedy

Y ES, there was no doubt about it — Mary Gilmour — Kirktown's
late minister's daughter, had been seen in Glasgow's Queen's
Park, wearing a blonde wig. Mrs Runcie's daughter, Jenny, in
her last year at Glasgow University, had seen her quite plainly. She
did think of saying hello, but had thought it might have embarrassed
the other girl. Anne had been with that girl who used to come regularly
to the manse. The two had been friends since schooldays.

Not that the womenfolk of Kirktown disapproved. There was no
doubt that a suitable wig could, at times, do something for a woman.
But it all seemed so totally out of character for Mary Gilmour. No-one
had ever thought of her as anything but the quiet, capable girl who'd

left school to run the manse, and look after her father and younger brother and sister when her mother died.

They could hardly wait for her to come back. But, as it happened, it was dark when Mary alighted from the last bus.

Unaware that she was the centre of interest, Mary Gilmour, back at home, made herself a cup of tea before unpacking her case. She'd had a lovely weekend with her friend.

Caroline Bryce was a real harem-scarem with plenty of fun and surprisingly enough, a shrewd business instinct that made her top buyer for Crabtree's, the large department store.

Right at the very top of the case lay the blonde wig. Mary picked it up and, shaking it out, let the curtain of gold spread itself across the bed.

The wig belonged to Caroline and it had been she who had dared Mary to wear it. She smiled at the memory. It had all been just a bit of fun and she had enjoyed every minute of the carefree weekend — it had been the happiest since before her father had died.

A T Caroline's suggestion she'd bought a new suit and shoes. Perhaps she'd wear the suit to church on Sunday or to the casting meeting of the dramatic society.

Caroline had persuaded her to keep the wig too and take it back to Kirktown with her.

"Did you notice the men who looked at you in the park?" Caroline had said, then.

Mary had simply laughed.

"It must have been your wig."

"No, it wasn't," Caroline said firmly.

"Do you have to stay in Kirktown?" her friend continued. "The men there must be blind or too old or they would have had a path beaten to the manse door long ago."

Mary couldn't help laughing at the picture conjured up by Caroline.

"Well, the path to the manse door was pretty well overgrown with weeds."

"Suffering from a distinct lack of eager male feet!" Caroline said with a sniff.

"You have to remember, Caroline," Mary said, in a more serious tone, "that most of the young men, and girls as well, have no choice but to leave and get work elsewhere."

"H'mm. I suppose you're right," Caroline said thoughtfully. "Come to think of it, last summer when I was staying with you, about the only presentable young man I saw was that artist chap, what's his name."

"David Holmes," Mary said, not looking at her friend.

"That's it," Caroline said. "He was mentioned in connection with an exhibition of paintings in the McLellan Galleries not long ago and had some good notices from the critics." Caroline eyed Mary thoughtfully.

"Nothing possible there?" she queried.

Mary laughed again.

"Why this desperation to get me married off? But, no, there's nothing possible there," Mary mimicked. "We know each other, of course, and Dad liked to visit him at his studio." Then, with an air of finality, "Now, will you give it a rest." She laughed.

Caroline held up an imperious hand.

"I shall have my say and you'll listen to it!" her friend commanded. "You have an attractive personality, classic good looks, and yet there isn't a man for you in Kirktown. Why do you stay?" She sighed exasperatedly. "It's all such a waste!"

Mary waited patiently until her friend stopped.

"Look, Caroline, I know what you're going to say. My brother, Angus, in Vancouver, has written and said more or less the same thing. He wants me to go out there. And my sister in London wants me to go and join her."

"Well, now I'm asking you to think of coming to Glasgow," Caroline answered.

"There's room for both of us here. You've got shorthand and typing . . . so I don't think you'd have much difficulty finding a job."

"Caroline, it's lovely of you to ask me, but I just don't know what I'm going to do yet."

Caroline sighed, obviously admitting defeat, and stood up to make them a cup of tea.

"Well, if the time comes and you decide to make a move — remember what I've said." She made one final request.

"I will," Mary replied, "and thank you."

A S she dressed in her new suit and shoes to go to the drama meeting Mary recalled Caroline's parting shot to her. She picked up the wig and held it in her hands, turning it this way and that. Somehow it had been fun wearing it when she had been with Caroline, but here, it just didn't fit in. She put it away.

There was more or less a full turn out of members at the dramatic society meeting.

The three-act play, "Miss Crawford's Dilemma," had been chosen some time ago and Mary knew that there would be some discussion as to who should fill the various roles.

Mrs Alice Fenton, who was president of the society and producer of its stage offerings, brought the meeting to attention.

"Well, now, you all know what the play is about. After reading it I've no doubt you've all had your own ideas about filling the various parts."

She paused and looked round and her words met with approving nods and murmurs.

"The difficulty about this play is that so much of it hinges on the portrayal of the character of Miss Crawford.

"She is not the simple, uncomplicated soul that could be suggested by external appearance. She is, in fact, a very deep, many-sided character, sometimes resigned to being simple Miss Crawford, sometimes frustrated to the point of rebellion, but always drawing back from the brink. It is when she has to make the most vital decision that could change the whole of her life that she cannot . . . and that is her tragedy."

"What about doing the part yourself, Alice?" someone asked. "You could do it well."

Alice Fenton laughed happily.

"That's kind of you, but, no. Miss Crawford is on the forty mark, just beginning to show the ravages of age, as it were. The best make-up man or woman could hardly knock twenty-five years off me." Her reply was light.

"Anyway, I enjoy the job I do," she continued.

"It's easier to make up a younger person to look the right age than vice versa," Alice resumed. "That's why I'm going to suggest Mary for the part."

M ARY barely heard Alice Fenton's words, so deep was she in a turmoil of thoughts, stirred up by Alice's summing-up of the character of Miss Crawford.

In a little while that could be me, she thought. I'd be living the part — I wouldn't be playing it. I wouldn't need make-up. There'd be no problem. I'd be Miss Crawford . . .

"Well, Mary, what do you think?" Alice asked. "Will you take the part? You'd do it well."

Alice Fenton's direct question jerked Mary out of her abstraction.

"No, no, I'm sorry, I can't take it." Her reply was quiet, yet seemed to echo round the room.

"I'm sorry to hear that." The coolness in Alice Fenton's voice betrayed her disappointment. "Perhaps some other part . . ."

"No, I'm sorry. I can't take any part at all. I may not be here! In fact, I'm pretty certain I won't."

"Are you thinking of leaving Kirktown then?"

The clipped tones brought her fully back to reality and to the blinding knowledge that, in the last few moments, she had made up her mind.

"Yes, I'll be leaving Kirktown." Her voice was calm now. "I'm not exactly sure when. There will be one or two matters to clear up first."

"Well, I'm sure all of us in the society will miss you, Mary," Alice said. "Indeed the whole village will. But I won't say any more at the moment. Now . . ." Her eyes glanced round the room.

"I think we'd better get on with our business."

Mary heard them go through the various parts and finally they reached agreement on how they would be allocated.

"Oh, and by the way, we have one other loss," Alice Fenton said after a spell. "You know how very good David Holmes has been about painting bits of scenery and so forth for us. We won't have him this time. He's got some sort of commission from a big art publishing company and I understand he'll be abroad for perhaps a year."

For a moment or two Mary wondered where David Holmes would be going. But his leaving would be only temporary. Luckily, he'd finished the house he had been working on for all of the seven years he'd been in the village so at least he'd have that to come back to.

As soon as she found the opportunity she slipped away from the meeting. Outside she felt cold and started to hurry, as if to leave the disturbing vision of Miss Crawford behind her.

She left the main street and without consciously thinking what she was doing or where she was going turned down the narrow, winding road that led through the older part of the village, past the old blacksmith's house and forge, which David Holmes had bought, and restored.

The road dwindled into a track and, finally, into a path leading to the wooden footbridge that spanned the river.

She walked on to the bridge and halfway across she stopped to lean on the rail and look down into the river. The wood of the bridge still retained a little of the warmth of the day's spring sunshine. As she leaned she pushed off the new shoes, delighting in the feel of the cool breeze.

It had been here on the bridge, when she was thirteen, that Archie Greig had suddenly kissed her. He had stepped away from her, his face growing redder and redder, silent in his embarrassment, and then he had turned and rushed off the bridge.

She smiled at the remembrance.

Life's Promise

LOVE is all, and all of living
   Not to heed, nor count the cost.
Of doing willingly and giving
   All in life. That means the most
To those, who either far or nearest,
   Want us, need us. For a part
In the life of those the dearest
   Of our loved ones, give the heart.

Muriel Wilson-Pinney

It had been here she had come when her mother died, and here, at the same time, she had said goodbye to a girl's dreams and plans and accepted the duty of looking after her father and brother and sister.

Eleven years — it was strange that in all that time her father, so gentle and kindly and understanding with others, had never seemed to wonder if his own daughter was giving up too much.

She shook away her thoughts and turned to her immediate problem.

"Well now, you've brought yourself to the point of having to do something whether you like it or not, you have to go somewhere, but where — Vancouver, London, Glasgow?"

She voiced her thoughts, looking down into the water.

ABOVE the murmuring of the river she heard the footfall on the end of the bridge. She turned and saw the man coming towards her — it was David Holmes. He stopped a yard away from her.

"Hello, Mary." He stood uncertainly. "I went along to the drama meeting after I'd finished some work . . ."

He stopped again and turned to half-lean against the wooden rail and look down into the water.

"Alice Fenton told me you're going away. Is that right?"

"Yes, it is," she replied, wondering why she felt so light-headed.

"Perhaps I shouldn't ask, but what's made you decide to leave?"

"It started with a wig," she said in a matter-of-fact voice.

He looked at her doubtfully.

"You're pulling my leg."

She shook her head.

"Not really. I spent a weekend with my friend, Caroline, in Glasgow. You've seen her sometimes when she came to stay at the manse. She started it off and tonight, well tonight . . ."

She halted and looked away from him.

"I don't know why I'm telling you this and you may think it all silly, but tonight in the hall I had a sudden vision of myself becoming, in real life, Miss Crawford, the central character of that play. Have you read it?"

"Yes," he replied. "A short time ago. James Ross asked me what I thought of it."

"Then I needn't try to explain," she continued. "So, I've made up my mind to leave Kirktown and, as the saying goes, start a new life."

"Where will you go?"

She shook her head.

"I don't know for certain." For some reason she felt uneasy in his presence.

"Then why don't you come with me." He said it quietly but his words startled her. For a moment she gazed at him.

"What do you mean?" She couldn't hide the surprise in her voice.

"A big art publishing company has asked me to paint a series of sunshine scenes for them," he explained. "I'll be going to France, Italy, Spain, Greece, leaving in about two months' time. When I come home in about a year there'll be an exhibition of my work. We could have a marvellous time."

She'd always felt attracted to him, but he'd never displayed his interest in her before. She felt panic rising inside her.

"Don't say any more . . . Please."

"But, Mary, it would be marvellous. I wouldn't be working all the time and we'd see wonderful places. Think of all the different people and all the sunshine . . ." His voice tailed away.

"Don't you understand?" she said, her voice high. "Suddenly I'm free, able to do anything I want, at any time."

The flash of spirit drained away and suddenly she felt tired.

"I'm sorry," she said, looking at his surprised expression. "I'm not moaning or wallowing in self-pity. I loved my family and I've done no more, I suppose, than hundreds of other daughters have done.

SHE started to laugh and had to take herself in hand.

"And no sooner am I free than you come along and ask me to go away with you for some private reason of your own." Suddenly she was weary of this conversation. "I don't need your pity, David."

"Pity doesn't come into it, Mary," his voice was angry, but then it cooled quickly.

"I'm not asking you to take on another minding job, I'm asking you to share an exciting trip with me," he reasoned.

"You're seriously asking me to go away with you?" She couldn't believe this was happening.

"Yes." His dark eyes crinkled with laughter. "But, of course, we'd get married first."

I N the gathering dusk they stared at each other. Then she stooped and eased on her shoes. As she straightened she half-turned from him. The whole situation was ridiculous, completely out of hand.

"No," she said, as much to herself as to him. "That would be too simple. Thank you for asking, but, no, it's impossible."

"Don't you understand what I'm trying to say?" He gripped her arm.

"I'm trying to tell you you're the most beautiful girl I've ever known. How often I've wanted to paint you . . . or to try to paint you. I'm telling you I love you, have loved you since the first day I saw you here in Kirktown."

He let her arm go and she turned back to look down into the water.

It was a long time before she could speak. "Then why didn't you tell me?"

"How could I? You were devoted to your father and brother and sister. Apart from that I'd nothing to offer you but a broken-down, old smiddy. Everything I earned, and sometimes that wasn't much, went into creating a place where I wanted to live and work.

"Then I discovered I wasn't really building a house for myself, but for you. Something that I could offer you. So, I was trapped by my love for you . . . Now, with the house just finished and this wonderful job . . . you're going away."

"Did you say you loved me?" she asked, her voice low, and trembling.

"Yes, I did." His voice was quiet, impersonal, as if he were standing a long way off and looking at himself. "I've made a bit of a hash of telling you, just blurting it out. But well. I . . ."

She put her hand over his.

"Please don't go on. I'm . . ." She stopped and laughed softly. "It's really wonderful."

She stopped again and her fingers tightened over his.

"But it may take me a little time to get used to the idea!" she finished.

"Then you will think about coming with me?" he said, after a little while.

She tilted back her head and laughed.

"What girl wouldn't think about a honeymoon in France, Spain, Italy . . . Greece . . ."

". . . And she wouldn't feel restricted, a slave?" his question was anxious.

This new, wonderful feeling took a bit of getting used to. Somebody loved her, and she could feel her attraction for this man deepening.

"No, you were right before, it would be a shared restriction. We'd find our own freedom — in each other."

Her words were no more than a secret whisper, caught and held for a moment before fading into the quiet of the spring night.

I Can't Believe It's True

by Grace Macaulay

ANNA CARMICHAEL wrinkled her slender nose in a gesture of disgust and dismay. Had she really gone away for the weekend leaving her flat in this dreadful state?

A few minutes ago, David Williams had hinted that he would willingly accept an invitation up to her flat; he was longing for a cup of coffee, he said.

Now, as she surveyed the disordered sitting-room and mentally viewed the rest of the flat, Anna was extremely relieved that she hadn't invited him up. And she hadn't for one reason alone — Ellis Rodgers.

Suddenly, as if on cue, there was a light tap on the door. She knew at once that it would be him, her next-door neighbour who occupied the flat across the hall.

"Come in, Ellis," she said with a sigh.

He put his head around the door.

"Not interrupting anything, am I?"

She made a wry face at him.

"What could you possibly be interrupting when you know very well that I'm just this minute home?"

His dark curly hair seemed to flop forward on to his forehead, as he blushed brick red and, still without crossing the threshold, said awkwardly, "I've just made tea. Would you like some."

"Thanks, Ellis, I would." Anna found herself smiling at him. "A cup of tea is just what I need." She could never be angry with him for long.

His anxious expression of uncertainty cleared into a smile. Without saying anything more, he disappeared from sight and she heard him enter his own flat.

As soon as he was gone her annoyance with him returned.

Really, it was getting to be just a bit much, she thought, as she went across to his flat. It seemed she no longer had any privacy. He was always popping up at awkward moments. She really must tell him, she decided, as she flopped into a comfortable armchair and relaxed in the familiar atmosphere of scholarly neatness.

Ellis was always either reading or writing. He had a radio and record player and a television. But none of them were ever on when she was in his flat. Sometimes she wondered if he ever used them.

NOW, as he handed her a cup of tea, Anna realised that for the time being she was the object of his undivided attention.

He was the perfect listener — interested, attentive, encouraging . . .

She gave a small inward sigh for she knew that she wouldn't be able to resist telling him all about her weekend.

"Well, how was your weekend?" Ellis was smiling, relaxed in the deep leather armchair on the opposite side of the fireplace. "Did you go to that dinner-dance last night?"

Anna nodded.

"Yes, my mother took me out, bought me a new dress in the afternoon, and I had my hair done," she told him, then stopped to take a sip of her tea.

Abruptly, she put her cup down. She didn't really want to talk about the weekend. At least, she didn't want to tell Ellis . . . too much. But it was hard to break an old habit. He was waiting to hear more.

"David drove me back," she said quietly, and added, "I'm going out with him tomorrow night."

Ellis digested both pieces of information in silence.

Anna picked up her cup and gulped down some more of her tea.

"It's a funny old world," she said, with an unsuccessful attempt at a smile, "I didn't even recognise David when we were introduced at Valerie's party last week. Then we got talking and discovered we came from the same town, went to the same school, even. And his parents and my parents know each other very well."

After a moment, Ellis remarked quietly, "So your parents approve of David, then?"

She found herself inexplicably shying away from the real meaning of his words.

"That sounds very old fashioned!" She laughed.

Ellis stood up and went to fetch the teapot.

"I expect you'll start going home more often now."

His words puzzled her.

She shook her head as he came towards her cup.

"No more tea for me, thanks, Ellis. I have to go. I really must clean up the flat."

He refilled his own cup and sat down again.

"Yes," he said, vaguely, not really looking at her, "I expect I ought to be getting on with my work. I was correcting essays." He gestured towards the books on the table. He was a very conscientious teacher.

She stood up — he was so very nice — but they were just friends. And yet she always felt he would have liked things to be different.

Anna crossed the room and put her hand on the handle of the door. But he didn't add anything more.

"Thanks for the tea, then, Ellis. Be seeing you," she said.

INSIDE her own flat, she tried to avoid thinking about anything except the work in hand. And there was plenty of that. It was almost midnight when she finally lay down to sleep.

She closed her eyes, thinking of David, letting her mind drift back to last night . . . on the way home from the dance.

It had been such a wonderful evening. They had talked non-stop, finding so much in common.

"Now that I've found you," he'd told her, "I hope we'll see each other often."

She couldn't quite remember what her answer had been. She'd been a little nervous, unsure of herself, wondering if he was going to kiss her, wondering if she wanted to kiss him; imagining what it would be like.

Then he'd said, "I like you, Anna, there's something special about you — you've got style."

Again, she couldn't recall what her reply had been. But now, she savoured his words.

She tried to think of how she would describe David. Stylish, yes, maybe; or at least he'd like to think of himself as smart, polished, modern, successful. He was very different from Ellis.

She frowned and opened her eyes and stared at the strip of light between the curtains. She hadn't meant to think about Ellis Rodgers. He'd no business whatsoever to intrude on her thoughts.

All right, so she liked Ellis, she admitted irritably. And he liked her. But what about that night that Ellis had asked her to go out with him? He had two tickets for a play, he'd said.

Anna's mind cringed away from the memory of the boredom she'd experienced sitting in the darkened theatre watching a play she had neither liked nor understood. Then the tete-a-tete supper in that dreary silent restaurant when Ellis had been eager to discuss the merits of the play, while she had tried to appear interested.

> ### Forget Me Not
>
> *N*OT dead but sleepeth." It's the tale of a fiddle once hung on the wall. An old man played reels and the songs and psalms of Scotland on it till his fingers grew stiff.
>
> The old man died and the fiddle lay silent. For the touch of a hand that was gone, it was condemned to the attic, unstrung and forlorn.
>
> Then a young violinist took it home as a gift and she brought it to life again. The fiddle awoke from its coma, and yielded again the sound of music.
>
> It hadn't died, it was only sleeping. And that's true of other things than a fiddle!
>
> The Bible today is not dead – only neglected. And reverence for God is not perished – only forsaken.
>
> Rev. T. R. S. Campbell

He hadn't asked her to go out again. But it had made no difference to their friendship. In the weeks which had followed the disastrous outing, they had met and talked and shared coffee or tea as often as usual.

Trying to be honest with herself now, Anna realised that both of them must have been disappointed, although neither of them had even come close to saying so. It was as if, by mutual consent, their date was never mentioned and never repeated. Why not? She pondered the question vaguely as she gradually fell into a deep and dreamless sleep.

Next morning at the office Anna was eager to tell her friend, Valerie, about her wonderful weekend and to exclaim again about the amazing coincidence which had brought David to that party the previous week.

"Maybe you were fated to meet again," Valerie suggested, "it must have been in your stars."

Anna smiled happily.

"Well, I don't believe in the stars. I much prefer to be grateful to you because you introduced us."

"But I didn't even invite the man," Valerie protested.

"He was a friend of a friend." She hesitated for a brief moment, before she added, in a quiet tone, "I asked quite a few folk to bring someone — maybe you didn't remember that I told you to bring . . . your nice neighbour." She paused again before the final three words.

But Anna didn't notice at the time.

"Ellis?" She laughed. "He never goes to parties! He absolutely loathes having to shout above music and noise and he simply never dances."

Valerie gave a small shrug.

"Still, maybe he would have liked to be asked." She went back to her own desk without waiting for an answer and began to pound her typewriter.

The smile faded from Anna's lips. She was bewildered. Valerie had met Ellis on a number of occasions at the flat, but she had never seemed particularly interested in him, or had she? Anna tried to think back. But there was nothing. All her friends knew about Ellis — the man across the landing who was always on hand in a crisis.

The other girls had teased her about him, but she couldn't remember Valerie ever commenting on him.

A FTER a while she spoke to her friend, apologetically.

"Valerie, I didn't honestly think you expected me to bring Ellis to your party."

Valerie's head turned but she seemed deliberately to look past Anna.

"Forget it! The party was last week," she snapped.

Anna bit her lower lip. Valerie had never spoken to her like that before. It wasn't so much that she sounded angry; it was more like contempt.

Anna was still puzzled and very hurt. She genuinely couldn't understand why Valerie should turn on her like this. Tears stung the back of her eyes as she tried to concentrate on her work.

She ought to be angry. But instead she was aware of an obscure feeling of guilt. The same sort of sensation as she had experienced last night in Ellis's flat.

Try as she might, she could not analyse her feelings for Ellis. Of course she liked him. But she was not, and never had been, in love with him.

Thinking of love, of being in love, turned her thoughts spontaneously to David. There was a mysteriously-magical enchantment about everything he said to her, every touch of his hand, every look he gave her contained a special meaning, one meant for her, and her alone.

It could only be love, she told herself, with a faint sense of wonder, counting the hours until she would see him again.

A T lunch-time Valerie had apparently forgotten her earlier mood. She didn't exactly apologise, but she said something about having got out of bed on the wrong side that morning but that, once she'd had a good lunch, she'd be her usual bouncing self again.

Anna was willing to forget the episode too.

We've been friends too long to let a man come between us, she told herself thankfully. And then a sobering thought came to her. The man in question was in no way between them. She had not deliberately tried to keep Ellis to herself. But Valerie thought she had.

On her way home from work, she hesitated outside Ellis's door. Somehow she felt that she ought to be honest with him. Last night she had wavered, wanting to tell him and yet unable to say aloud the words which clamoured in her heart.

She still couldn't, she decided, going into her own flat to get ready for her date with David.

He had said that he would call for her around eight, and at precisely eight o'clock there was a firm knock at the door.

Anna's heart was fluttering as she hurried to open the door.

But it was no illusion. When their eyes met, it was exactly the same.

In his arms, with his lips against hers, Anna could have been floating down a rainbow.

"It doesn't seem possible in such a short time, but I think I'm falling in love with you."

She couldn't believe she was hearing this. It was just too wonderful to be true. She raised her mouth to reach his ear.

"I feel exactly the same," she said softly.

David drew her closer, kissed her again, then stepped back.

"I'm afraid we'd better go, darling. I know it's unromantic to say so, but I had to double park the car. I've booked a table at the Amber House," he added, with a smile.

Anna hastily picked up her scarf and bag.

"That sounds lovely," she said, "I've never been there."

He took her hand as they went out.

"Yes, I know, you told me."

She gave him a smiling glance.

"Does that mean you remember everything I've told you?"

"Every single thing," he assured her, stroking her cheek gently.

Over a candle-lit meal and to a background of soft music, they talked, discovering so much about each other and repeating the words of love they had spoken so cautiously earlier on. But now they were more confident and the promises they made to each other were firm and certain.

"I have to go north tomorrow morning," David told her, "and I couldn't imagine going away for three whole days without telling you of my feelings, without knowing how you felt, if you loved me . . . ."

Anna smiled at him and nodded.

"Not knowing was frightening while it lasted, wasn't it?"

"Terrifying," he agreed, and he confessed, "I pictured myself telling you how I felt and you saying something absolutely shattering like, 'Don't be silly, I hardly know you'!"

They giggled softly, holding hands, dreaming, gazing into each other's eyes, until they reluctantly realised that the music had stopped, and it was time to go home.

Three whole days seemed to be an eternity stretching ahead of them, but now that they were sure of their love the skies ahead seemed cloudless.

A NNA'S head was still in the clouds next morning as she set off for the office. But when she opened her door, she came face to face with Ellis Rodgers.

For a second, she was startled, then quite naturally, she said, gaily, " 'Morning, Ellis. Isn't it a glorious morning?"

He didn't smile but his face wore a look of amusement as he replied. "Depends how much you like rain."

"I love rain," she assured him, and then unable to contain her wonderful news any longer she told him, "Ellis, I'm in love, I'm going to be married!"

"Congratulations." He was smiling now. "I hope you'll be happy."

Now there was no awkwardness between them. "I was going to tell you on Sunday," she said simply. "But you see, David hadn't actually said anything . . . so I couldn't very well."

Ellis nodded understandingly and they exchanged a smile.

"See you!" Ellis said cheerfully, as they hurried their separate ways through the rain.

Anna was surprised by his reaction — and pleased. She had thought he might be upset. But he obviously regarded her as just a friend. So perhaps there was hope for Valerie.

She wanted everyone to feel as happy as she did.

In fact, she thought, I'll give a party . . . and first on the invitation list will be Valerie. Then she'd be able to tell everyone her news and introduce Valerie and Ellis too.

She issued the invitation as soon as she saw Valerie. Neither girl mentioned Ellis Rodgers. But they both knew that he would be there. Anna could only guess at Valerie's secret hopes and wishes.

Valerie and Ellis would certainly meet at the party, Anna thought dreamily, and then it would be up to them. Perhaps they would fall in love, perhaps not. She giggled. It was all in the stars.

She still didn't believe that they could foretell the future. And yet she knew that meeting David had somehow seemed pre-ordained.

Then she remembered he would be phoning her at lunchtime. Her heart gave a flutter. She'd never been so happy, had so much to look forward to, so much to plan. The future was like a bright star, twinkling in the heavens.

A Certain Kind Of Magic

by Kate Mortimer

C AROL fixed the folding chair so that it faced the lake, and turned to her friend.

"Not even you could get involved in other people's troubles here," she said.

Jane flopped gratefully into the chair, and rested her plastered right hand and arm.

"Other people's troubles? Me?" She looked up at her flatmate and colleague with a grin.

"Yes, you!" Carol said, then as an afterthought, "I hope I didn't bully you into coming here when you wanted to stay at home. You didn't want to stay in, in case Brian called, or telephoned, or . . ."

Jane smiled brightly.

"I didn't. Brian won't. And you, poppet, couldn't bully anyone, even if you tried!"

"Bless you," Carol said warmly, picking up her handbag from the grass. "You know, Jane, you really are incredible. There you sit, an elegant five-foot nothing who looks as if she couldn't say boo to a goose, and yet . . .''

"It was an oil-soaked gull on a cliff, remember?'' Jane replied, "and don't start nagging again!''

"You need to be nagged, and learn how to stop getting involved — for your own sake,'' Carol told her firmly. "Just think what you've done the last few days.''

She held her hand up and counted on her fingers.

"You gave up your place in the tennis tournament to go down to the coast to look after Brian's kid brother while his parents were away.''

She moved on to the next finger.

"You see a wrecked tanker, the oil slick, and the gulls, so you decided it was your responsibility to climb down the cliff to the rescue.''

"Now, Carol, be truthful,'' Jane interrupted, good humouredly. "You'd have gone down that cliff, too, You know you would.''

"I daresay. But having come an almighty cropper, broken my arm, fingers and a budding romance, I'm sure I'd do as I was told and sit back and relax. But not you, oh dear me, no! If I hadn't put that gang from the upstairs flat in their place, you'd have been running after them right, left and centre.''

"Be fair,'' Jane said, trying to reason with her friend. "They were only excited. They've just started a group and, of course, they wanted to go and rehearse.''

"They are selfish opportunists,'' Carol said firmly. "They were using your troubles for their convenience. They're always on the borrow — time, groceries or whatever. They needed a lesson and . . .''

"O.K. O.K., you've made your point. You've done a noble deed, rescuing me and bringing me here while you do the shopping on this gorgeous Saturday morning,'' Jane replied. "But don't forget you've got a hair appointment, and if you miss it, your Bill will arrive to find a very bedraggled girlfriend!''

Carol looked at her watch, and then back at Jane.

"Now, Jane, promise on your honour that if anybody falls in the lake you'll stay right here — and let them fend for themselves.''

"Scram!'' Jane said, and laughed as Carol turned away and hurried across the park to the road, where the Mini they shared was parked.

"It's tempting fate to say things like that,'' she called after her.

Then, turning back to face the lake and the ducks, she rested the book she had brought on the strong wooden arm of the chair.

WHAT'S the use of thinking about Brian, she told herself stolidly. Whether he ever came, wrote or telephoned, there was nothing he could say or do that could make any difference to his attitude to those wretched gulls.

Their friendship had been fun while it lasted, but it hadn't lasted long. There's a lesson in disillusion, she decided philosophically, bending her head and turning to the first page of her book.

Carol was right. This was just what she needed.

A Certain Kind Of Magic

"Excuse me, miss!" Jane jumped as a hand touched her shoulder.

"Oh! I'm so glad it's you." There was relief in the new arrival's voice.

Jane instantly recognised a former cashier from the supermarket checkout. She looked at the baby in the pram and then at the pretty girl with her.

"So that's why I haven't seen you lately," she said with a smile. "She's absolutely gorgeous."

It was then she saw the small boy, bloody but unbowed, and liberally spattered with mud, hiding behind his mother.

"He . . . he just walked into the lake to see how far he could go," his mother explained. "I'd only turned away for a minute.

"I . . . you wouldn't mind keeping your eye on the baby while I take him to the loo and clean him up," The young mother asked.

"Of course not," Jane replied instantly.

"She's ever so good, really." The woman's voice sounded relieved. "And so's Lulu."

"Lulu?" Jane murmured. As if on cue, a big shaggy dog, of very dubious ancestry, shambled forward from behind the pram, to which he was securely tied.

The dog sat down on her bottom, and looked up at Jane with large brown eyes clearly announcing her complete and utter innocence, as young mother and filthy boy scuttled across the grass towards the toilets.

"Gaaaaa," the baby gurgled, dark eyes sparkling, as she held out a friendly little fist.

"Goo goo goo," Jane burbled, grasping the tiny fingers.

The little curly head fell back on to the pretty floral pillow and two lively diminutive feet kicked a gollywog on to the grass.

Jane was just reaching to retrieve the golly, when the peace was suddenly shattered by a fiendish yapping.

Lulu's docility disintegrated in an instant and she began to bark with the full power of her lungs, leaping about at the same time. The baby started to wail, frightened by the noise, and the rocking of the pram.

"Stop it, Lulu! Down," Jane shouted helplessly. But the dog continued her excited barking.

Jane turned a furious gaze on the cause of all the trouble — a big, scruffy dog with an ancestry as varied as Lulu's. He was clearly telling the world in the only way he knew how, that Lulu was his chosen — for the moment, at least.

IN half a minute the peaceful corner of the park had become a canine battlefield in which no holds were barred.

Desperately, Jane tried to hold the pram steady with her left arm, telling herself not to panic. Of course the pram wouldn't fall over . . . Of course the baby wouldn't fall out.

Valiantly, Jane tried to make her voice heard above the crescendo of barks, yelps, growls and infant cries.

She was just deciding on the desperate step of releasing the almost-demented Lulu from the pram, when a deep, strong and authoritative voice sang out.

What it said was unrecognisable as human speech. But such was its tone and power of command that within thirty seconds the battlefield was cleared, the abandoned Lulu was sitting on her bottom as if she'd never so much as moved a muscle. And the cause of all the trouble was squatting at the feet of the peacemaker, looking at him, adoringly.

Jane hardly even looked at the peacemaker. She was much too occupied crooning to the infant in an effort to calm her.

Only when the child was lying back contentedly sucking her thumb did Jane look up and see the young man. But she was in no mood to be impressed by his height, nor his rugged charm.

In a few icy words she told him what she thought of people who allowed dangerous dogs to race around parks unleashed.

"He's not dangerous," the peacemaker said calmly. "He's only full of the joys of spring . . ."

"This isn't funny," Jane said coldly. "Heaven knows what would have happened if the pram had gone over."

"But it didn't. And anyway, I take a very poor view of a mother who ties a dangerous dog to her baby's pram handle."

"Lulu is *not* dangerous." Jane flushed. "And, anyway, it isn't *my* baby," she added cuttingly.

"Ah! I was thinking you looked as if you'd have more sense," the man said calmly. "And as a matter of fact, this is not my dog."

Jane was momentarily deflated, stunned into silence.

"Then how did you make him stop?" she said when she recovered her breath. "And why . . ." she broke off, seeing with relief that the young mother and cleaned-up small boy were running across the grass.

"Thanks ever so much," she burbled. "She's been a good girl?" It was a statement, not a question.

"Of course," Jane murmured.

"And Lulu?" the girl said, with the same confidence.

Jane took a deep breath while noticing out of the corner of her eye that the peacemaker had withdrawn from the scene of operations.

"They've both been absolute angels," Jane said, with a smile.

A S mother and children, with Lulu, sauntered away, the peacemaker returned.

"What *did* you say to those dogs?" she asked him.

"Oh! Abracadabra, sort of!" He grinned down at her, and then added blandly, "I just happen to be a vet. I had to come into town for some supplies and decided to have a look at the park."

"Oh, I see."

"I've just joined my father's practice out at West Rilham."

Carefully he took her left hand and shook it.

"Roger Simpson, at your service," he said.

"I'm Jane Martin, and I reckon your service is top notch. Seriously —" she looked up into the laughing, grey eyes — "I'm eternally grateful. Goodness knows what would have happened if you hadn't come along when you did. I wouldn't have known what to do."

He looked at her plaster reflectively.

"Looks like you've been in some sort of fight, lately, too."

Jane explained about the gulls.

"The plaster just proves I'm no cliff climber."

"It says a lot for you trying anyway," Roger said. "Did they survive?"

"Only one," Jane said, sorrowfully. "There was a bird sanctuary and the couple there were great when I went to them . . ."

Jane stopped, remembering that blazing row with Brian. How he had argued, raged about driving her there. They hadn't any time to waste, he'd said, and what were a few seagulls anyway?

"It must have been horrible for you." Roger's eyes darkened with sympathy and understanding. "Looks like you are the sort of person things happen to!" he added with a smile.

"You can say that again!" Jane said.

SUDDENLY Jane started to laugh, to giggle.

Roger Simpson bent over her and took her left hand again.

"What you and I need now," he said firmly, "is a good strong cup of coffee."

Instantly Jane stopped giggling, and looked at him in astonishment.

"It works with humans as well as dogs!" she whispered. "I mean your brand of abracadabra."

"Talking of dogs," Roger said, picking up her book and handbag and helping her to her feet, "the sheepdog trials are on at West Rilham tomorrow . . ." He left his words dangling in mid-air.

"It's an awful admission," Jane said, as he tucked her arm in his and walked her carefully across the grass, "but I've never seen sheep dog trials."

"Ah!" Roger Simpson murmured. "Then over that cup of coffee, we can discuss filling in the educational gap. I wouldn't think even you could come to grief, quietly watching sheep dog trials with a vet!"

"Don't be too sure, Mr Simpson," she replied with a giggle. "You've a lot to learn about me."

And they walked off happily, arm in arm.

J OEY! Joey! How's Joey then?''
    Emily Bowden pulled the cover off the cage and gazed at the
    budgie.

''Wake up, Joey, spring's here . . . I think.''

She turned to the window and looked out to where the sunshine was lighting the row of houses opposite. Soon the doors of those houses, replicas of the one where Emily lived, would open and the young men and women who lived there would spill out.

There were one or two people of Emily's age but she hadn't had a chance to meet them yet, well not to get to know them.

''Perhaps it was a mistake, Joey. Perhaps I should have stayed in the place I knew.'' She gazed at the bird, who tilted his head and gazed right back at her.

''Stupid bird!'' Emily cried, taking the water container from the cage to fill it.

''Why won't you talk? The man in the shop said you'd soon learn. Heavens! It's not as if I don't talk to you enough. Too much, if you ask me. People will think I'm a bit peculiar, talking to myself.''

But you've got to talk to someone, she thought. Should I have stayed?

126

N A FRIEND by Phyllis Heath

Yet how could she? The old house where she had lived all her married life had been too big for herself alone. There'd been an excuse to stay when Jill had married and visited often with the three children. Even when Mark had left home for college, he'd come home bringing several of his friends with him.

But eventually Mark left college and went to live down south in his own flat. Jill's family grew past the baby stage and her husband felt an urge to see the world.

"We're going to Canada, Mum," Jill told her one day. "It's all arranged. We didn't say anything when we were only looking into things, no sense worrying you."

Emily saw the way her eyes watched her anxiously.

"Worrying me? Why do you and Mark think I'm going to be perpetually worried by the things you do? I stopped worrying when he went into long pants and you got yourself a boyfriend." She laughed.

But of course it wasn't true, one always worried about them.

"My, but it's a grand idea — the best thing you could have done," Emily had said, enthusiastically. "Tell me all about it."

So Jill had poured out all her excitement and Emily had kept the eager look on her face, damping down her own concern. When Jill and her family had gone home later that evening, Emily had walked through the empty rooms and come to a decision. She would find a nice flat somewhere. Somewhere that she too could start a new life.

S O Emily had been very practical — selling the large house and finding this two-roomed flat on the ground floor of a similar house the other side of town.

I suppose I've not really pulled up my roots, she'd thought, settling in that first day some months back. Just stretched them a little. But I'll make new friends here. There'll be different shops to go to, different places to see. I'm quite looking forward to it.

She said the same sort of things to her son and daughter and they settled to their own new lives reassured that she seemed so happy.

"Which is just how it should be, Joey," Emily told the silent bird.

Joey peered back at her, cocking his head, his bright eyes gleaming.

"Stupid bird," Emily said crossly. "Why won't you talk? Fat lot of company you turned out to be."

E MILY began to wash the breakfast dishes, watching the sunshine through the window as its rays began to cross the pavement towards her own side of the street.

"Sun looks lovely, Joey. Going to be a nice day. I think I'll go for a walk." Her gaze went to the waste bin where she'd just deposited the crust from her toast.

"I could feed those ducks in the park."

She rescued the crusts, thrusting them into a paper bag.

" 'Bye, Joey. Back for lunch . . . See, I can't stop talking to you even if you don't answer. Stupid bird, stupid Emily."

It wasn't much of a park, just a stretch of grass, a few swings for the children, and the duck pond. Emily stood near the edge and tossed the crust into the water. Instantly the ducks came to life, swimming frantically towards her, fighting over the pieces.

Emily took a step or two back as they began to clamber out of the water and the next handful fell short.

But as she bent to pick them up a black and white bundle of rather tatty fur rushed under her arm and gulped down the bread.

"Scamp! Scamp! Here, boy!" A man's voice shouted behind her. "Bad boy!"

Emily turned, seeing the man on the bench for the first time. She smiled at his apologetic expression.

"It's no use, he's eaten the lot. Don't you feed him?" She laughed.

"Of course."

The man smiled back, and Emily stuffed the bag into her pocket and strolled towards the seat. Scamp followed, nudging her hand hopefully.

"There's nothing left," she told him, and sat down. The dog crouched at her feet, tail thumping, ears pricked and tongue lolling expectantly.

Scamp then moved to lay his head upon the man's knee and he no longer looked so happy.

"Why's he looking so miserable now?" she asked.

The man shrugged, hunching his shoulders, and just when Emily was about to give up he turned to her, ruffling the dog's coat affectionately.

"He's a grand chap, but like you say, mischievous. No malice, mind you, but full of life, even though he's no youngster."

"He must be good company," she ventured.

"Yes." The single word gave nothing away.

"Especially if you're on your own . . . ?" she said, inquiringly.

"No." There was another silence.

"No, I don't live alone. It'd be a bit awkward really," he added, and nodded towards the foot which twisted uncomfortably. Then Emily realised that he had never taken his left hand from his pocket.

"I've had a stroke, you see," he explained.

Milly grunted her sympathy and waited for him to say more.

"Not that I'm complaining. Far from it. I live with my daughter and her husband — they're good to me. Let me bring some of my own bits and pieces, and Scamp too. Right good to us they are, aren't they, lad?"

He fondled the dog's ears and the dog licked his hand affectionately.

"He seems very fit." Milly wondered if perhaps the dog was ill and this was the reason for the man's unhappiness.

"Yes, he's fit enough. Not like your old man, eh, Scamp? They won't have to put you in a nursing home while they go on holiday, will they?"

EMILY was saddened by the man's attitude. Surely he didn't resent his daughter taking a holiday? They had evidently made arrangements for him.

"I expect they need a break," she tried.

The man's eyes turned to her accusingly.

"Don't you go thinking I begrudge them a holiday. Why, my Dorothy's been very good to me! But she needs a break, and then there's the kiddies. Of course I want them to go. It's just Scamp."

Emily watched the soulful look Scamp gave his master, almost as if he understood.

"Can't you get him into a kennels. You'd like that, wouldn't you, Scamp?"

The dog, hearing his name, came to push his cold nose into her hand.

"He's a friendly soul," Emily said, patting the rough head.

The man stared at her in amazement.

"He's taken to you, that's for sure. I've never known him like this, he's a one-man dog, generally."

Emily laughed.

"I expect it's cupboard love, he thinks I've got some more titbits for him."

"Maybe," the man sounded unsure.

"But there'd be no-one to give him a bit of coddling in a kennels. Oh, I don't say they'd be unkind. The one they've chosen seems very good, but it's not like home. And I know he'll miss me. He pined so when I was in hospital.''

''Do you live near?'' she asked, to change the subject.

He nodded towards a small car parked beyond the grass, which Emily hadn't noticed before.

''That's mine. It's fixed up so I can drive it. I can get around on my own two feet, but not too far. That way Scamp and me can get out into the country, can't we, old lad?''

''The country? Mm! That sounds lovely.'' Emily sighed.

''Scamp'll miss our days out,'' he said.

''But it won't be for long.'' Emily's tone was sharper than she meant it to be and the man's face flushed.

''I must sound selfish.'' He straightened his shoulders and smiled at her.

''I'm a bit grumpy this morning. You know how it is sometimes . . .''

''Don't I? I was the same earlier, just because my silly bird won't learn to talk.''

She went on to tell him of Joey's lack of conversation.

They were back where they'd started and Emily thought it was time she went before the man started to worry again.

''Time I was off. 'Bye, Scamp. 'Bye, Mr . . . ?'' Emily waited for him to supply his name.

''Tom, Tom Bradley. Been nice talking to you.''

Emily nodded.

''I'm Emily Bowden. Yes, it has been pleasant. I — I shouldn't worry too much about Scamp.''

She moved away and then found that the dog was close behind her.

''Go back, you silly animal, I've nothing for you.''

Tom Bradley scratched his head.

''Now, I'd never have thought it. Come here, boy. He's never done that before.''

Scamp went back but he gazed after Emily until she reached the main road again. I don't know about him being a one-man dog, maybe he's a one-woman dog too, Emily thought, secretly pleased.

N EXT day Emily found herself putting on her coat as soon as her chores were done.

''I don't recall saying I'd go out, Joey. Do you know what's got into me?''

Joey cocked his head and then went to look at himself in the tiny mirror. Emily laughed.

''Now who's being stupid? Fancy asking you questions. 'Bye, Joey. I'll be back for lunch.''

She made her way to the little park again, wondering if Tom and Scamp would be there. Now she realised that she had been thinking of her two new friends all night. They both had the same expression in their eyes, trusting and friendly. An idea was forming in her mind.

''It'll only be for a couple of weeks,'' she said, as she waited at the crossing.

"And it would be a sort of trial. I'd find out if I could manage a dog. There is that bit of land behind the house."

Scamp raced towards her before she was halfway to the seat where Tom was sitting. Emily lost no time in making her offer.

"I'm sure he'd be all right with me. I know he'll miss you, but we are friends now, aren't we, Scamp?"

Tom laughed.

"I always said he had brains, that one. I think he knew what he was doing yesterday. Are you sure it will be all right? I know I'd be easier in my mind . . ."

He didn't wait for Emily's assurances.

"He isn't much trouble. I'd bring some biscuits and meat for him." He pushed the dog playfully.

"You're a sly one, aren't you? But you knew when you were on to a good thing, didn't you? You certainly like a bit of spoiling."

Scamp sat back on his haunches and grinned as if he was enjoying the joke, and when Tom handed Emily the lead to see if he would indeed go with her, he wagged his tail enthusiastically. Nor did he pull back when she walked him round the tiny park, or even when she took him out on to the road.

"It's very good of you, Mrs Bowden," Tom's son-in-law said when he called with Scamp's basket and feeding bowls.

The Blackbird

REGARDLESS of my watchful eyes,
He tries the water dish for size.
And, head inclined, he meditates
Upon the ripples he creates.

Then swiftly generating power,
He makes a silver sequinned shower,
And bobbing, dancing, carries on
Till every drop of water's gone.

Sylvia Hart

"Dorothy needs a break, but we knew Dad was fretting about the dog."

"Don't give it another thought. And," Emily looked up at him, "Tom understands. He thinks a lot of both of you, and didn't want you to know how he felt."

The young man smiled.

"I know, but we guessed. Those two have hardly ever been separated." He hesitated.

"I'm glad he's found a friend that he seems to enjoy talking to."

When Emily brought Scamp back to her flat she let him off the lead to sniff around the rooms and then into the little walled garden.

The days simply flew along and Emily found she was dreading the end of Scamp's stay. He was as mischievous as Tom had warned her and she knew now that she could never start with her own dog.

"At least you're always in the one place," she told Joey.

"I'm always falling over Scamp — but he is more company, despite that."

Emily's eyes went to the postcard on the mantelpiece. Though Tom had written only about Scamp's welfare it had been a friendly gesture to write at all.

WHEN the day came to hand Scamp back, Emily clipped on his lead with a heavy heart. Scamp seemed to sense some of her unhappiness.

But the rapturous greeting he gave Tom dispelled any such ideas.

"My, he's looking fit. I hope he hasn't been any trouble."

"He's been fine. I've enjoyed having him."

"You wouldn't get your own dog, though?" Tom asked, and supplied his own answer. "They are a trouble to rear from a pup and it's not every full-grown dog that takes to people the way Scamp does."

Emily hid a smile. So Scamp wasn't a one-man dog any longer.

"We could, well, sort of share him," Tom said cautiously.

"I've got a new car now. I can take a passenger."

His eyes slid to Emily.

"That's nice," she said.

"I was thinking, in there, maybe you'd come out sometimes, just to give Scamp a run, you understand. I'm sure he'd like you to come."

Emily bent to pat the dog's head, hiding the blush which rose to her cheeks. It was a long time since she'd been invited out by a gentleman.

"Well, we can't disappoint Scamp, can we?" she asked, and smiled into Tom's face.

BACK at home it seemed quiet with no scrabbling paws and welcoming whines.

"But I've made a friend, Joey. Two friends actually."

Joey rang his bell and chirruped noisily. It was clear he was glad Scamp had gone.

"Have I been neglecting you? Well it's your own fault. I told you you should talk."

She busied herself making her tea and sat down to eat it. The corner where Scamp's bowl should have been seemed empty, and she found herself listening for the patter of his paws outside the door.

Joey ruffled its feathers, and began to preen.

"Aye! I suppose I've still got you." She grinned, pushing a piece of millet through the bars.

"We're all right together, aren't we?"

Joey accepted the offering and ran to look at his reflection. He cocked his head and turned to look at Emily. When Emily smiled back at him he seemed to glare round the kitchen.

"Scamp! Scamp!" he cried, just as she had called the dog many times.

"Well! You old fraud! You can talk." Emily sat down and gazed up at the bird. "I've got my bit of company after all, and I've got a friend to boot. *And* I'm going for a drive tomorrow. Now what do you think of that, you clever fellow?"

Joey looked to where the millet was lying on the floor of his cage.

"Stupid bird! Stupid bird! Stupid bird," he cried.

A Man To Avoid

by
Ruth Sinclair

THE canteen with its mingling smells of bacon, fish and chips was no place to be on such a lovely day.

Amanda and Iris, in common with most of the younger members of the staff, usually ate their main course quickly so they could sit outside in the pleasant garden grounds bordering each unit of the industrial estate.

Amanda, newly graduated from the typing college, loved every minute of the new job. Mrs Russell, the pool supervisor, was very fair and the soul of patience. All the girls both liked and respected her.

"Here he comes again," Iris Semple announced loftily. Since Amanda joined the firm, she had taken her under her wing, initiating her into the mysteries of the duplicating and Telex machines, introducing her around the various departments with a few comments thrown in about one or two personalities.

"Who?" Amanda asked.

"Mike Inglis," she had informed the new girl shortly after the introduction, "is the pushy type — and always joking. You just never know when to take him seriously."

Mike, who worked in the drawing office, seemed to be a daily visitor to the typing pool, and usually a great deal of hilarity accompanied his visits.

He had even serenaded Amanda when Mrs Russell was out of the room, earning some applause from the other typists. Conscious of Iris's disapproval, Amanda had looked rather solemn.

THAT night they caught the same bus to town and Mike made sure Amanda and he sat together.

"My car's off the road at the moment," he told her. "The old boneshaker, I mean — costs a fortune in repairs, but I just can't run to a new one, yet."

"Well, there's always next week," she returned lightly.

"There certainly is," he agreed. "Are you free next Monday?"

"Sorry," she said coolly. "I'll be busy that night."

He nodded, in no way downcast by her refusal.

"I'm not surprised," he replied. "I expect you're out every night. How do you like working in Mellors, Amanda?"

"Very much," she said, glad to be on more impersonal lines. "Have you been with them long?"

By the time they reached the bus station, she'd learnt he'd served his draughtsman's apprenticeship in Mellors, was keen to make a success of his profession, and equally enthusiastic about enjoying himself.

"So you really don't have the time to go out with me?" he had finished, helping her down from the bus in the station.

"No, I'm sorry," she retorted, smiling.

"Excuse me, I must dash or I'll miss my bus home," she said, avoiding his eyes.

Trying to forget the look on his face, she ran for the outgoing bus that would drop her at the corner of her street. How did he manage to make her feel as though she had let him down in some way. But if what Iris had told her about Mike Inglis was even half true, it would have been silly to get involved and possibly end up hurt, like the others.

SHE was soon to discover that he was not so easily brushed off. Next morning as she walked to work, a delapidated car drew up and the owner offered her a lift.

"Good as new, well almost," Mike assured her. "At least, it'll save you walking the last hundred yards or so."

"Thank you," she said, determined to be no more than civil.

And when he asked if he might wait and run her home in the evening, she refused politely.

"So you're getting the romantic treatment now," Iris remarked one day, spotting a bunch of violets on Amanda's desk.

"I suppose he's taking you to the theatre and dinner in town."

"What if he is?" Rose Hennessey put in from an adjoining desk, with a sympathetic look at Amanda. "What's it to you, Iris?"

"I don't want to see her getting hurt, that's all. Remember how it was with . . ."

"Please don't fall out over me, girls. There's absolutely nothing between Mike and me, and that's the way I want it. So, can we please drop the subject?" Amanda said.

The little attentions continued, however. Every morning when she uncovered the typewriter there would be a poorly-typed line or two, the obvious result of Mike's overtime working the previous night.

Hello, Amanda! There's a very good film on at the Odeon this week.

Each day there was a different message.

Surely you must have a free date sometime soon.

By now, the typewriter cover was usually off long before Amanda reached the office, for the rest of the girls were keen to discover what the latest message might be.

"Nothing's private with you lot," the girl said, pretending to be annoyed. And though she wouldn't have admitted it to anyone, she was as interested as everyone else to read each little note from Mike Inglis.

One morning, much to everyone's disappointment, there was no message, but Rose pointed out the possible reason.

"There's a board meeting this morning and usually the directors come round the offices on a tour of inspection."

E VERYONE seemed a little on edge waiting on the visitation. When it came, the directors seemed pleasant enough.

One of the visitors had a sheaf of board papers in his hands as she passed Amanda, he asked if she had a paper clip.

"Yes, certainly," she replied, quickly.

Diving into the top drawer, she picked a clip from the tin that held them, and before the fascinated gaze of a dozen pairs of eyes, a veritable necklace of clips came with it.

"Just one will do," the director remarked, a little mystified, while Amanda fumbled to disentangle the chain, and Mrs Russell looked on with a reproaching expression.

Later, having seen the visitors safely out, she returned to the room, quelling the giggles erupting around her.

"If you've time to play around with paper clips, Amanda," she said, pointedly, "I'll obviously have to see you get more typing to do."

"I'm awfully sorry," Amanda apologised. "It won't happen again."

Another of Mike's silly pranks, she thought angrily, stabbing the typewriter keys. Well, he had gone too far this time.

Her chance to put Mike in his place came a little later that day, when Mrs Russell sent her to the Buying Department to take dictation from one of the section leaders.

The Drawing Office was on the floor above and she made her way there with firm deliberation.

Mike was sitting behind a large sloping desk on which lay the drawing he had been working at. It was her first visit to the Drawing Office and the initial impression seemed to be of a vast hall flanked by windows and flooded with sunshine.

"Hi, Amanda!" he called, looking surprised and yet obviously pleased. "Something I can do for you?"

"Yes." Her voice was cool. "Will you please leave me alone and stop annoying me with silly, time-wasting pranks like this." Pulling the paper-clip chain from her pocket, she threw it before him on to the desk with a little more emphasis than she had intended. To her horror she saw it career across the neatly-lined drawing, tip over a bottle of Indian ink, and produce a huge blot.

She was too horrified to say anything immediately, but then she found her voice.

"I'm terribly sorry," she said in a horrified tone. "I didn't mean . . ."

"The next time you feel like coming here with your accusations, perhaps you'll give us fair warning," he said, sharply. "That way, we can hide everything that might get spoiled."

"I've said I'm sorry." She was angry now. "What more can I do?"

With flaming cheeks she turned and ran from the room, conscious of the silence and the curious glances sent her way by Mike's colleagues.

What a fuss to make over a little spilt ink, she thought defensively.

Iris tried to console her by saying it was as much as he deserved after making her look ridiculous that morning, but there were no words of comfort from Rose, who looked grave when she heard of the mishap.

Next morning there was no message on the typewriter — Amanda hadn't really expected there to be one.

She hadn't been able to stop thinking about the drawing, all the work he must have put into it, and how quickly she'd spoilt it.

THERE were no more offers of lifts to and from the works, but the car was still in the workers' parking lot and it looked as though Mike was clocking in earlier than usual and leaving later in the evenings.

Then she was sent by Mrs Russell to take dictation from Purchasing.

"Can you go along to Personnel, please, Amanda," the supervisor directed. "I think Mr Watson may ask you to deliver the letter he's about to dictate. In that case, you can leave after it's been typed."

"Yes, Mrs Russell, thank you," Amanda said.

"It's to one of the cleaners," the Personnel Officer explained. "She's had to give up her job for a spell because her husband's in hospital, and the envelope contains back wages. Mrs Russell and I didn't think you'd mind handing it in, since the lady stays in your area. It wouldn't be any bother, would it?"

"Not in the least," the girl assured him quickly, glad that they trusted her with such a job.

Once the letter had been typed up and signed, she covered her machine, got her things together, and explained the early departure to Rose.

"Will you let Iris know I'm away, please?" Amanda asked.

"Yes, of course. It'll be nice for you to get away early, Amanda."

Rose seemed to be hesitating as though she wanted to add something else, and Amanda waited, smiling encouragement.

"Was there something else?"

"I've been trying to get an opportunity to speak to you on your own," she said cautiously. "But I'm not quite sure how to put it, actually. I don't want to seem as though I'm talking behind anyone's back, but . . ."

"But . . .?" Amanda prompted gently.

"I like Mike Inglis!" Rose stated baldly.

"You do?" Amanda looked a bit astonished at the unexpected confession.

"And I like you, Amanda." Rose's voice softened. "I was so pleased when you both seemed attracted to each other."

"But how did you . . .?" Amanda started.

"You didn't have to tell me, I knew how you felt," Rose interrupted.

"Much good it did me," Amanda said, letting her true feelings show for the first time.

"Don't worry — it'll work out," Rose said sympathetically. "But don't let Iris influence you. You see, at one time she was in love with Mike. You know how charming he is to everyone . . ."

Amanda nodded.

"Yes, well Iris thought he was in love with her, so she felt very hurt when she realised he wasn't. And now when anyone new comes to the office she feels she has to warn them about him."

"Thank you for telling me this, Rose," Amanda said, gratefully. "It's probably too late now for Mike and I but, at least I know how things really are."

O N the way to deliver the letter, her mind was full of what had been said. By the time she reached her destination her head was aching and she was glad to turn her thoughts to something else.

She was warmly welcomed by Mrs Parker, whom she recognised as one of the office cleaners on her floor.

"I was sorry to hear your husband was ill," Amanda said, sincerely.

"It'll mean a long spell in hospital, I'm afraid," the woman said with a sigh. "I did hope to be able to keep on my job, taking Sandy along in the evenings, but I soon realised that was out."

Seven-year-old Sandy sat nearby concentrating on a giant jig-saw, but when his mother opened the letter from Mellors, he ran to her side.

With a whoop, Sandy grabbed the paper clip attaching the cheque to the letter and put his hand in his pocket and produced, before Amanda' startled gaze, a number of clips all strung together in chain form.

"One of the reasons I gave up the job," she told the girl, "was because this son of mine wouldn't leave the office equipment alone, especially paper clips. No matter what I said or did to him."

Sandy grinned unrepentantly.

"In the end, I bought him a box of clips to play with at home," she explained.

"Well, I'd better be getting home now," Amanda said, dazedly.

The row with Mike was crowding into her mind again, but this time along with it came the dreadful realisation that she had accused him of something he just hadn't done. What a mess!

Well, the least she could do was seek him out and make a proper apology.

OUTSIDE, a faint drizzle was falling and she pulled up her coat collar against the chill to hurry homewards.

"Care for a lift, lady?" she heard a man say.

Recognising the voice, she swung round, her face aglow.

"Mike! The very person I wanted to see," she exclaimed.

"Well, that makes a nice change." He sounded delighted. "I was expecting to get the cold shoulder again."

"And yet you still came?" she amazed. "How did you know where I was?"

"Rose mentioned it when we bumped into each other in the corridor. She told me you'd gone away early, and after all the overtime I've done recently, I felt I could ask to leave early myself."

"You didn't have to do extra work because I spoilt that drawing, did you?" Her concern was genuine.

"Stop worrying about that, Amanda," he reassured her. "It was an accident that could have happened to anyone. I kept away, thinking you needed time to cool off. By the way, did you ever find out who was sabotaging your paper clips?"

"Yes, it was a young man called Sandy Parker," she explained. "He's seven years old and heading for a great career in paper-clip construction."

They laughed happily together.

"The car's parked right over there." Mike indicated. "Let me give you a lift home — please."

"I'd like that." She smiled.

On the journey home they found they had many things in common — including their sense of humour. And when Mike asked her out that night Amanda was only too pleased to accept.

She knew there would be a lot of good-natured teasing in the office next day and from now on, but somehow she felt sure if Mike could take it, so indeed could she.

Loch Linnhe lies at the south-western end of Glen More — the Great Glen — a natural cleft that runs north-eastwards across Scotland to the Moray Firth. The Great Glen lies along the line of a fault, on which movements can still be felt and which provides the route of the Caledonian Canal.

The trip from Oban up Loch Linnhe to Fort William is quite breathtaking, passing some of Scotland's most picturesque scenery and places of historic interest.

LOCH LINNHE : J CAMPBELL KERR

THE NEW FOLK IN TOWN

by

KATHLEEN KINMOND

The New Folk In Town

STEVEN RITCHIE opened the official-looking envelope with fingers that shook a little, then hugged his wife in delight.

It was theirs! After years of hard saving, their offer for the corner shop in the little town of Muiryton had been accepted — in a month's time they could take over.

"Well, we've done it, love," he said exuberantly, "the shop is ours. I just can't wait to get started!"

"Me too, Steven," she said excitedly in her gentle, melodious Welsh voice, "I feel exactly the same, but we'll have to remember it's not the end — only the beginning, with lots of hard work if we're to make a success of it."

"I know, but we're both still young and we'll be working for ourselves now, which will make all the difference," Steve agreed.

It was indeed an achievement for Steven. Not so long ago he'd been an N.C.O. in the Army Catering Corps. He'd met and married Dilys when stationed in Wales.

After he'd left the Army they had worked together in hotels but their goal had always been to own a little shop — and now their dream had come true.

But in the little town of Muiryton the people of the community were feeling slightly apprehensive about the change of ownership. After all, it had been a focal point in the district where Mr Porteous had served them faithfully for over thirty years.

"I don't know why he needs to retire," Miss Laird said crossly to Willie Smith as they left the shop together one day, "he's still a comparatively young man.

"I'll never get anyone to keep my special brown bread until I feel able enough to come for it."

Willie Smith smiled to himself, knowing that he and Porteous, both in their mid-sixties, must seem mere boys to Miss Laird's seventy-odd years. He said so afterwards to the shopkeeper, who shook his head over the irascible old lady.

"She's not a bad old girl, really," he said mildly, "but she's never been the same since she and Agnes Soutar fell out over something or other a year or two ago."

"Yes, that was a great pity," Willie agreed, "I heard they'd been friends since school days."

"I've seen them brush past each other in this very shop. It seems very silly to me but I tell myself it's none of my business," Mr Porteous commented.

Another member of the town to feel depressed about the departure of Mr Porteous was seventeen-year-old Lesley Middleton. Now the old man's nephew, Arthur Dewar, would no longer come every weekend to help his uncle with the Saturday-evening rush and the sporting papers.

Lesley was a regular customer to the shop to collect her father's evening paper, and she had been falling more and more in love with the handsome young student but he just didn't seem to notice her. And now the shop was changing hands and she'd probably never see him again.

Mr Porteous stayed on for a week in the shop to show the Ritchies the ropes and then they were on their own.

I N less than a month Steven had taught himself the names of all the customers and always greeted them as they entered the shop.

"Why do you call some folk by their christian name and some by their surname?" Dilys asked curiously, one day.

"Because some people prefer one way to the other," he replied logically.

"But how do you know which to choose?" She was still curious. Her husband grinned and hugged her affectionately.

"Haven't you noticed? Whenever I discover their first name, I try them out by calling them by it and if they like it that way, they answer by calling me Steven. It's quite simple, really, my love," he concluded.

"I call everyone Mr or Mrs," Dilys said, disengaging herself from her husband's embrace when the door bell jangled and Miss Laird entered, her expression disapproving.

"Good afternoon, Miss Laird," Dilys said politely, disappearing into the back shop and leaving the old lady to Steven.

She could hear the mumble of their voices, then she heard her husband's calling her.

"Can you bring some sugar for Miss Laird, sweetheart?" he said.

She gathered up a few bags in her arms and carried them through to the front shop, where the old lady was quickly putting her purchases into her shopping bag. As Dilys passed behind her, she lifted her eyebrows enquiringly to Steven, who gave an almost imperceptible shrug.

Miss Laird nodded her abrupt thanks and as she was leaving, met Willie Smith crossing the street.

"Well, how are you taking to the new people, then?" he asked.

"Not at all," she snapped, "it's quite out of place the way they address each other in the shop — 'sweetheart' and 'dear' and 'darling.' A piece of nonsense."

Her attitude annoyed Willie intensely. He still missed his wife a great deal and would have given anything to hear her soft voice, calling him dear.

"And why shouldn't they?" he snapped. "They're obviously a happy couple, and personally, I find them a pleasure to deal with." And with that he marched off, leaving Miss Laird gazing after him in astonishment.

The Ritchies had heard Mr Smith's raised voice and noticed his heightened colour but made no remark about his encounter with Miss Laird.

By now he was feeling a bit deflated after his outburst and asked for his items almost diffidently.

As Steven tallied them up, Dilys felt she had to voice her concern.

"Are you all right today, Mr Smith?" she asked.

"Yes, yes, I'm fine, thank you. Why do you ask?"

"I was wondering if maybe you'd caught a cold or something," she said tentatively.

"I did see you working in the front garden the other day without a jacket and it was very cold . . ."

Willie looked at the young woman in surprise.

"I — I was wearing my cardigan, though," he mumbled, picking up his purchases, but as he returned home he felt a warm glow of pleasure. It was nice to know that someone cared.

A S the spring days lengthened into summer ones, the little corner shop became more of a focal point of the community than ever, with the Ritchies' good nature and happiness reaching out and enveloping everyone who knew them.

Whenever Willie felt a little weary, he'd pop over on some pretext or other and was sure to return home, feeling better. He would time his visits to the quieter times of the day when for a few minutes Steve and he could chat about their Army days. Willie had been in the R.E.M.E. during his wartime service.

Another elderly woman had begun shopping at the corner shop and it was only when Mr Smith addressed her one day as "Bella" that they learned from him she was Miss Soutar, the lifelong friend of Miss Laird until their quarrel.

"Yes," Willie nodded his head wisely, "two silly old women. They won't make it up at all. It has changed Miss Laird, too. She gets more and more irritable every day."

"Did Miss Soutar come here a lot, too?" Dilys enquired.

"Oh, yes," Willie replied. "But she changed to the supermarket, when they quarrelled, in case she bumped into Agnes Laird here."

"What's made her change her mind now, then?" Steve was curious.

"Well, I met her in the town the other day and she said she was getting tired of the supermarket. Everyone was always too busy to chat, while here, there's always somebody coming or going. She'd heard you two are always willing to exchange a friendly word, too. It means a lot when you're on your own."

Dilys and Steven exchanged pleased glances and then he said, "Didn't Mr Porteous try to get them together again?"

"No, no. He's a bit of a shy man. He once said to me it was none of his business anyway." Willie said, in a matter-of-fact voice.

"Well, I may be interfering," Steve exclaimed when Willie had left, "but I'm not going to have these two old dears passing each other in my shop."

"Oh," Dilys said in an anxious voice, "do you really think you should? Look, see, maybe Mr Porteous was right." Dilys' Welsh accent was always more pronounced when she was worried.

"I don't know what I'll do exactly." Steve was thoughtful. "I'll just have to wait and see."

Contrary to what she'd prophesied, Steven kept Miss Laird's brown bread exactly as Mr Porteous had done, and once when she hadn't called in he had dashed along with it himself, to check up if she was all right. And sometimes when Lesley Middleton was in for her father's paper, he'd ask her to deliver it.

ONE day, Lesley came in, hoping as usual that Arthur would appear from the back shop, as he'd used to, and yet knowing this was impossible.

Steven had actually put his hand into the glass cupboard where the bread was kept, when he saw Miss Soutar at the door of the shop and quickly withdrew it.

It was fortunate that after Lesley had left, there was only Bella still in the shop, putting her groceries into her shopping bag.

"Oh, dear!" he exclaimed, "Miss Laird's brown bread is still here. You pass her house on your way home, don't you? Would you mind handing it in? It would save my wife or me a walk before going home."

Miss Soutar began to say no, then decided it would be churlish to refuse. And, anyway, he wasn't to know of their feud.

After she left the shop with the bread among her purchases, Steven and Dilys hugged each other in delight.

"So far, so good," Steven said. "I wonder what'll happen now."

What did happen next was that on their next visit to the shop, the ladies were together, talking quite naturally as if they'd never been apart. And it was obvious they'd only been waiting for a nudge in the right direction, to make them renew their friendship.

As the summer passed, and autumn then winter visited the little town, the Ritchies celebrated their first anniversary as owners of the little shop. Their endeavours had paid off and to their delight their accountant was well pleased with their progress.

THE snow came early that year and a heavy overnight fall made the pavements impassable. While Dilys organised the paper boys, Steven went out to clear the pavement round the shop, then decided to clear Willie Smith's doorway, too. It could be very hazardous for old folk.

By the time Willie appeared, the traffic on the main road had made it passable, and so to his surprise, was his pavement.

Knowing who'd been responsible, he popped over to the shop to thank Steve.

"Who knows, perhaps someday I might be able to return the favour," he said sincerely, never suspecting that he'd have his chance, very soon.

A few days later, Dilys, who'd been helping a child cross the road, caught her heel on the kerb, and fell heavily.

Steve heard her cry and rushed out. As he tried to help her up she said with a groan, "My ankle, Steve, I've twisted my ankle!"

And looking at it, Steve could see that already it was very swollen. Although he carried her through to the back shop, very carefully, she was still very white and shaking when he lowered her on to a couch.

The New Folk In Town

He'd always been told not to move a person who'd had a bad fall, but his commonsense told him that lying on a cold pavement could be just as harmful.

He settled her as comfortably as possible, then rang for the doctor. By now the shop was filling, mostly with men buying their weekly cigarettes and tobacco, and waiting for the Saturday-night sporting papers.

Steven was dashing about, madly, when the doctor arrived and he had to let himself in by the side door.

Willie Smith was among those who were in the shop and heard the doctor tell Steven his wife would need an X-ray — they'd have to phone for an ambulance to take her to the cottage hospital.

"Wait a minute," Willie Smith broke in, "what's happened? Is it necessary to get an ambulance? I'd be very willing to take her to hospital in my car, if that would be possible."

Dilys, listening from the back shop called out, "I'd like that, please, if Mr Smith can take me."

"And what about you, Mr Ritchie?" the doctor said. "You'd really be better to go with your wife, but what about the shop?"

The papers had still not arrived and among the customers waiting were Lesley Middleton and Mr Porteous who still ordered newspapers from his old shop.

The doctor, who'd brought Lesley into the world and had known her all her life, looked at her expectantly

> ### Search For Serenity
>
> *T*AKE *to the woods thy fretted spirit, for woods have healing hands.*
>
> *Are they not sanctuaries enclosed within the solid masonry of trees, whose stems are soaring pillars and whose leaves form the tracery of their vaulted roofs.*
>
> *The muted wind that breathes is like an organ softly playing, and bird-song is the sweet singing of the choir.*
>
> *Step into a city Church, withdrawn from the traffic's roar, to bathe the fretted soul in God's serenity. But neglect not Nature's Cathedral, where the abiding, solemn trees give the air of an ancient, holy place.*
>
> *And know that peace is in the heart of God, as calm as in the depths of a wood.*
>
> Rev. T. R. S. Campbell

"I'm sure you could help, Lesley, until Mr Ritchie gets back?" he inquired.

"Yes, of course, I'd be glad to," she said willingly.

"I'd have been delighted to help, too," Mr Porteous said quietly to Steven, "only my wife and I are going out as soon as I get back, but my nephew might be able to help."

Steve agreed rather hazily.

After the Ritchies and Mr Smith had driven off, Lesley found herself confronted with a huge pile of newspapers, and her heart quailed, but luckily, everyone waiting was more than willing to help.

By the time the shop cleared, she was feeling breathless but triumphant. If she'd stopped to think when Dr Braid asked her to look after the shop she'd probably not have done it. But now she was glad she'd tried. The doorbell clanged and she turned to serve her next customer, only to come face to face with Arthur Dewar.

She hadn't heard the conversation between the two men and could only stare in astonishment at Mr Porteous' nephew.

"My uncle phoned to say that Mr Ritchie needed some help. I — I used to help my uncle here sometimes when he had the shop."

"Yes, I remember," she said at last.

Just then three customers arrived and Arthur went behind the counter with Lesley. Of course, everyone wanted to know where the Ritchies were.

When Arthur and Lesley closed the shop at eight o'clock, they felt they had known each other for years.

"Where are you off to now?" he asked Lesley as they locked up.

"Nowhere really. Dad came along to see what had happened when I didn't return home with the paper and said he'd phone my friends and explain why I couldn't meet them tonight."

"Oh, good," Arthur said enthusiastically.

"Well, what I mean is," he explained when she gave him a strange look, "if you're not going out anywhere, why don't you come with me to the Union Disco. I'm on my way there now."

"If you'll give me half an hour to change, I'd love to come."

STEVEN and Mr Smith arrived home from the hospital, tired and weary after their long wait.

Steve, who was tired mentally and physically, allowed himself to be led into Mr Smith's house.

In no time at all, he was served with piping-hot bacon, eggs, sausages and fried potatoes. with lashings of strong black tea.

Dilys had to remain in hospital for a few days, as it was more serious than was at first thought. When the pressure of business prevented him getting in to see her, the neighbours and customers organised a rota of visitors so there would always be someone there.

"Miss Laird and I were wondering if you'd like to come to her house tonight for a meal when you come home from the hospital," Miss Soutar said one day as she put her change into her purse.

"We understand you won't want to stay too long for you've such an early rise, but we would like you to come."

Steven, who'd been about to decline politely for just the reason she expressed, felt he couldn't possibly now refuse and was thankful he hadn't when he saw the trouble the two old ladies had gone to.

Steak pie with feather-light pastry by Miss Laird was followed by a luscious trifle made by and served by a beaming Miss Soutar.

"I don't know how to thank you both," Steve said when at last he sat back from the table, almost unable to move.

"My dear man, it's we who have to thank you," Miss Laird said.

"We don't suppose you realise it but if it hadn't been for you asking Bella to deliver my bread, we could have gone on for the rest of our lives never speaking to each other."

"Did I really do that?" Steve replied in well-feigned surprise.

All the time his wife was away, he was bombarded with invitations for meals and offers to run him into the hospital. Housewives brought offerings of home-made soups and pies.

WHEN it leaked out that Dilys was coming home, his tins at home were soon filled to overflowing with home-baked biscuits, shortbread and cakes.

Willie Smith, of course, immediately volunteered to go to the hospital for Dilys, in Steve's lunch break.

Between them, the two men helped her up the path and into the house, Mr Smith almost as excited as Steve at having her home again.

Steven had laid the table so that the three of them could have a cup of tea and some of the home-made goodies given to them by the customers.

Dilys was amazed at Miss Laird's gift of a cream sponge cake.

"It was very nice of her to think of us," Dilys said, delighted.

"That's nothing," Steve said, proudly fetching and opening more of the tins.

"Look what we got from Mrs Spence and Mrs Taylor and Mrs Buchan."

Dilys' eyes filled with tears.

"Why has everyone been so kind?"

"My dear." Willie Smith put his hand gently on her arm. "You shouldn't be surprised. You cast your bread upon the waters and hasn't it indeed come back to you?"

Steve and Dilys smiled at each other contentedly. It looked like they were home.

The Right Decision

by Jean Murrie

L INDA stopped and gazed down at the rock pool. How quiet the
water lay. It was difficult to believe that only a few moments ago
it was part of the sea, crashing and frothing as it drew itself back
towards the horizon.

She envied the little pool its tranquillity. Just now, she felt she had
more in common with the turbulent tide.

Continuing her walk along the sea edge, she reflected how fortunate
that even an attack of flu should prove to have a silver lining. For some
days she had been quite ill, but as she recovered, the enforced stay
in bed had given her the opportunity to think. And it always seemed
to be Terry's last conversation with her that ran through her mind.

Pick me up.

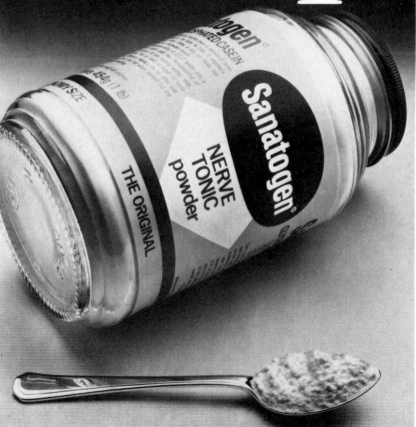

At the time, she hadn't been able to give her full attention to what he had been saying, important though it was, for she had felt so ill. He'd told her again how much he loved her, but noticing the unnatural colour in her cheeks, he'd stopped in consternation.

"You're not feeling well, are you, Linda?" he'd asked.

"To tell you the truth I feel terrible. I just want to go home and curl up with a hot-water bottle," she'd replied with a shiver.

His grey-green eyes had looked at her tenderly.

"Then that's just what you'll do."

Linda had looked up at him in consternation.

"I've really spoiled the evening for you, haven't I?"

"Don't be silly. You know how much I like being with you, even if it's just for a little while." He smiled then.

"There will be plenty of other times to . . ." He broke off.

"To what?" she asked, knowing that tonight was to have been the night when he would propose.

"Oh, nothing," he'd replied enigmatically.

But she knew she was right. She'd been expecting this moment for a while now and was becoming more confused about what answer she would give.

She knew this evening was to have been a special one. Terry had planned her birthday celebration so well, taking her for a meal at a restaurant which could conveniently conclude with a moon-lit walk home, along the riverside.

"We're going to celebrate this birthday of yours again," Terry had said, "just as soon as you are up and about."

Now the time had come. Tonight, Terry would want his answer and this morning she had decided to spend a day at the seaside. These few hours alone would afford her the opportunity to make sure she was making absolutely the right decision.

SHE had known Terry for as long as she could remember. In fact, Terry's mother and her own had grown up together, married about the same time, and remained close companions. As they had watched their children grow, they had laughingly told each other how nice it would be if their offspring married. The remarkable thing was that, when they were about seventeen, that friendship had turned to romance. All had been well for a while until Terry told her he had applied to a university down south.

"It must be all of two hundred miles away," she had said. "You'll have to live away from home and we'll hardly see each other!" Linda's voice had risen incredulously.

"But it's the best one for the subjects I'll be taking." He ran his finger gently down the side of her face.

"I'll be home in the vacations, and anyway," he'd paused, searching for the right words, "we've let ourselves get into a rut. I do love you, but we've got to give ourselves the chance to discover if we're completely right for each other."

Linda had struggled from his close embrace.

A Great Smoke and a Good Deal More.

Club King Size with 10 coupons.

KT105

"You're tired of me." Her voice had been hurt, angry. "I'm just not clever enough for you. All right, go and find yourself another girl. I'll buy a cat and help old Miss Draper take collecting tins round the doors!"

And yet, despite her words, she knew he was right.

Sundays Of Yesteryear

OH! how I wish that I could spend,
One Sunday in the past.
With just a radio at hand,
And not the television's blast.
When Mother aired the parlour,
With musty timber logs,
And Dad wore his Sunday shoes,
And put away our clogs.
He stacked them in the pantry,
One pair, two pairs, three.
When Auntie Flo and Uncle Jim,
Were coming round to tea.
We children wore our Sunday best,
But tongues were never free,
Not to speak unless spoken to,
When auntie came to tea.
With the special meal time over,
And "May I leave the table" said,
We would gather round the glowing fire,
Until it was time for bed.
Oh! yes I long again for a Sabbath,
Of the old fashioned kind,
With family love and kindling logs,
And bearing God in mind.
But now it's anoraks and shopping bags,
And hamburgers deep frying,
Supermarkets open,
And the Sabbath day is dying.
Elsie Collinge

Their circle of friends had narrowed as they had become more absorbed in one another. But this knowledge couldn't prevent the childish outburst or the tears from flowing.

Then Terry had pulled from his pocket a little box, lifting from its nest of tissue a silver locket. He drew Linda tenderly towards him and fastened the delicate chain round her neck.

"I was planning this as a going-away present," he said, "but I want you to have it now. Perhaps you might forgive me enough to carry my photo inside it."

Linda managed a tremulous smile as she thanked him.

"It's beautiful and I don't deserve it after all the mean things I've just said. But I shall miss you so much." She sobbed.

Terry gently kissed her tears away.

"Cheer up. You'll be too busy when you start your nursing course next month to give me more than a passing thought, I bet!"

"Not true." She replied cheekily. "Still, I do hear there are some very nice doctors at the General!"

she taunted, snuggling deeper into his arms.

THE years passed quickly enough, busy as they both were with their studies. Letters passed between them, fast and furious at first, slowing down only as they progressed towards their final exams.

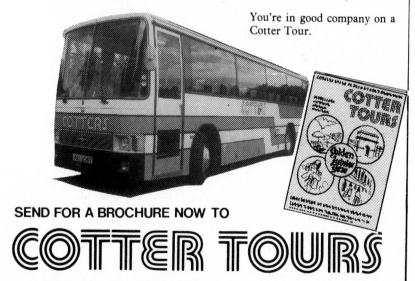

Terry hadn't managed to be at home as much as he had intended as he found a regular vacation job near to his college. But at last he qualified and came back home to work, and everything was as it had been before. Well, almost the same. Both were more sure of their feelings for one another. This time they felt there would be no more partings.

They had accomplished what they had set out to do, widened their circle of friends, tested their love and found it had survived. To become engaged seemed the next inevitable step.

Yet now Linda wondered whether her doubts had ever really been dispelled. It was all too perfect, too much like the ending to an old-fashioned fairy tale. She recalled the words of an old friend, Marion, whom she had visited a few days previously.

"No-one marries childhood sweethearts these days — that's old-fashioned," she'd said, dismissively.

"I know Terry's smashing but look at all the fabulous men there are around."

"And I've got to know some of them, too," Linda had retorted dryly.

"But he was always at the back of your mind," Marion replied. "You never really gave yourself a chance to forget him."

Linda had admitted to herself that the ever-perceptive Marion might just be right.

She paused in her tracks, fingering the little locket she always wore, looking at the dancing water without seeing it. It would be cruel to raise Terry's hopes yet again. She couldn't think of marrying him with all these doubts still in her mind.

Linda shook her head in despair. The glimpse of a red telephone kiosk on the promenade strengthened her resolve. She would ring him now.

The prospect made her feel sick and panicky, but she made her way quickly to the box, concentrating on the words she would have to say. She fished a ten-pence piece out of her bag as she ran, knowing if she wasn't prepared she might lose courage.

As she reached for the telephone receiver she saw the purse. It was lying nearby, partly hidden by grass. With only a moment's hesitation she picked it up and opened it. Inside were a couple of pound notes, a few coins, a pensioner's concessionary fare ticket.

She would return the purse to its owner as soon as she had been in touch with Terry. But a senior citizen might already be worrying about her loss. What she had to say to Terry could wait a little longer. There was an address on the ticket and the first person she asked was able to direct her to the street.

M INUTES later she was standing in front of a small terraced house. Linda had hardly taken her finger from the bell when an elderly woman pulled open the door. She stared blankly at the girl for a moment.

"I thought you were the ambulance man," she said, a little agitated. But then that would have been a mite quick," she said, sighing.

How many times a year could you use an extra bank account?

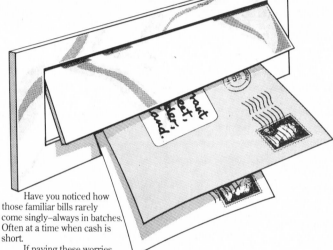

Have you noticed how those familiar bills rarely come singly–always in batches. Often at a time when cash is short.

If paying these worries you–and it worries some people–we believe we have the solution–another Bank Account–SCOTBUDGET.

Ask at BANK OF SCOTLAND about SCOTBUDGET.
Then you could be worry free. All the year round.

✖ BANK OF SCOTLAND

Linda shook her head.

"Are you Mrs Sarah Ross?" Linda asked. And when the woman nodded, Linda replied:

"Well, I've found your purse. It was in the phone box. It is yours, isn't it?"

"Yes, it just goes to show. I didn't even miss it." Mrs Ross turned to the hall behind and it was then that Linda noticed an old man sitting on the bottom step of the stairs, leaning awkwardly against the wall.

"My husband, he fell, and seems to have hurt his shoulder," Mrs Ross explained, in a worried voice.

"I was phoning Dr Turner and he told me he would send an ambulance straight to the house. He said they would need to take X-rays at the hospital anyway."

Mrs Ross had moved back into the house again to her husband's side, and Linda followed, concerned for the old couple. The old woman turned.

"I didn't even thank you for your honesty and trouble," she said, dismayed.

"The kettle is on. I'm going to make a cup of tea for Albert and me. Please have one with us."

"Better not give Mr Ross anything," Linda advised. "They might have to give him an anaesthetic at the hospital. I'm a nurse," she explained quickly, seeing the older woman's puzzled expression.

"Have you a rug or a blanket? That will help to keep him warm."

REFLECTIONS

*O**NCE** I saw a tiny painting of a bee which had alighted in an artist's studio on a summer's day. It was so real! Imagine the skill of the painter who could make his canvas a mirror and reflect accurately the image of a bee.*

Once the ancient Greek master, Zeuxis, painted a bunch of grapes. They were so real that the birds pecked the canvas.

Parrhasios deceived even Zeuxis with a painting ostensibly covered by a fine curtain.

"Pull aside the curtain!" Zeuxis was asked. But the curtain was the painting!

Is our Christian role to imitate Christ? To make the canvas of life a mirror, reflecting faithfully His way?

Or are we more than artists portraying Christ?

In us the living Christ is made alive!

Rev. T. R. S. Campbell

WHILST Mrs Ross made her husband more comfortable, Linda brewed the tea and brought two cups into the hall. Mr Ross leaned back against the wall, obviously in pain. His wife covered his hand with hers.

"He was trying to change the light bulb," she explained. "I told him to wait until Bob, that's our son, comes tomorrow, but no, independent as always."

STOP AN ACHING BACK BECOMING A PAIN IN THE NECK.

The aches and pains you sometimes get from everyday activity needn't be too much of a problem anymore.

Because of Lloyd's Cream.

It contains a really effective analgesic (Diethylamine Salicylate) which helps to relieve muscular pains quickly as you massage.

It's different from most other treatments because it's odourless, painless and leaves your skin its natural colour.

You'll also find that it's non-greasy and easily absorbed into the skin.

As well as relieving the everyday "backaches" Lloyd's Cream is an ideal aid to relieving rheumatic pain, lumbago and fibrositis.

It'll stop a pain in the back becoming a pain in the neck.

LLOYD'S CREAM ⊕

MADE IN BRITAIN BY RECKITT & COLMAN PHARMACEUTICAL DIVISION, HULL.

Mrs Ross glanced proudly round the hall, smiling the whole time.

"He painted this lot, last year. And the year before that decorated the sitting-room, all on his own. And he'll be eighty-six next birthday."

Linda genuinely admired her immaculate surroundings.

"How long have you lived here?" she asked.

"Nearly fifty years," the old woman said proudly. "This was one of the first houses the Council built here. Bob was only a baby when we came here, Jessie and Mary not much older."

Linda let her talk on, seeing some of the anxiety disappear as happy memories seeped back.

"Mary's been in Canada for years now, but she and her family are saving hard to be with us for our sixtieth wedding anniversary." Lost in her memories, she continued:

"We were all set to be wed in nineteen-fourteen and then the war started and Albert went off with the other young men. Oh, it was such an age to wait! At times, I didn't think he would ever come back. Those lists of dead and missing and the terrible moments till I was sure his name wasn't there. Then at last it was all over and he was home."

Sarah Ross laughed.

"How we saved then! That chair you're sitting on cost only five shillings and it's still as strong as ever. You can't get stuff like that nowadays."

A S she talked, Linda imagined the girl of long ago, her heart sore for the loved ones of those who would never return, but leaping too, because the name she sought was not amongst them.

She thought of the young man, enduring the miseries of the trenches, his only joy the memory of the sweet girl waiting back home. No doubt in their minds, no suspicion that their first choice of partner was not the right one. Playing the field would never have entered their heads.

How would Albert have felt if he knew his Sarah was walking out with other men as he endured the dark, terrible days in France? Sarah was one of the lucky ones. There were many who weren't — Miss Draper, for instance, filling the lonely years with acts of kindness for others.

Albert Ross roused himself.

"Don't go on so, Sarah. The young lady doesn't want to hear all our life story."

"Oh dear, I do tend to ramble." Sarah was apologetic. "I'm sorry, my dear. We're holding you back and you've been so kind to us."

She eyed the locket round Linda's neck. "I expect you're going out with your young man. That's very pretty — very like the one Albert gave to me more years ago than I care to remember. Would you like to see it?"

A glance from Albert stopped her from rising.

"There I go again!" At the deepening colour in the girl's cheeks, Mrs Ross smiled and added softly:

"If you are thinking of marriage, I hope you don't have to wait

for your wedding day like we did. The country's not at war, thank goodness, but it doesn't seem any easier these days for young ones wanting to get married, what with the price of houses and so on." She sighed, then turned to Linda with a smile.

"Life always tends to be difficult for those in love."

THE arrival of the ambulance cut short any more conversation, and amid hurried goodbyes and thanks, Linda took her leave.

She felt chastened by what she had heard. Oh, she and Terry had been wise to give each other space, and time to realise their feelings, but she had searched for obstacles where there were none. For countless couples, throughout the years, the path of true love had been far from smooth, yet hers had been so well surfaced that she had almost slipped away from Terry altogether.

Now she was in no doubt that he was the man for her, always had been, always would. She was even grateful for an old man's stubborn independence and his wife's forgetfulness, for through their paths crossing she had gained from them the reassurance she had been seeking.

Her heart warmed towards them and she prayed Albert would soon be fully recovered. The least she could do would be to send them a piece of wedding cake when the time came.

Meanwhile, all she wanted was to be with Terry again, yet this evening was still so far away. Then she spotted the phone box. In just a few minutes she would hear his voice . . .

As she walked towards the box she started to rehearse the words she'd say. She was so excited she didn't want to spoil this very important moment. After all, she had taken long enough to make the right decision.

She entered the phone box and stood for a minute, savouring this new happy feeling. There was so much to look forward to now. And the most immediate was simply the sound of Terry's voice.

She lifted the receiver and dialled the number. When Trevor's deep voice interrupted the ringing she hurriedly pushed a coin into the box.

"Trevor," she said. "It's Linda . . . About the other night . . ."

ENGLISH PAINTED ENAMELS
The Charm of Kate Greenaway

Kate Greenaway was one of the most beloved illustrators of children's books in the last century. Crummles & Co. have produced a short series of enamel boxes depicting a selection of her drawings delicately handpainted to commemorate her work. The price of each box is £19.67 and they are available from selected outlets throughout the country.

Stockists:

Jamieson & Carry, Jewellers,
ABERDEEN
R. D. Finnie Ltd., Jewellers,
ABERDEEN
James Young,
BANCHORY
The Posthorn,
CASTLE DOUGLAS
R. L. Christie, Jewellers,
EDINBURGH
David Irons & Sons Ltd.,
FORFAR

R. W. Sorley, Jewellers,
GLASGOW
Thomas Love & Sons Ltd.,
PERTH
Smalltalk,
PITLOCHRY
Victoria Violet,
NAIRN
Graham Bell Gallery,
GRANTOWN ON SPEY

Enamel
Box
Makers

Crummles

Special
Commissions
accepted

CRUMMLES & CO. 2 Cromer Road Poole Dorset England

L

It's So Hard To Say You're Sorry

by MARY LEDGWAY

THE postcard dropped through the letter-box, landing noiselessly on the soft carpet. As I carried my tray into the living-room I saw it lying there, glossy side up. Idly I wondered which of my friends were lucky enough to be able to go in search of the sun.

But when I finally looked at it I saw it was an old one.

"Please come, Mum — I need you!" it read.

It was my first contact with my daughter, Marion, for nearly three years. I sat on the stairs, huddling into the warm cosiness of my dressing-gown — remembering.

The Domestic Help

Cojene®

helps relieve
rheumatic pain

Remembering the tension that had gradually mounted between Graham and Anne; how I came home early one evening and heard raised voices. They had stopped shouting when I walked in. Marion, pale and tense, made to leave the room, but at the door she paused.

"I'll be out all day tomorrow with Ross."

Then she hesitated, looking at us both, her eyes filled with bewildered pain, which I was at a loss to understand.

"We're going to some friends, so we'll probably stay the night."

Unlike Marion, Graham was flushed with rage, his breathing heavy.

I knew Graham disapproved of Ross, with his casual dress, and hair that was usually flopping over his eyes. The boy had just finished college and was looking for a post in engineering.

Knowing better than to try to talk things over until he had calmed down a bit, I went into the kitchen to make some tea.

I had a bad night, and the next day, Saturday, we both slept late. When we got up, Marion had already left. I started on the chores and Graham left for a round of golf, and, I suspected, to lay on a couple of bets.

It didn't worry me, though, as Graham had always put his home and family first, and my money was always there when I needed it.

It was nearly lunchtime when they rang me from the golf club — Graham had collapsed!

THE nurse opened the curtains and pulled a chair forward. It was a strange, unfamiliar Graham who lay there.

While the doctor was with him I rang Ross's home, but they didn't know where Ross and Marion were, so I sat alone by Graham's bed, just staring at him.

And when the doctor asked to see me there was no need for him to break the news to me — I could tell from the sympathy in his eyes that there was little hope.

But I couldn't cry. A numbness had crept over me.

That dazed feeling stayed with me even when I returned home. I had a bath, changed and sorted out some things for Graham.

When I was nearly ready to leave, Marion and Ross appeared. Ross's arm was round her shoulders. I knew what they had to say even before Marion held out her left hand with the new circlet of shining gold.

"Be happy for us, Mum." And she looked around her, a little apprehensively.

"Where's Dad?"

"Your father's in hospital!" Worry made my reply terse.

I climbed into Graham's dark-grey saloon and drove off.

There was only one hospital in the small town. Marion soon followed and sat opposite me.

When, in the early hours of the morning we said our last goodbyes to the man we had both loved for so long, and walked out to the car, we both held our grief tight in our hearts.

She stayed with me till the funeral. Ross helped her when he could, but returned to his own home at night.

The relatives at the funeral obviously put Marion's quiet wedding down to Graham's illness, and neither of us explained. If they thought my manner strange, they attributed it to grief and shock. Strangely it was from them I learned that Ross had gained a post at Ambleside.

When everyone had left, Marion started to clear up but I stopped her.

"Don't bother — you've done your duty — observed the niceties! I can manage now."

My voice sounded hard and sharp, even to my own ears.

"Haven't you done enough?" My voice was shrill. "If it hadn't been for you, this might never have happened! Graham might have —"

"Come on, Marion. You mother needs to be alone." This was a new Ross. Quiet and dignified. A man caring for his wife.

"Here." I handed her a cheque. "This will help with the flat."

"No thank you, Mrs Carter. We can manage," Ross said. "We've left our address near the telephone. If you need us any time —"

"If *I* want *you*! You'll need me long before that happens." I walked into the lounge. Through the net curtains I watched them walk away.

Nightmare months followed. I found that Graham had indeed been gambling. He had borrowed from friends, neglected bills, and even taken out a small mortgage on the house. I sold what I could and paid what I could. Then I turned the spare bedroom into a work room and went back to my old trade of tailoring.

N OW, three years later, I was solvent, and had even managed to buy an old, but reliable Mini.

But loneliness and regret for the way I'd treated Marion haunted me.

Back in the present, I gazed down at her plea for help, and knew what I had to do.

I telephoned tradesmen, cancelled fittings, packed a small case, and found the address still in the telephone book.

Then I glanced at the map, deciding on the quickest route. Two hours later I was turning off the A1 towards Hawes and Sedbergh, and the sky was heavy and overcast.

I knew I should stop for coffee, but an inner determination drove me on. Not until I saw the rainbow did I ease off the pedal.

As I poured the coffee, I could almost hear Marion's childish voice.

"Daddy — Daddy — a rainbow, a fairy rainbow! Tell me about it again, Daddy, please?"

And Graham would tell her again about the fairies with their magic paints preparing the glorious arc of colour for a special party.

Suddenly I felt relaxed, confident that my journey would end happily. The rainbow was an omen — a good one. I drove on.

Soon I was in Ambleside. The flat wasn't hard to find, but when the landlady, Mrs Drayton, opened the door she looked at me in surprise.

"But Marion left here, nearly two months ago. I needed the rooms for my married daughter."

She must have seen how deflated I felt.

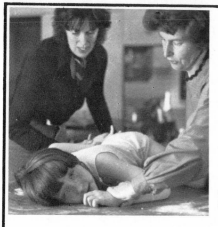

"Look, dear. Come in and have some tea. I've got her address."

I thanked her but refused the tea. We knew the Lakes well, it had been our favourite holiday place and I didn't relish the drive over Kirkstone Pass.

M Y fears proved well founded. As I climbed higher and higher the car was enveloped in clinging, impenetrable mist.

Then, as so often happens in the Lakes, the fearsome wall of threatening grey phantoms was left behind.

A few miles later, I was there.

The cottage had a forlorn, neglected look. A plump, untidy woman opened the door and stared at me, her blue eyes vacant.

"Mrs Green? I'm Esme Carter, Mrs Fairburn's mother — you were expecting me?"

The loose lips parted in what was meant to be a smile. Putting an arm out she pulled me into the dark, dingy hall and pointed upstairs.

I ran up the steep steps. The door at the top of the stairs was open. Marion lay, a tiny figure in the huge double bed. Then I was holding her close.

"Mum, oh, Mum, I wanted you so much!" I stroked the tangled hair as she went on. "I'm so afraid — I don't want to lose my baby, not again!"

"Marion love!" I gasped. "You mean . . ."

"Yes, last year — then it nearly happened again this time. The doctor says I have to rest," she finished.

"But Ross," I asked. "Where is he?"

"His firm got this contract for Saudi Arabia. The money was good and we're saving for a deposit. He didn't know about the baby or he wouldn't have gone. I didn't know what to do. Sally does her best. She's willing enough but a bit slow. Not quite, well — with it.

"Her parents left her this cottage and she muddles through. She can't

Self Inefficiency

To cut the cost of living
    Fruit and veg. I meant to grow,
But after all my efforts
    I haven't much to show.

The bullfinches looked pretty
    As they fluttered in the trees,
Devouring the fruit buds,
    So my only crop was leaves.

The lettuces were promising,
    Until a neighbour's rabbit
Escaped to eat them all,
    As it got to be a habit.

The birds ate the blackcurrants.
    Marked washing on the line,
In derision at their victory
    In stealing what was mine.

The weather was against me.
    It forgot to rain,
So I'll put the garden down to grass,
    And buy my food again.

P. R. Mason

It's still the tobacco that counts

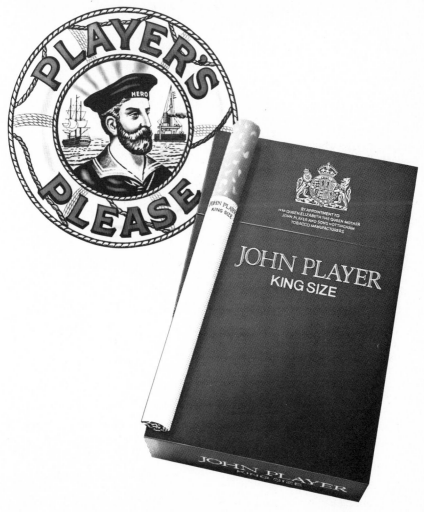

JK24PF

read or write so I couldn't ask her to phone. I thought if I wrote you might —

"I might not open the letter," I finished for her as she hesitated.

We looked at each other, each aware of the suffering we had both endured so needlessly.

"So I tore the card out of an old album and just hoped she would post it.

She lay back, and I saw her cheeks were flushed.

"Be quiet now, love, you've talked enough. I think the first thing is to get you into a clean nightie, and fresh sheets. You look most uncomfortable."

SOON she was back in bed between clean sheets, her dark hair neatly tied.

I heated soup and cut fingers of buttered toast. Marion ate well.

"I'm all right now you're here. It's just that I was frightened, and alone." Then she looked at me and smiled. "You were right, you said we'd need you first."

"But I was wrong — so very wrong, I needed you so much — only I was too proud. I'm sorry, Marion, for everything."

We were interrupted by a peremptory knock on the door, and a tall, angular female breezed into the room.

"Well, I must say you look a lot better, young lady!"

"I feel better. Doctor, this is my mother, Esme Carter. Mum, this is Dr Williams."

"So you finally made it —"

"Doctor, I'm sorry, but —"

"No need to be. I didn't mean to criticise, and you've certainly made a big difference since you got here. You do realise Marion must rest, I mean complete rest, for at least another week. You can stay?"

"Well, actually, we haven't had a chance to discuss it yet. I was wondering if I could take Marion home —"

I glanced anxiously at my daughter, but Marion's expression left me in no doubt that the plan was more than agreeable to her.

Dr Williams walked across to the window.

"And where might home be?" she asked.

"A market town near Harrogate."

"And that's what you propose to use?" The doctor pointed to the Mini.

"Naturally, it happens to be the only car I have!" I retorted.

She laughed heartily.

"You mustn't mind me — it's just my manner. But no way can Anne travel in that. She must be able to lie down.

"Look, leave it with me. I'll be back later." She was gone as swiftly as she had come. I sank into a chair.

"Is she always like that?" I asked, amazed.

Marion laughed.

"Yes, but don't get her wrong. She's caring, and so gentle. Oh, Mum, it would be lovely to go home, but . . ."

If you can't eat, you should turn to drink.

Make yourself a lovely, warming cupful of Bengers.

It's tasty, it's nourishing and it's easy to digest.

The natural enzymes in Bengers pre-digest the milk protein and wheaten food in the cup.

It's food for thought, especially when you've lost your appetite for solid food.

BENGERS MAKES NOURISHING MILK EASY TO DIGEST.

"I know, you don't want to give up the flat. Well, we won't. We'll pay Sally for the next few weeks and see how things go. I do hope the doctor can fix something up."

Dr Williams was back in a couple of hours.

"It's all fixed up. Leslie Sanders, a neighbour, has an estate car. He will call for you both at nine o'clock. His friend, Ron Woodley, will leave earlier than that in your car, so you'd better give me the keys. They're both going to a conference.

"Here's a note for your own doctor, and some pills for Marion. Give her two before you leave and she'll sleep most of the way." Her eyes were gentle as she bent over the bed.

"You're going to be all right, love, and so is that baby."

Curtly she brushed away my thanks.

"Just doing my job," she insisted, and then she left.

We had a nice tea, then Marion talked. She told me about Ross's job, the baby they had lost, and the home they were saving for.

Then I asked a question.

"But the money you had from your grandmother? Wouldn't that have paid the deposit?" There was a short silence.

"Dad borrowed it. He said he was going to double it, but . . . That night you came home he wanted more and there was hardly any left. That's why we married as we did. I knew there was no money for a big wedding. I tried to talk to you afterwards, but —"

"But I wouldn't listen," I finished for her.

"And I was so sorry — for all those horrible things I said." My voice was low. I felt so ashamed.

"I knew you didn't mean it, Mum. You were so upset, I hated leaving you. I knew there'd be money worries as well. How did you manage?"

But I had seen the shadows under Marion's eyes and I shook my head.

"I'll tell you later — we've talked enough now. You needn't worry though, I'm managing fine."

And soon Marion was asleep.

PROMPTLY at nine o'clock Leslie Sanders drew up outside the cottage. The back seat was let down, a travelling rug and soft pillow, even a hot-water bottle, already in place. Tears of gratitude blurred my vision.

Marion slept most of the way. Leslie and I were soon on christian-name terms. He told me about his family, his trips abroad and the conference he was attending.

Marion gave me a little hug as she snuggled down contentedly in her old bed. I was glad I'd kept her room ready, just the way it was.

I made coffee for Leslie before he left. As I moved round after he had gone, preparing a light meal for Marion and myself, I realised how much I had enjoyed his company. It was the first time I had spent any length of time with a man since Graham's death, and it made me feel younger.

The next morning our own doctor assured Marion that complete rest was all she needed, and we spent a happy coffee break planning for the

You'll get on better with The Royal Bank.

For a start there are more Royal Banks to get on with.
Almost 600 in Scotland, 11 in London.

More Branches than any other Scottish Bank.

For one simple reason. There's more demand.

Compare the services we offer. Compare our attitude, and you'll understand why.

Make an appointment with your nearest Royal Bank Manager.

He'll show you what we mean.

There are more Royal Banks to get on with.

baby. Then as Marion slept, I did some baking, singing while I worked.

Just after lunch, Leslie telephoned.

"I promised to pick Ron up at your place at three, but I've been held up. Can you tell him to hang on till I get there?"

A little later, the doorbell rang, and when I answered it there was a tall, middle-aged man, standing on the step.

"I'm Ron Woodley." His voice was low. "You must be Marion's mum."

Over a glass of sherry, Ron and I talked, immediately at ease.

He told me about the death of his wife ten years earlier, and their sadness at having no family. I recognised a loneliness beyond my own. I, at least, had a daughter.

At four o'clock when Leslie still hadn't come I went to make some tea, suddenly glad of my baking session. When I came back with the tray he was looking at one of my books.

"Dales Walks for the Motorists," he read out.

"Tried them all?"

"A few," I answered.

"I was wondering — about Sunday?" he said, hesitantly. "The conference finishes on Saturday, but, as Leslie is visiting friends on Sunday I'll have to stay on. And as there's nothing I enjoy more than walking in the fresh air in beautiful countryside, I think I'd like to try the one around Semerwater."

> ## *Late Autumn*
>
> Last gay roses, falling leaves,
> Golden glow of garnered sheaves,
> Dusky evenings falling soon,
> Silver light of harvest moon.
> Changing moods and changing scenes,
> This is what the Autumn means.
>
> *Elsie Campbell*

"It seems pretty easy going to start with. That is, if you fancy the idea and can leave Marion."

"Oh, Marion's no problem now," I said quickly. "Her friends are already rallying round, and, yes, I would like it very much."

We looked at each other. Two middle-aged people, suddenly shy, not knowing what to say next. Fortunately the bell rang and Leslie walked in.

"Ah! See, I smelt the tea! Sorry I've kept you waiting, Ron, but I'm sure Esme's looked after you well."

I poured his tea, aware that he was regarding us both with a twinkle lurking in those deep-set eyes under the shaggy brows. Had he really been delayed, I wondered?

I passed him his tea and he winked at me, a slow, deliberate challenge. I knew then the delay had been of his own making, but I was suddenly glad.

Suddenly life was worth living. My daughter and I were friends again, and the future seemed bright and exciting. As I passed the scones I winked back.

I thought of Marion's rainbow fairies. They must have been very busy since my journey to the hills.

7 Good Old Fashioned Remedies from Pickles.

FIERY JACK

Suffering from Rheumatism? Remember Fiery Jack. The friend to thousands. For sufferers from rheumatism, fibrositis, lumbago, and general muscular aches, remember Fiery Jack. It's strong, hot, penetrating action loosens stiff joints, restores circulation and quickly soothes away the pain.

Lipgarde

Puts back what winter takes out of your lips. Prevent chapped, cracked lips from spoiling your looks this winter with Lipgarde, the time-tested lip protector. It's natural ingredients – pure vegetable oil, lanolin and wheat-germ oil – protect your lips from the effects of wind and frost, whilst moisturising them, to give a natural healthy sheen, whatever the weather. In translucent pink or white, Lipgarde can be worn under ordinary lipstick or in place of it.

SNOWFIRE

The little healer that works as hard as your hands do.
Hard-working hands need Snowfire. It's the time-tested remedy for chapped hands, chilblains, stings, bites, abrasions and cuts – all the minor accidents which happen in the home. Soothing and healing.

Pickles Ointment

The time-tested remedy for painful corns and hard skin. Thousands of sufferers over the years have searched for a remedy that really works, and discovered Pickles Ointment. It's soothing, healing action eases away the pain and discomfort by quickly removing the cause. Discover Pickles Ointment for yourself and join the thousands of others who've benefitted from it.

Snufflebabe

The vapour chest rub that's specially for the very young. When your baby has a cold or irritating cough, use Pickles Snufflebabe, like thousands of other mothers. Specially formulated for the very young, combining the natural ingredients of Camphor, Menthol, Thyme, Pine and Cedar in a gentle, effective vapour rub that helps to clear both stuffy noses and the bronchial tubes.

S.C.R.

The safe, gentle treatment for baby's Cradlecap.
Pickles S.C.R. has been specially formulated to treat Cradlecap – the greasy looking plaques that can sometimes be seen lying at the base of the hair on a baby's scalp. S.C.R.the effective, yet gentle treatment for Cradlecap.

COLSOR

Cold Sores? Use Pickles COLSOR cream. A tested, proven remedy.

Remedies that over the years have brought help to thousands. Giving real value for money, all Pickles products are available from most leading chemists

Good Old Fashioned Remedies from *J Pickles & Son*

Pickles House, Church Lane, Knaresborough, Yorks.

All You Have To Do Is Dream by JEAN McDOUGALL

WITH her usual knack of getting the most out of things, Petra thoroughly enjoyed the wedding. Looking over the photograph proofs circulating at the reception, she was relieved to see she wasn't a bad-looking bridesmaid for her cousin, Emmy, the lovely bride.

Petra had been delighted with the lovely pink crepe dress and head-dress of tiny roses, and especially pleased that her mildly curling fair hair looked tidy for once.

Simon had told her several times during the dancing how she outshone every other girl in the room, and held her tightly whenever an old-

LET US COACH YOU

Q. *What do outings, holidays, and express travel have in common?*

A. *A coach from the Eastern Scottish fleet of Scottish Omnibuses Ltd.!*

More and more people are coming to this conclusion — be it club secretaries organising a night out, or family heads arranging their holiday travel.

We have coaches for outings, tour holidays, and daily express services linking Edinburgh, Glasgow, Aberdeen and Fife with London. A network of express services is available from Glasgow and Edinburgh to most parts of England.

If you have a travel problem, phone us. You'll find the answer in a coach from :

SCOTTISH OMNIBUSES LTD.
St Andrews Square Bus Station, Edinburgh

Private Hire—031-556 7040.   Tours—031-556 2126.

fashioned number like a waltz or quickstep gave him the chance.

"It'll be your turn next," Emmy had forecast as she was changing out of her wedding finery.

"Have you and Simon talked about marriage, yet?" her cousin queried.

"Well . . . no." Luckily, Emmy was too excited about getting away from the reception to notice Petra's slight hesitation or press for an explanation, but when the moment came for throwing the bouquet, she aimed it in her cousin's direction and it found its mark.

Blushing a little at the applause coming from those standing nearest, she looked across the room for Simon, to see if he had noticed.

But Simon and her grandfather seemed to be in a small group of two, deep in some discussion that apparently eliminated all the others at the reception and completely disregarded anything they might be doing.

Feeling somewhat deflated, she passed the bouquet on to her mother, who promised to place it somewhere cool till it was time to go home, and smiled encouragingly.

T HERE was an upsurge of interest amongst the guests when they saw that bride and 'groom were about to take their leave, with the usual hilarity and joking, the decorated car and the cascades of confetti.

"Good luck and God bless." The good wishes rang in everyone's ears.

Forgetful of the chill evening breeze, Petra had run out with the others to wave off the bridal car and now that it was a disappearing fleck on the roadway, she shivered and made her way back to the hall, where the musicians were tuning up for an Eightsome Reel.

Well, if anything could be guaranteed to set the circulation going again, surely it was that.

Before she had taken two steps into the hall, she had been claimed by Emmy's brother, Hal.

"No excuses, mind," he warned, grinning broadly. "This is about the only dance I can manage, so consider yourself booked."

"With pleasure, Hal." She laughed. Across the room she spotted her grandfather, as eager as the young people to enjoy the festivities, but Simon seemed to have disappeared.

She consoled herself with the thought that perhaps he too had gone out to speed the newlyweds on their way, and was still enjoying a breath of fresh air. She would go in search of him after the eightsome was over.

All the way through the lively dance she kept a smile on her face, but her thoughts were elsewhere.

The two most important men in her life, Simon and her grandfather, were right here in this hall with her, and the fact ought to have made her very happy. Instead, as on the few occasions before, when they met, she had been left with the impression that deep down, under the polite conversation, they did not really care much for each other.

When she'd mentioned it to her mother she'd been quite rational. "Your grandad has always been slow to make friends."

We couldn't save this horse!

It had to be put down. We didn't get there in time.
But with **your** help we could prevent more suffering.
Will **you** help? Help us to fight cruelty and to prevent suffering?
As Scotland's largest animal welfare organisation we must provide
SPCA services in eight of the country's Regions and in the three Island Areas.
But we receive no State Aid. We need **your** help.
Will **you** help by joining our Society or by sending us a donation?

Scottish SPCA, 19 Melville Street, Edinburgh, EH3 7PL.

I enclose Cheque/P.O.for £   payable
to The Scottish S.P.C.A.
NAME _____
ADDRESS_____
_____

I wish/do not wish to become a member.
Please send details.   PFA

SCOTTISH SPCA

Scottish Society for Prevention of Cruelty to Animals.

"But he's a great mixer," Petra protested.

She had seen him in lots of different kinds of company and had always admired his facility for meeting people on their own territory.

Most of her friends liked him enormously and he was always very polite even to those with whom he privately felt he had little in common.

But surely that couldn't apply to Simon — Simon who was so very friendly and could, when he set his mind to it, be very charming.

THE reel finished to enormous applause and finally the groups dispersed to leave the floor clear for an energetic cha-cha-cha.

She finally discovered Simon seated in an alcove with an ashtray of half-smoked cigarettes before him.

"Hello," she said, sitting down beside him.

"You're still with us then?" She tried to sound light-hearted. "I thought you'd gone home."

"Hi, Petra! No, I didn't attempt the eightsome — too much like work." He gave her a quick smile.

"Poor old you!" Petra replied. "Goodness knows what you'll be like at sixty," she teased, and was surprised when he sighed loudly.

"I hope by then I'll have learned not to poke my nose into other people's business."

The solemn expression gave way to a grin when he saw Petra's face.

"I'm sorry, love. Just ignore me!" He kissed her cheek.

"Tea or coffee?" she enquired, seeing the trim waitresses make another appearance.

"No thanks." He still sounded dispirited, or was it bored? She couldn't quite make up her mind, but being Petra, and Sam Hamilton's granddaughter, she believed in speaking her mind.

"What's wrong, Simon?" She was anxious now.

"You seemed to be enjoying the wedding, then all of a sudden, you changed. Was it something to do with my grandfather?"

He looked at her warily.

"I suppose it was." Taking a deep breath he said, "He wanted to know my intentions."

Petra tried not to giggle, but the situation was too much for her.

"And you got annoyed?" She was incredulous. "I can't believe it."

"Well, I couldn't help it. I felt like telling him it was none of his business."

"And neither it was," she agreed mirthfully. "Except of course, he probably feels responsible for me since Dad died."

Her eyes took on a sombre faraway look, and he reached across the table to clasp her hand.

"Sorry I spoilt the day for you, Petra," he apologised sincerely.

"I've been a bit of a wet blanket."

"Oh, nonsense! You could never . . ." She wanted to tell him that he had made her day just being there, and except for the last hour of the reception when his mood seemed to change, she had enjoyed sharing her family and friends with him, and even wondered if he felt the same sort of awe she had known during the marriage ceremony.

She would have liked to have been sitting beside him during the service but, of course, her place was next to Emmy, holding the bridal bouquet while the ring was placed on her cousin's finger.

"It's still early," he was saying with renewed enthusiasm. "Let's finish off the evening by going to see a film."

"With me dressed like this?" She fingered the pretty crepe dress doubtfully. "OK, then," she decided. "But I'll have to check that Mum and Grandad have transport home. Give me a few minutes, will you?"

MR HAMILTON was staying with them for the wedding, though he had made it very clear he would be returning to his house the following morning.

"Yes, of course, we'll manage home. Off you go and enjoy yourselves, my dear," her mother said warmly, while her grandfather gave something that sounded suspiciously like a snort.

This was Petra's cue. Two of a kind, the old man and granddaughter faced up to each other.

"What have you been saying to Simon, Grandad?" she challenged.

"Precious little," he responded with a wry grimace. "He's none too communicative, your latest."

"Grandad! My latest, indeed," she said indignantly. "Anyone would think I brought home a new boyfriend every other week or so. And if Simon's not very communicative to you, maybe it's because you two hardly know each other."

She relented a little, then went on.

"Look, why don't I bring him to the cottage some afternoon soon, so you can really get acquainted."

"Yes, of course," he said readily enough, tugging at his neckwear. "I can't wait to get out of these monkey clothes."

"Saturday all right?" she asked.

He nodded, smiling as she kissed his cheek.

"Be nice to him, Grandad." Her voice was soft.

"Aren't I always?" he said cheekily.

THE FESTIVE TABLE

CLOSE the curtains on a drab, dying day. Enjoy the mellow light and warmth within. The family has all arrived: the ritual of exchanging gifts is over. Men gather round the fire; children display their presents; women-folk are busy in the narrow kitchen.

Places set about the table – the flurry of passing round laden plates. Time to pull crackers; time for leisurely relaxation over coffee while the children cluster round the television.

A family enjoying Christmas dinner, together in their parents' home, together in mutual affection. Because it's Christmas, the birthday of the Christ who came. Who bound man to strive towards a day, when all nations shall be happy as one.

As happy as a family at Christmas when they gather round the festive table.

Rev. T. R. S. Campbell

The Gathering of the Cans

CANNED FOODS

Richmond Bridge, Galston

The Murray Brothers Collection.

SEND FOR IT TODAY.

A range of traditional Scottish daywear that will amaze you with its quality and value for money.

Made, in most cases, from pure new wool, the Murray Brothers collection will delight you.

Send for our free full colour brochure today.

Murray Brothers

Free Post, Dept. PF80, Tower Mill, Hawick, Scotland.

He was chuckling when she left and the sound cheered her considerably. They had always been close, and understood each other perfectly. Now he knew how she felt about Simon, surely he wouldn't place any more obstacles in the way or bring about that gloomy obstinacy in Simon's face again.

She found her boyfriend tucking in heartily to a plate of sandwiches and cream cakes.

"Well?" he enquired. "Got yourself permission to leave, have you?"

With an effort she bit back a sharp retort.

"All present and correct, sir," she said, instead. "Where are we going?"

He suggested a film they had both expressed a wish to see, and with a final goodbye to her mother, they hurried off to catch the beginning of the film.

On the way, she asked about Saturday, if they were meeting, or did he have something else to do?

"We could go dancing, or did you have something else in mind?" he replied.

Choosing her words carefully, she put forward the suggestion they might call on her grandfather in his cottage. Simon looked a bit taken aback. For a moment he didn't speak.

"If that's what you want, Petra," he said eventually. "But you've only just left him and he's been staying with you and your mother all week. Will he be expecting you to drop in so soon?"

"Oh, I checked with him first," she said gaily.

B Y the end of the evening, the film, which really was excellent, had put him in a better mood, and both were in high spirits on the way home.

"It's been a great day, Petra. I've enjoyed it, and it was really nice of your cousin to invite me to her wedding — usually I hate these kind of affairs."

It was on the tip of her tongue to ask whether it was family gatherings or simply weddings he didn't like. But she managed to stop herself in time. Somehow she didn't want to know.

N EXT day, as she was still on holiday, she escorted Grandad back to the cottage. Both mother and daughter had pleaded with him to stay a little longer, but Mr Hamilton was quite firm.

"Jem Ormond's doing a job for me, putting up some shelves in the kitchen. He said he'd be today and Jem always keeps his word."

T HERE was no sign of his old friend, Jem, at the cottage, though, towards the end of the journey.

"There!" Petra pointed out. "We needn't have hurried after all. Let's go inside and make us a nice pot of tea."

The sound of music from the back garden reached their ears, and Mr Hamilton said shortly:

"Now who can that be? Some of these youngsters have no respect

REMEMBER THE LIVING WAR BLINDED
AS THEY GROW OLDER

Our dead from the Wars are remembered every Armistice Sunday and Lawrence Binyon's poem is read at many a Cenotaph:

"They shall grow not old as we that are left grow old:
Age shall not weary them, nor the years condemn:
At the going down of the sun, and in the morning,
We will remember them."

Linburn, the residential centre and work shops for Scottish War Blinded ex-servicemen and women, has a constant need for money, for essential and urgent improvements to meet the needs of the disabled, as they grow older.

Will you now remember the disabled living, blinded in the service of their country, by giving a donation, deed of covenant or legacy to:

The Scottish National Institution For The War Blinded,
38 Albany Street, Edinburgh EH1 3PW.
Tel: 031-556 6894.
also at NEWINGTON HOUSE and GLASGOW.

The safe way to the top

Safety and quality. The two things you look for when you want to buy a ladder.

They're the first two things you find when you consider a Ramsay. And it doesn't stop there.

Take the A1 Model Loft Ladder. It's made completely of lightweight aluminium and disappears in seconds. The non-slip treads are $3\frac{1}{2}''$ wide with a $1''$ nosing and are fitted at a standard $10''$ rise. And we can supply a safety handrail if required.

BRITAIN'S FINEST LADDER

Registered Office and Works:	*Edinburgh Depot:*	*Glasgow Depot:*
61 West High Street,	**8 Baileyfield Crescent,**	**6 Castebank Crescent,**
FORFAR, Angus, DD8 1BH.	**Portobello,**	**Castebank Trading Estate,**
Phone FORFAR 0307 62255	**EDINBURGH EH15 1TA.**	**GLASGOW G11 6DE.**
Grams: "Ladders, Forfar"	*Phone 031-669 5721*	*Phone 041-339 3083*

ALSO AT LONDON, LEEDS AND COVENTRY

at all for private property, but, don't worry, I'll soon sort them out."

One solitary young man stopped strumming a guitar as they emerged from the back door and got to his feet, smiling in friendly fashion.

"Mr Hamilton. My great-uncle can't manage to do any carpentry for you today — the old pain is playing him up, so I volunteered to do what I could."

"Thanks, but I don't want any hit-and-miss efforts," the old man said curtly. "I'll wait till Jem can come himself. Who did you say you were?"

"Bill Ormond," the young man replied. "My grandmother's spoken of you to me many a time."

"Has she indeed?" The old man couldn't hide his pleasure.

Feeling a little sorry for Bill Ormond, Petra interrupted with an invitation to join them for a cup of tea.

"Thank you," he said, relaxing a little. "That would be just great."

Mr Hamilton lost some of his reluctance to accepting the deputy joiner when he proved how knowledgeable he was.

Grudgingly, he conceded.

"Well, I suppose you can go ahead, but mind you finish the job by Friday. My granddaughter's got a special friend coming. We can't have the place looking like a shipwreck."

One of the reasons Petra had arranged to spend so long at the cottage today was to tidy up generally with Simon's projected visit in mind.

Since she had to work in the kitchen preparing a light lunch, it was natural to stop and chat with Bill Ormond.

At one stage, he resorted to the guitar once again and sang a verse or two:

If I could meet a girl like you,
I'd walk for many a mile.
A girl with eyes of speedwell blue,
A bonnie dimpling smile.

"What's that?" she asked interestedly. "Is it a new record?"

"I should be so lucky." He grinned. "I make them up as I go along."

"Young man." Grandad's grey head was round the kitchen door. "You're here to see to the shelving in the quickest possible time. We can do without the music."

"Yes, sir. I just have to wait a little till the glue sets under the Formica. How do you think the shelving looks, Mr Hamilton?"

"Not bad." The old man's approval was grudging, and catching Petra's reproachful look, he chuckled a bit shamefacedly. "It's actually a first-rate job, Bill. Jem himself couldn't have done better. He's taught you well."

"It's always been a hobby of mine," the younger man told them during the lunch break. Although the joinery was completed, he had already volunteered to wash the windows.

"Well, you want the place looking its best for the Saturday visit, don't you?" he pointed out when Petra protested.

"Yes, I do, but that's no reason why we should take up your precious time."

"I'm on holiday — till the university term starts again," he

explained. "Did I tell you I was hoping to qualify as a language teacher?"

He was an unusual young man, she thought, seeing him off at the front door, tool-bag and guitar tucked firmly beneath his arms.

"Hope everything goes all right for you," he said with a kindly smile. "Maybe I'll see you again when you're visiting your grandad sometime. 'Bye."

THE little haunting melody stayed with her for quite some time, as she drove home, and even that evening as she told her mother of the day's events.

There was a phone call from Simon around nine o'clock.

Would she mind very much, he asked, if he called off the Saturday trip?

"No, it doesn't really matter. Has something come up?"

"Well, not exactly. I still think he needs time to get used to me."

It was very obvious what was wrong — Simon didn't want to get involved.

"No." She knew that her voice was firm.

"I hope you don't feel I'm letting you down?" His voice sounded strangely formal.

"Simon, I understand. I really do. There's no need to explain."

He would always be a loner, forever fearful of being trapped in marriage. It was odd that it had taken her so long to see it, when Grandad apparently sensed it right from the start.

There was no reason why they couldn't go on being good friends, but when that night she sat again on the edge of the bed nursing the bridal bouquet, it was no longer associated with Simon.

One day she would carry such a bouquet and throw it in the direction of her bridesmaid. Before that, she would walk up the aisle.

The 'groom waiting down there, turning to smile proudly as she advanced to him, was still a shadowy figure, but one day the features and the form would be crystal clear.

Was it a sign for the future that as she drifted off to sleep "The Wedding March" seemed to have the haunting sound of a guitar accompaniment.

Printed and Published in Great Britain by D. C. Thomson & Co. Ltd., Dundee, Glasgow, London and Manchester.
ISBN 0 85116 194 4

TROUTBRECK, NEAR LAKE WINDERMERE